The Coffin in the Wall

A DI Emma Christie crime thriller

M J Lee

The Christmas Carol

The Missing Father

The Irish Convict

The Salford Sioux (2024)

When the Night Ends

What the Shadows Hide

What the Dead Want (June 2024)

Other Fiction

Samuel Pepys and the Stolen Diary

Tuesday, October 24

Chapter ONE

'Shhhh…' Kevin placed his finger across his lips. 'Did you hear something?'

All three of them crouched silently behind the hedgerow, listening to the noises on the wind.

A dog barking in the distance. The low hum of traffic. Another noise, a strange scratching noise, like something being dragged along the ground, followed by muffled hammering.

'What's that?'

Kev popped his head over the wall, taking a quick look at the ruins of the south-eastern chapel of St John's Church just one hundred yards away. Even in the dim lights mounted on the walls, the ancient ruins looked frightening and ominous, as if a thousand secrets were hidden in the shadows.

He slumped back down and whispered to Dan, the smaller of the two boys who were with him, 'It's nothing, probably just the caretaker wrapping up for the night.'

'You had me scared for a moment,' laughed the largest and toughest of the three, known universally in school as Big Dave.

'Look,' said Kev, speaking to the smaller boy. 'This is what you have to do. The lights are on a timer and they will go off in a moment. When they do, you need to move as fast as you can. You have to go to the ruins and write your initials beneath the coffin. It's as easy as apple pie. Don't try and trick us because Big Dave will check it out tomorrow to see if they are there. And he won't be a happy camper if you lie to us, will you, Dave?'

'The unhappiest camper you've ever seen,' said Dave, shaking his head menacingly.

Kev paused for a moment to let the threat sink in, before handing Dan a small lump of blue chalk he had nicked from school that morning.

'I don't know...' Dan stammered. 'It looks pretty scary to me.'

Kev punched the smaller boy's arm. 'That's the whole point, dummy.' He rolled his eyes extravagantly. In the dark, they seemed like white ping-pong balls in the middle of his face.

'Yeah,' interrupted Big Dave, 'what would be the point of an initiation that wasn't scary?'

'But it could be haunted...'

'Of course it's haunted, stupid, it's an old, abandoned church. Everybody knows these old places are always haunted by the ghosts of the past.' Kev nudged Big Dave. 'It's said an old monk dressed all in white wanders the ruins at night, rattling his chains.'

'My mate said he saw him once,' said Big Dave.

'And what happened?' whispered Dan.

'Dunno, never saw him again. Wonder what happened to him?'

Dan peered around the edge of the wall. The lights illuminating the ruins cast dark shadows in the corners where the walls met. Anything could be hiding there; boogeymen, the white monk, a zombie ready to infect him with a single bite, or worse – a Medusa ready to turn him into a stone gargoyle.

A violent shudder ran down his backbone, looking for a way out.

He slumped back against the wall. 'Couldn't I do something else, like nick a car?'

'Listen, if you want to be part of our gang at school, this is the initiation ceremony. Me, Little Hoss, Stevie G., Charlie, even Big Dave, we've all done it before.'

'I didn't. I nicked a car,' piped up Big Dave.

'Well, everybody else has. And so will you.'

'Stevie G. did it?'

'Even better, he wrote "Kilroy was here" on the wall and signed "Stevie G" underneath.'

'He didn't sign it as Kilroy?'

Kev frowned. 'Why would he sign it as Kilroy? His name's Steve Godfrey.'

'Cos he wrote "Kilroy was here".'

'Never mind,' said Kev slowly, shaking his head.

'What if I—'

Before Dan could finish his sentence, the lights at the ruins went off.

'Time for you to go.'

Dan popped his head around the side of the wall once more. Without the lights, the ruins looked even more frightening, the walls bible black against the orange glow of Chester. Even the shadows had shadows.

'One last thing. Don't look at the coffin.'

'Why?'

'If you do, you'll be turned to stone. At least, that's what the legend says.'

Dan took three deep breaths, desperately trying to quieten the heart beating wildly in his chest.

'Of course, we could go home now and I'll tell the whole school how you chickened out…'

Dan turned back quickly. 'No, don't do that. I'll go, just give me a second.'

He pulled up his socks and retied his trainers, taking three more deep breaths like his mum had taught him to do when he was feeling stressed.

'Are you going to do it or not?'

He stood up, glanced quickly on either side – not seeing anything in the dark – and took a few steps forward before stopping and listening.

'Hey, dopey, you forgot this.'

Kev was holding up the blue chalk.

Dan retraced his steps, looking over his shoulder back at the ruins.

'Good luck,' said Kev. 'You're gonna need it.'

Big Dave chuckled.

Dan shut his eyes and took three more breaths before turning to face the ruins and walking forward. Behind him, he could hear more laughter.

Idiots. He would show them.

He moved more quickly now, his feet brushing through piles of leaves collected by the autumn winds, rustling with every step. His eyes had adjusted to the lack of light and he could see the angular shapes of the ruins rising above him, dark as hell.

A shudder went down his spine.

'Got to keep going, I'm not afraid,' he said aloud, to soothe his nerves. He was sick of being bullied. At least in Kev's gang he'd be safe. Nobody would touch him if they knew he was part of the gang.

He'd googled the ruins as soon as Kev had told him what the challenge was. It was old, very old, founded in 767 by the Saxons, according to Wikipedia. He'd studied the period at school. King Alfred and his cakes, the Venerable Bede, and the Vikings, all lived about the same time. He liked the Vikings but his mum wouldn't let him watch the TV series. 'Far too much violence,' according to her.

'But that's the whole point, Mum. The Vikings *were* killers.'

She didn't listen, she never did. Not since Dad left, anyway.

A loud noise on his right. A car door shutting? Who was here too?

He stood still and listened to a strange sound, like an electric motor with a weird rumbling in the background. The sound seemed to curve right past, going into the park and carrying on behind him. A slow, monotonous sound.

He didn't move for a while. Off to his left, another sound. A slight hissing and bubbling. He tilted his head. What was it?

The river.

The River Dee speaking to him, telling him not to be afraid.

He walked on, stepping over some branches lying on the ground, reaching the metal fence. Kev said there was a gap he could squeeze through along here, somewhere.

He moved along the fence, searching for the slight bowing of the metal rods where he could slip through and down into the sunken lane.

Here it is.

He turned sideways, just managing to shimmy through the small gap. Two steps across the lane and up on to the embankment. The ruins closer now, looming over him.

He stopped for a moment, listening again. It was amazing how acute his hearing had become in the last few minutes. It was as if he could hear everything happening in the world. Of course, the loudest noise was the sound of his own breathing.

He took three deep breaths again, trying to calm himself.

'Right, here goes.'

He scrambled over the low fence and rushed towards the old ruins, pressing his back against the walls, feeling the hard coldness of the sandstone. How long since anybody had felt the touch of these walls? What secrets had they seen, or heard, or witnessed in the time they had stood beside the river?

He edged to his right, feeling his way along the wall to a place where it had collapsed and the stone had been removed to leave a jagged edge. He rounded the corner and knew he was in the main body of the ruined church now. Three walls rose high above his head, etched black against the orange glow of the city lights.

For the first time, the wind rustled the leaves on the paving stones. The wall with the coffin embedded in it lay in front of him. In olden days, this was where the altar would have been. A priest saying mass, holding the host above his head as the congregation looked on in wonder.

He used to go to church with his family on Sundays, but they didn't bother any more. Not since Dad went away.

The coffin was on the right-hand side, high up in the wall. He edged towards it, blue chalk in hand.

He decided he wasn't going to write his initials, he was going to leave a message: 'Daniel Sangster was here and wrote this.'

Let Big Dave see it when he came tomorrow. He was going to show them how brave he was.

He moved towards the wall. His heart was pounding, his hands sweating. The coffin in the wall was above his head now, but he wasn't going to look at it. He didn't want to turn into stone.

He began writing in large block capitals: D-A-N-I-E-L

The chalk slipped from his fingers and fell to the floor. As he bent down to search for it, he accidentally looked up at the coffin.

Then he heard a sound like a car alarm, loud and screeching, cutting through the still air of the autumn night and rebounding off the old stone walls of the church.

The sound was coming from him, Daniel Sangster.

He was screaming.

Chapter TWO

Detective Inspector Emma Christie of the City of Chester Constabulary was enjoying herself. Most of her colleagues hated filling in police forms but she took a certain satisfaction in doing it well.

The office was quiet at the moment. Generally, working the night shift was a good time to get all the paperwork done, and this week it was Emma's turn to take the graveyard shift.

The form she had on her computer was a Section 8 – a search warrant looking for evidential material. In this case, ill-gotten gains from a series of burglaries in houses in Cheshire. They had arrested two likely lads a week ago, but without any concrete evidence neither had admitted guilt. A tip-off from an informant revealed they used a lock-up on Sealand Road to store their stuff until it could be fenced. In order to look inside the garage, the police had to get a magistrate to sign the form so they could mount a raid.

She'd reached the fourth question with its two constituent parts.

4. Premises to be searched which CAN be specified.

(a) Address or other description of the premises:

(b) Why do you believe that the material you are looking for is on those premises?

She tapped out the address using her index fingers, like two voracious woodpeckers hammering into the keys, mouthing each word as she went along. She'd always wanted to learn how to type properly but never had the time.

One day, one day.

She glanced at the next question and thought about writing the truth: 'Because some snout down the pub told us about it when we gave him twenty quid.' But instead she wrote:

Based on reliable information from two reputable sources, including the owners of the facility who have reported suspicious activity, we believe this lock-up is being used to store items from burglaries in the Cheshire area.

That should be enough for any magistrate. She didn't want to go into too much detail on the form. The vaguer it was, the better. After all, she just needed a signature for a search, not an agreement to prosecute the case.

She was about to complete the next question on the form when there was a knock on the door. Through the smoked glass, she could see the familiar imposing shape of John Simpson, a civilian researcher with the force.

'Come in,' she shouted.

'Have you completed the warrant yet, boss? It's just that the duty magistrate is Tony Fellows and he'd sign his life away to the devil, but he likes a few drinks so you should catch him before he's out for the night.'

Emma glanced at the clock on the wall opposite. 10.10 p.m. Cowboy time. She laughed to herself, remembering one of her dad's jokes. 'Just doing it, John, won't be long.'

John Simpson stared at the two index fingers poised to strike the keys. 'You want me to do it for you? Wouldn't take me long.'

John's fingers were like greased eels across a keyboard. Watching him always turned Emma bright green with envy.

'No thanks, I have to work this out as I'm doing it.'

'We have a template, boss, you could just follow that. Tony Fellows never reads them anyway, he just signs on the dotted line.'

Emma sighed. 'I know, but I still want to get this one right. I don't want some sharp brief getting our slags off on a technicality.'

'Your choice, boss.'

'Aye, it is. Don't you have anything to do, John?'

'Lots, boss, but this warrant is the priority at the moment.'

'Has Davy Jones put you up to this?'

The civilian researcher stared down at his feet and mumbled his words. 'The chief inspector did mention before he went home it had to go out tonight.'

'It's coming, but the longer you stand in the doorway hassling me, the longer it's going to take.'

DC Anna Williams joined him in the doorway, obviously out of breath. 'A call's just come through, boss, some kid's found a body in the ruins close to St John's Church.'

'Suicide?'

'Dunno, boss, doesn't look like it.'

Emma Christie was on her feet in seconds. 'Where's Harry?'

'In the canteen, I think.'

'Drag him away from his cheese toastie and get the car out front. Who's at the scene?'

'A Sergeant Harris, according to the dispatcher.'

'Good, Tom Harris knows what to do. Well, what are you waiting for? Go and get the car, chop-chop.'

'You want me to finish the warrant, Emma?'

The DI looked regretfully at the computer as she packed her bag, making sure her notebook and warrant card were safely tucked away. 'You'd better, John. But let me see it before it goes out.'

'Davy Jones won't be happy, boss.'

'Bugger Davy Jones and his happiness.'

'Is that an order or just a request, boss?'

'A bit of both, John.'

Chapter THREE

Outside, the Vauxhall Cavalier was already waiting with the engine running when Emma came out of the main entrance, DC Harry Fairweather standing at the open door of the car.

'Sorry to drag you away from your toastie.'

He patted his baggy suit pocket. 'No worries, I brought it along in case it could be a long night.'

'Hope not, my dad's carer finishes at six tomorrow morning.'

'How is your dad?'

'Good days and bad days.' She shrugged her shoulders. 'You know how it is.'

'Yeah, my mum went the same way.'

Emma was joined in the back by Anna Williams. Harry put a blue light on the roof and started the siren as they pulled out from the car park.

'Harry, I don't think the good citizens of Chester want to be woken at this time of night by a screaming police car racing through the centre of town,' she shouted above the noise. 'And if it is a dead body, getting there thirty seconds earlier isn't going to bring it back to life.'

The noise stopped. 'Sorry, boss. ETA in six minutes… without the siren.'

'Bloody thing always gives me a headache.' She turned to Anna. 'Anything else from the scene?'

'Not a lot. Sergeant Harris is sealing the area off.'

'Good. Who found the body?'

'A kid. Daniel Sangster.'

'What was he doing there at this time of night? Shouldn't he be at home sleeping or playing World of Wizards or something?'

'Dunno, boss.'

They raced through the quiet, neon-lit streets of Chester. At this time on a weekday night there weren't many people or cars around. St Oswalds Way and its innumerable roundabouts were easy to navigate, most cars pulling over when they saw the flashing blue light in their rearview mirror.

'Slow down, Harry, I want to arrive in one piece not as another road traffic statistic.'

The car immediately slowed.

'The body was found in the church?'

'Not exactly in the church itself, actually in the ruins beside it.'

'The ruins? Next to Grosvenor Park?'

'That's the place. I don't know what the kid was doing in the ruins.'

'Or what a body is doing there, but we're going to find out.'

Harry swung round The Bars and raced along Grosvenor Park Road, accelerating to a stop behind two parked patrol cars with a tall, bearded sergeant leaning on the roof of one of them. Next to him, a younger copper was being violently sick in the gutter.

'You were here quick, we only called it in a few minutes ago,' the sergeant called to Emma as she squeezed her way out of the car.

'Heard it was you in charge, Tom, came as quickly as I could.'

'Glad you did. I can't stand working with that old tosser, Riggs. He's a waste of oxygen.'

Detective Inspector Riggs was the head of the other detective team in the City of Chester Police. It was no secret that the two DIs didn't like each other and therefore led different teams.

Taking a large black ledger from her bag, Emma said to Harris, 'Take me through what we've got.'

She opened the pad to the first clean page. Official updates on any case were kept in the computer logs; these case notes were hers and hers alone, written in an unruly scrawl that leant heavily to the right, the problem of writing using her left hand.

They were personal, her impressions of a scene or a witness, and questions that she needed to ask herself moving forward. It was a technique advocated by her father: 'You discover more from how you felt about a scene than any photograph can tell you. Trust your instincts, Emma – worth more than half the police courses at Bramshill. Maybe, just maybe, it'll be one little detail you've written down that helps break the case down the line.'

The sergeant saw her pen poised over the paper and began to speak. 'There's the body of a young male, aged around fourteen, placed in the coffin on the wall. I've not seen anything like it, not in twenty years of coppering.'

They began walking to the ruins of the church, leaving the bright lights of the street behind. Emma closed her book and pulled out a flashlight.

'I remember coming here on a school trip once,' she said. 'Didn't like it, gave me the willies.'

They reached the outer wall.

'It's inside and it's not pretty.'

They stepped in. Tom Harris's torch moved from the ground to illuminate the far wall. On the left, about ten feet up, was an upright wooden coffin embedded in the wall.

Inside the coffin was the small, fully dressed body of a young man, jammed inside the small space.

'Why didn't he fall out?'

'I think somebody nailed him in.'

'Nice.'

Emma Christie was joined by her two detective constables.

'What the...' exclaimed Anna Williams. 'What's happened to his eyes?'

'He hasn't got any,' answered the sergeant.

They advanced slowly over the rough paving stones, stopping when Emma pointed to a lump of blue chalk on the ground. 'Don't go any closer, don't want to contaminate this crime scene.'

They all stood still, their flashlights illuminating the body. Around the boy's neck hung a hand-written placard inscribed with a message in block capitals:

NOT IN MY CITY

They all stared at the sightless eyes for a few seconds before Harry Fairweather spoke in his broad Liverpool accent. 'Well, at least he won't be needing glasses any more.'

The joke shocked Emma Christie out of her inertia. 'Right, Anna – get on to the coroner, we need the duty pathologist here asap. Let's hope it's David Anstey.'

'On it, boss.'

'Harry, get a CSI team here. I want the whole area cordoned off up to the road, including the park and the church next door.'

'The local vicar ain't gonna be chuffed.'

'Tough, we've got a young boy who died painfully in his ruins. You know the procedure – nobody comes in or out of the cordon without signing in. And make sure we keep the papers away; I don't want to see pictures of this poor soul on the internet.'

'We're going to need more warm bodies, Emma.'

'I'll authorise the overtime, Tom, but don't go over the top.'

'It's a big area, Emma.'

'It's also a major crime scene. Where's the boy who found the body?'

'I put him on a bench in the park with a PC. Tried talking to him but he made no sense. He stopped a woman and her boyfriend on the street and they rang 999.'

'You were first on the scene?'

'We were in town when we got the call.'

'You and the vomit merchant outside?'

'He's new, Emma, first dead body.'

'Won't be the last if he stays on the force.'

Just then, Anna Williams appeared by Emma's side. 'The boy's mum has arrived.'

'Which boy?'

'The one who discovered the body.'

'Right, we'd better have a chat with him. Tom, make sure nobody goes anywhere near the crime scene until the pathologist and the CSIs get here.'

'Leave him there like that?'

'For now.' She turned back to stare at the young boy standing upright in the coffin. 'Somebody put this poor soul's body here as a warning. It's on display, Tom.'

'Why?'

Emma Christie shrugged her shoulders. 'I don't know… But I'm going to find out.'

As she finished her sentence, her mobile rang. She checked the name. 'It looks like God has woken up.'

She pressed the answer button and walked away from the scene. 'Yes, sir.'

'I've heard a body has been found.'

'Correct, sir. The body of a young man in the ruins next to Grosvenor Park.'

'Murder?'

'Looks like it.'

'Shit. Just what I didn't need when Riggs is away.'

'I can handle it, sir. We're just waiting for the pathologist and the CSI team to arrive. We've already cordoned off the area.'

'Okay, you handle it for now, but no cock-ups like last time. Do it by the book, Emma, understand? We'll decide how to proceed in the morning.'

'Right, sir.' The phone went dead in her hand. 'Thank you for the vote of confidence.'

Chapter FOUR

'I told you not to leave the house. Your job was to look after your sister…'

The mother was standing over the boy as he sat on the park bench all alone. His head was down, staring at the ground, hands together as if in supplication.

There were more police cars and vans lining the road and its approaches now. A small crowd of onlookers had begun to gather, held back by a thin yellow line of police tape.

'…but did you listen? No. You never listen, just like your father…'

'Mrs…'

'Sangster,' Anna Williams whispered quietly in her DI's ear.

'Mrs Sangster, my name is Detective Inspector Emma Christie from City of Chester Police. I'd like to speak to your son, if I may?'

The mother turned away from the boy to face the DI. She was wearing a thin coat over her light blue NHS uniform, her lank blonde hair swept up in a loose chignon. Around her eyes, an immense tiredness from lack of sleep, anger and stress.

'Be my guest. See if you can get any sense out of him. He's not saying a word to me.'

With a flick of her eyes, Emma Christie indicated she wanted the woman moved out of earshot.

The detective constable took the mother's elbow and steered her away from her son. 'Would you like a cup of tea, Mrs Sangster? I'm sure we could rustle one up from somewhere, even at this time of night.'

Emma Christie knelt down in front of the boy, bringing her head to the same level as his. 'It wasn't a very nice thing to discover, was it?'

The boy shook his head but didn't say a word.

'My name is Detective Inspector Emma Christie from City of Chester Police. My job is to find out what happened here, what happened to that young lad. Will you help me?'

The boy nodded slowly.

'Good, that's a start, hey. Now, Daniel—'

'It's Dan. Only my mum calls me Daniel.'

'Mums. Can't live with them, can't live without them, hey?'

The boy looked up for the first time. 'She's not bad, just hasn't been the same since Dad went away.'

The boy's head went down again.

'So your dad's not living at home at the minute?'

The boy shook his head.

'Where is home, if you don't mind me asking?'

'Blacon. Harris Road, just near the minimart.'

'I know it well. Grew up in Blacon, I did. Is the chippy still on Western Avenue?'

The boy looked up again. 'Nah, it's closed. A curry house now.'

'Shame, I used to love their haddock and chips on a Friday. Used to get extra scraps with it. Nothing better than scraps.'

'I like them too, between two slices of bread and lots of vinegar.'

'Can't be beaten.' She paused for a moment, looking round the park. 'You're a long way from Blacon tonight.'

The boy nodded.

'Why did you go into the ruins of the church?'

The boy remained silent.

'Look, you won't get into trouble, but if I'm to catch whoever did this, I need your help. Understand?'

The boy nodded slowly.

'So why did you go into the ruins?'

'It was a dare, a challenge.'

'Who set the challenge?'

'I can't say. They'll kill me if I tell you their names.'

'Are they from the same school?'

The boy nodded.

'And they were with you here tonight?'

'Not all the gang, just two of them.'

'Only two?'

'Kev and Big Dave.' The boy's eyes flared as he realised he had said their names.

Emma carried on as if nothing had happened. 'But they didn't go with you into the ruins?'

'They stayed in the park.'

'Where? Where did they stay?'

The boy pointed. 'Over there, behind the hedge.'

Emma stood up. 'Can you show me?'

They walked together across the park. Next to the ruins, the CSI team, dressed in their all-white Tyvek suits, were already setting up lights and screens to surround the ruins.

'We sat here.'

Emma could see the grass had been trampled at the base of the hedge. 'Where are your friends now?'

The boy shrugged his shoulders. 'They must have run off when the cops arrived.'

'Not very good friends, are they? Leaving you in the lurch.'

'They're not bad, just…'

'So they set you a challenge before you could join their gang?'

The boy looked up at her, surprised she understood. Before he told her.

'We're all set challenges, Dan. I had to pass one before I could join *my* gang.' She indicated with a wave of her hand the coppers and CSIs surrounding the ruins. 'There's always strength in numbers. What did you have to do?'

'Write my initials on the wall beneath the coffin.'

'In blue chalk?'

Again, a surprised look appeared on the boy's face.

'There's a stick of blue chalk on the ground in front of the wall.'

'I must have dropped it when I saw…' His voice tailed off.

'Tell me what happened, right from the beginning,' she said brightly, changing the mood. 'What time did you get here?'

'Around nine thirty, I think. We took the bus from Blacon.'

'How did you get in? The gates are locked.'

'We hopped over the fence, it's pretty easy.'

'And then what happened?'

'We sat down here and waited. We could hear the caretaker moving around in the ruins but Kev knew he would leave and the lights would go out at ten.'

'Did they go out?'

Dan nodded. 'That's when I started walking towards the ruins. It was pretty dark and scary.'

'Did you see anything or anybody?'

'No, I couldn't really see anything.'

As he spoke, two arc lights switched on, illuminating the ruins. The entrance was now covered in a screen so nobody could see inside.

'Let's retrace your steps. Try to remember everything you did or heard or saw.'

They took a few steps forward before stopping.

'I had to go back and get the chalk from Kev, I'd forgotten it.'

'Good, I'm glad you remembered.'

They walked forward a little further.

'I thought I heard something now, and I was scared.'

'What did you hear?'

'A sort of scraping or dragging noise, followed by a sort of soft hammering, if that makes sense. I didn't know what it was, so I stood still.'

'There were no other noises?'

The boy thought for a moment. 'Nothing for a minute or two. Then I thought I heard another noise, like the whirr of a motor and a squeaking sound.'

'Was it a car? Did you see it?'

The boy shook his head. 'I didn't know and I couldn't see it from where I was.'

'So what happened next?'

'After the sound stopped, I squeezed through the metal fence, dropped down into the lane and up on the other side.'

'You didn't see anything or anybody?'

Dan shook his head. 'I took a few steps to the wall, touching it with my fingers. I followed it round to the main body of the church and went inside.'

'It was empty?'

'I think so. I didn't see anybody else but it was dark. I edged up to the wall and started to write, but then I dropped my chalk and looked up to see…'

'That's great, Dan. You've been a great witness. Anything else you remember? Anything at all? A noise? A smell? Anything you saw?'

Dan thought for a long time before shaking his head and looking back to where his mother was standing with DC Williams.

'Do you want me to have a chat with your mum?'

'Nah, I'll handle it.'

'No… we'll do it together. Remember, you're part of my gang now.'

Chapter FIVE

'You can take Dan home now, Mrs Sangster, but we need to arrange for him to come in to give a formal statement in the next couple of days.'

'Right, you're grounded, Daniel. After this little episode, no Xbox for the next month and you're staying in the house from now on, no going out on your own. This evening, because of your little shenanigans, I've had to get a neighbour to look after your little sister *and* I've had to leave work early...'

'About that, Mrs Sangster,' Emma interrupted, 'there's no law which determines what age you can leave a child on their own, but it is an offence to leave a child alone if it possibly places them at risk. The rule of thumb is that children under twelve are rarely mature enough to be left alone for a long period of time, while children under sixteen should not be left alone overnight. How old is your daughter?'

'Nine.'

'And were you planning to leave her in the care of Daniel overnight until tomorrow morning?'

'What am I supposed to do? I'm a single mum who has to work shifts to feed and clothe my kids. Do you have any kids? Do you know how hard it is to take care of them?

Feed, clothe and wash them? What would you do in my place?'

'I don't have kids, no, but I think I would arrange childcare for them when I wasn't there.'

'Do you know how expensive it is to arrange a babysitter who stays overnight? More than I earn on the whole bloody shift. It wouldn't be worth working if I did that every time I was working the night shift.'

Emma did know how expensive it was. She had arranged for a nurse to look after her father while she was working the night shift this week. It had cost her an arm and a leg and another arm on top of that.

'All I'm saying is that Daniel has suffered a traumatic experience this evening but has handled it in a mature and responsible way. He is a good example of a bright young boy and if I were you, I wouldn't be too harsh on him.'

'A good example who left his nine-year-old sister on her own.'

'She was playing next door with her school friends, Mum. I planned to pick her up at ten thirty.'

'But you didn't tell *me* your plans, did you, Daniel?' Mrs Sangster sighed. 'You don't know how hard it is bringing up kids on your own.'

Emma stepped forward and placed her arm around the other woman's shoulder. 'It's tough, I know. But you're raising him well, he's a good kid. Because he told the police what he found, we may be able to put away whoever did this before they kill another child. You should be proud of him.'

The woman nodded through her tears.

'Now let me organise a lift back to your home, it's the least we can do.' Emma reached into her wallet. 'And, Daniel, here's my card. If you think of anything else, just give me a call at any time, okay?'

'We're going to ride back in a police car? Can we have the siren on?'

'Yes, you'll get a ride in a squad car, and no, we won't be using the siren.'

She took another card and gave it to Mrs Sangster. 'If you need anything, or just want somebody to have a chat to, give me a call. It's good to talk.'

For the last two minutes, Harry Fairweather had been hovering on the edge of the group, desperate to say something.

'What is it, Harry? You hover like a kestrel ready to take a mouse.'

'Boss, the pathologist has arrived.'

'You've taken him into the ruins to see the body?'

'Already there, boss.'

'Good. Can you arrange a lift back to Blacon for Mrs Sangster and Dan? Use the BMW and Dan can switch the siren on for ten seconds, but no longer. The good citizens of Chester don't need to be woken up too often.'

She turned back to Mrs Sangster. 'I do mean it. Call me if you want to chat at any time. We'll see each other again when Dan comes in to give his statement. Let Harry here know when it is convenient and we'll send a car to pick you up.'

Chapter SIX

'What have we got, David?'

Both the pathologist and Emma Christie were now dressed in white Tyvek body suits to prevent contamination of the scene. The DI had struggled into hers, protesting all the time. 'Why don't they make these bloody things easier to put on?' She zipped up the front and put the hood over her head, ensuring all her brown hair was tucked beneath. Finally, she struggled to put on the overshoes; bending down and touching her toes was always a major achievement.

She then picked up her ledger and a pen. When Dr Anstey spoke she always found it useful to take notes.

They both stepped through the screen into the ruins. The body, still in its coffin on the wall, was now illuminated brightly by two arc lamps pointed directly at it. The empty holes where the eyes should have been were now even more stark in their horror. In the middle of the ruins, a photographer, also in a protective suit, was moving around taking pictures.

Dr David Anstey, the pathologist, strode up to the wall, placing his medical bag carefully on the ground. He spent a long time examining the body before climbing the ladder placed at the side to look at it more closely.

'I'd say what we have here is a young male, aged fourteen to fifteen. It's always difficult to tell somebody's age visually. I can be a little more exact when we X-ray him, but even then it's difficult. People develop at different rates during puberty.' He pointed to the face of the corpse.

'See, there's a thin down of hair on the top lip, suggesting he had certainly started puberty.'

'You're going to X-ray him?'

'The hands, teeth and clavicles. They should give us a good idea of an age but it will be a ballpark. I could explain what we're going to do but I doubt you'd have the patience to listen.'

David knew her too well. They had worked together often in the past. She had found him precise and professional in his work but a little too given to long, verbose explanations using medical terminology. Words that hid as much as they explained.

'When will we know?'

'As soon as I've finished the post-mortem. It's fairly straightforward to give a rough estimate. If you want something more exact, I'll need to work with a forensic anthropologist, but that will cost you.'

'Let's see if we can identify him first. Cause of death?'

'Let's get him down and I can examine him more closely.'

He indicated to two of his assistants to step forward. They placed a plastic sheet on the ground and two stepladders next to the coffin in the wall.

The pathologist leant across the body, examining it close-up. 'So that's how it was done.'

'What was done?'

'The body is upright in the coffin. Somebody has used masonry nails through the shoulders, just below the clavicles, to keep it in place, and then glued the back of the head to the coffin base so it wouldn't slump forward.'

'The perp wanted the body to be upright, looking out with sightless eyes. Horrific.'

'It is rather gruesome.' He called his assistants forward, instructing them to cut away the hair to release the head, and used a saw to cut through the masonry nails close to the wall.

'Does this look religious to you?'

'The fact we are in a former church would seem to indicate that, but the hands weren't pierced nor are the arms outstretched in a typical Christ-like pose. I can't totally rule out religious iconography, but I believe the nails had a much more functional use – they kept the body upright.'

After ten minutes of painstaking work, the small body was taken down and laid out on the plastic sheet.

'He may be a little younger than I thought; thirteen to fourteen. His body is small and relatively undeveloped.'

'Cause of death?'

'I'm coming to that,' Dr Anstey said peevishly. 'You're always rushing me, Emma. Remember; more haste, less speed.'

The pathologist often used these epigrams when he wanted to admonish the detective inspector. It was as if he had a whole library of them filed away in his brain, ready to appear when needed. Today, as in the past, she just ignored him. He would give her an answer quickly enough.

'From the bruising on the neck and the possible broken hyoid bone, I'd say he was strangled. Shame. Without the eyes, I can't check for petechiae.'

'Peti-what?'

'Small blood vessels in the eyes. They burst during strangulation. A classic sign. I can't see anything else at the moment to be the cause of death, so you'll have to wait for a definitive answer after the post-mortem.'

'Right. But this is a murder, not an accidental death or suicide?'

As soon as she asked the question, Emma knew she would get a witheringly sarcastic answer from Dr Anstey. But she had to ask for the record.

'Nobody takes their own eyes out and then glues their head to a wall accidentally. And I can think of far easier ways to commit suicide; the river is less than fifty yards away.'

'Thank you, I just thought I'd ask.' She made a note.

'Ask and you shall receive. Or not, in this case.' The doctor checked the boy's head along the hairline. 'A small mark with the beginnings of a scar here. Probably caused in the last week or so.' He then moved down to the hands. 'That's interesting – I can't see any visible signs of dirt under the nails and the hands look like they've been washed. We'll bag them up anyway and check them back at the lab. One last job.' He began going through the boy's pockets, checking for any ID. 'Nothing. We officially have a John Doe until you can identify him. Do you want to bag up the sign before we take him away?'

'Yeah, it might help. Jane, can you place that in an evidence bag for me?' Emma pointed to the sign with its block capital letters.

The crime scene manager came forward with a large transparent evidence bag. Carefully she removed the sign from around the head of the young man and placed it in the bag, marking a number on the front.

The doctor stood up from the body, motioning his assistants forward to take it away. 'And before you ask, time of death was at least twelve hours ago.'

'You took the words out of my mouth. Can you give a more exact time? And before you say "I'll know more after the post-mortem", give me a rough estimate.'

The doctor sighed. 'I'll know more after the post-mortem…' A long pause. 'But from the general morbidity and, at this time of the year, I'd say he's been dead for about eighteen hours, give or take six hours.'

'That's probably the most exact you've ever been in all the time we've worked together.'

'What can I say, your devastating repartee talked me into it. You can let the CSIs rip now, I've finished. I'm calling the time as 1.37 a.m. for your log. I'll have a wee nap and start the post-mortem at two tomorrow— Sorry, *this* afternoon. You are, of course, welcome to attend with any of your minions who haven't yet seen what the inside of a dismembered body looks like. Remind them to eat their lunch afterwards, though.'

'Thank you, Dr Anstey. As ever, it is a pleasure doing business with you.'

'As it is with you, DI Christie.'

'Oh, one last question – how did it get up there? The coffin is at least nine feet off the ground.'

He glanced up at the coffin. The famous painted words on the base, written in an old-fashioned script, were now clearly visible:

Dust to dust

'I think that is for you to ascertain rather than me, but if I were a betting man, I'd say he got up there in the same way we took him down.' He tapped the stepladders.

'Wouldn't have been easy for one man.'

'But not impossible. The young man doesn't weigh very much. Anybody larger wouldn't have fitted in the coffin in the first place.'

'A sad end.'

The doctor stared down at the body as it was being zipped up into the bag and then looked all around the ruins. 'Ashes to ashes, dust to dust. Call me superstitious, Emma, but I have a bad feeling about this one. I don't think it will be our last.'

Chapter SEVEN

After Jane Eastham, the crime scene manager, had been briefed, Emma took a short break to call Hortensia, her father's carer.

'How is everything?'

'All quiet, Mrs Christie. Your father is sleeping now and I gave him his meds.'

'I hope he wasn't too much trouble.'

'He's an absolute dear. Bit of a charmer is your dad.'

Hortensia was a West Indian nurse Emma had recently discovered by putting an ad on the parish noticeboard. Once every three weeks, she looked after Emma's father when Emma was on the late shift. She'd been a bit nervous introducing them at first. Her dad was totally unpredictable with people. Sometimes he just hated them immediately without any reason, becoming aggressive and demanding. With Hortensia, however, he'd just said, 'You're black.'

Hortensia had replied, 'And you're white, Mr Christie, but I ain't complaining.'

Her father had stared at the nurse for a long time before saying, 'Call me Ted,' and the two of them had hit it off, becoming friends immediately.

Every three weeks, Hortensia took over from Mrs Lockwood, the woman that looked after her dad during the day. The service cost Emma an arm and a leg but there was nothing to be done. Davy Jones had made it clear that if she wanted to work in Major Crimes, she had to do her share of the shift work; it went with the job.

She checked her watch. 'It's two forty-five now. I should be back before you leave at six a.m., but if I'm not, just check on Dad and shut the door when you go. He doesn't like to get up before ten anyway, and Mrs Lockwood will be back in at nine.'

'Right-oh. Is there anything you want me to do before I go?'

'No, just check he's asleep. As I say, with a bit of luck I'll be back before you leave and we can have a cup of tea together.'

'Boss.' Anna Williams was standing in front of her. 'The caretaker for the building is here. We finally got him to come in.'

'Right, Anna, I'll be with you in a minute. Sorry, got to go, Hortensia.'

'See you later, Mrs Christie.'

Emma clicked off her phone. 'Right, Anna, where's this jobsworth?'

'He's here.'

A small, nondescript, mouse-like man with a brown beard and unkempt hair crept out from behind the detective constable.

'Are you the caretaker?'

'That is my position at St Johns. But I do resent being called out in the middle of the night to come down here. My wife was most upset.'

'Can't be helped, Mr…?'

'Henry. Arthur Henry.'

'Right, Mr Henry, can you tell us what time you locked up tonight?'

'Why, what's happened?' The caretaker looked over her shoulder to see the lights and activity in the ruins of the old church.

'Just answer the questions, please, Mr Henry. What time did you lock up?'

'The usual.'

Emma sighed, long and loud. It was going to be one of those sorts of interviews. 'What's the usual?'

'I lock up at the same time every night. Eight p.m. Always the same time, every day of the week, including Sundays.'

'Did you notice anything different in the church?'

'Different?'

'Unusual?'

He shook his head. 'No. I did my rounds, checking all the doors in the main church were locked before padlocking the gates.'

'Did you go into the ruins?'

'No, why would I look into that place? Nothing to lock up there.'

'You didn't see anybody hanging around? Anything out of place?'

'It was empty. It usually is at that time of night. The lights were on and all of them were working.'

'What time do they go off?'

'Exactly ten p.m. They're on a timer. We used to keep them on all night. The church and the ruins look beautiful in the small hours of the morning, but the parish decided to save money, electric being the price it is these days.'

'Tell me about it. When do the lights come on?'

'At this time of year? At seven thirty p.m. But we change the time as winter closes in.'

'And how many CCTV cameras do you have?'

'Just the two over the main doors of the church. But they're not working at the moment. Some vandal broke them a couple of nights ago. Young people these days, no respect for property…'

'Oh?'

'We caught him on tape. A man in a balaclava just walked up and smashed them with a hammer and then he cut the power cables too. We're insured, of course, but I'll never understand why people do such random acts of violence.'

'Perhaps it wasn't so random,' Emma said under her breath. 'That reminds me – Anna, can you pull all the traffic camera footage for the area and, tomorrow morning, get somebody to wander round all the shops, banks and local homes to get copies of the CCTV footage before it's deleted.'

'What are we looking for, boss?'

'I won't know till we see it.'

She turned back to face the caretaker. 'So, just to be clear, Mr Henry – you locked up at eight p.m. as usual but didn't see anything unusual around the church or in the ruins?'

'No, it was just a normal night. I did my rounds, locked the church and went straight home to the wife. The snooker was on TV.'

'What time did you get back?'

'It must have been eight thirty or so. I rode my bike home, it's much quicker than waiting for a bus.'

'Right, thank you, Mr Henry. And sorry for getting you out of bed in the middle of the night.'

'What's going on?'

'Earlier this evening, just after ten o'clock, a body was found in the ruins of the old church.'

His hand went to his mouth. 'But that can't be. I was walking around there just a couple of hours earlier. Was it the man in the balaclava? I bet it was the man in the balaclava.'

'It's far too early to speculate, Mr Henry. Thank you once again for coming in. I'll get somebody to take you home. Tomorrow, one of my officers will visit you to take a formal statement. Please give your details to DC Williams.'

'I could have been killed. What would have happened if I'd wandered in just as the man in the balaclava was committing the murder?'

The caretaker seemed to wobble slightly on his feet.

'Please take him home, Anna. It's getting late, or getting early – I never know which it is at three in the morning.'

Wednesday, October 25

Chapter EIGHT

Over the next few hours, Emma was busy with the various jobs of a senior investigating officer of a major murder inquiry.

Photographs of the body in the coffin had been shot by the police photographer as well as close-ups to aid in identification. Fingerprints were taken before the hands and head of the young man were bagged. The coroner's officer was notified that a potential homicide investigation was in progress. And finally, a Major Incident Room was set up in a spare section of the Chester Civil Justice and Family Centre building, close to St John's Church.

By seven o'clock the sun was just starting to creep up over the Chester Meadows, the Groves and the River Dee and, for the first time, Emma Christie could see the whole crime scene in the cold light of day.

She gathered her team in the Incident Room. They had been joined by three young constables from the crime task force. The log had already gone round for everybody to note down their names, ranks and telephone numbers.

'Right, this is the centre of operations for the foreseeable future. Until we have the results from the post-mortem, this is classified as a suspected homicide. I repeat, a suspected homicide. Our victim is an as-yet-unidentified male aged thirteen to fourteen. Tom, when are you handing over to the day shift?'

'It's Ron Tarrant, and he's due any minute now.'

'Make sure you brief him to keep everybody away from the crime scene, particularly the press. I don't want some nosey reporter queering our pitch.'

'Will do, boss, but it's a big area. You want to keep Vicar's Lane and Little St John Street closed? I've already had the hotel manager complaining that his guests can't get entry to the hotel.'

'Tough, they'll have to walk. The roads stay closed for the moment. You three, what are your names?'

One of them pointed to his chest. 'I'm Gleason, and that's Rowlands, and the one at the end is Rafferty, Detective Inspector Christie.'

'On my teams, we only do first names. Try again.'

'Richard, Mo and Gerry.'

'Gerry Rafferty? Your dad like his music, did he?'

'Nah, me mam,' said the young constable, in a broad Liverpool accent. 'You see, we lived on Baker Street in Speke when I was born and me mam was listening to the song all the time she was up the duff with me…'

Emma held up her hands. 'I just want your name, not your life history. Anyway, I want you two—' she pointed at Richard and Mo '—to quickly canvas the neighbourhood, see if anybody saw anything suspicious, or anything at all between nine and eleven o'clock last night.'

'Will do, Detective Inspector Christie.'

'And I'm "boss" or "guvnor" and occasionally "Emma" when I'm in a good mood. And you, Gerry Rafferty, Mr Baker Street, I want you to work with Detective Constable Anna Williams and check for CCTV. Grab a map of the area and mark the location of all the possible working cameras. Ask for the footage straight away, I don't want any fool to erase the recordings. If anybody gives you trouble, tell me.'

'Right, Detective— boss.'

Emma turned to the crime scene manager. 'Jane, when are your lads going to be finished with their work at the crime scene?'

'It's quite a big area, but we should be done by the end of the day.'

'Great. Can you check on Little St John St, particularly in front of the church and the lane between the ruins and the park? Our witness said he heard an engine starting up just before he found the body. The only places they could park would be on those roads.'

'I'll check it, boss.'

'Anna and Harry, take a break – you've been working all night and you might want to get your head down for a couple of hours. I'm off home to take a quick shower. I'd like us all to meet back here at noon for a briefing and next steps. Any questions?'

One of the young constables, Richard Gleason, put up his hand. 'Are we going to search the park, boss?'

'Not yet, we'll decide at the noon meeting.'

'What about resources?' asked Sergeant Harris.

'I had a phone call from the assistant chief constable half an hour ago. To quote him precisely, "no expense is to be spared to find the perpetrator". Does that answer your question, Tom?'

'I'll work everything out with the local nick, Emma.'

'Great. Anything else?'

'What about PR? Has anybody called them?'

'Thanks for the reminder, Anna, I'd forgotten. Can you give them a call and invite them to the noon briefing?'

'Will do, boss.'

'Right, I'll see you all back here at noon. But if anything comes up in the meantime, do not hesitate to call me. We have a particularly nasty killer out there, people, and I want him put away before anybody else disappears. Understand?'

Emma glanced at her watch. 7.25. Damn, was that the time? Hortensia will have already gone, leaving her father alone. She'd better go back and check on him.

'Tom, can you get somebody to give me a lift home? My car's at HQ.'

'Is Stewart Riggs coming back to take over the investigation?'

'I don't know, Anna, that's a decision for Davy Jones. Until we hear from our fearless leader, we are running this case and we are in charge. Is that clear?'

'Yes, boss,' came the answer from the assembled detectives.

'Right, you all know what you have to do. Let's meet at noon.'

Chapter NINE

In the squad car going home, Emma closed her eyes, going over the process she had followed since last night.

Had she missed anything?

Had she forgotten to do something which might jeopardise the investigation later?

After last time, she had to make sure there were no silly cock-ups. Davy Jones was watching her every move with his beady little eyes.

In her mind, she ticked off the boxes from the police SIO investigative manual. She'd completed the PIP II course four years ago, and it wasn't her first investigation, but still the nagging fear remained that she had forgotten something.

For the moment, she dismissed her worries. She'd check the manual before the next briefing but she thought she had laid the foundations for the investigation. Those golden hours, the short time after the discovery of a murder, was always the most important time. It had been rammed into them again and again in SIO training that any mistakes made at this time would come back to kick their arse in the future.

She opened her eyes again. It was a bright, clear October day, one of those wonderful days when summer had to be dragged kicking and screaming out of the way of autumn.

They were getting close to her dad's home. She still called it his, even though she had been living there for three years, ever since her partner, Colin, had passed away in the car crash. She had moved back into the large semi-detached house, bought when Dad was promoted to inspector back in the eighties. A place where she'd grown up and had loved. A place of safety.

They turned right off Stocks Lane and immediately were faced with a large, bright red fire engine parked outside the house. Before the police car had properly stopped, she had the door open and jumped out, running towards her home.

'Dad, Dad…'

A group of firefighters dressed in their yellow and black uniforms were milling about. She ran past them and up the driveway, still shouting, 'Dad, Dad…'

Just as she was about to enter the house, a firefighter came out, blocking the door.

'You can't go in there, love, not till we've checked it over.'

'But Dad, he—'

'Your dad's okay, he's just having a mug of tea.' He pointed back towards the group of firefighters. At the centre was her father, standing out because of his height and the baldness of his head.

The breath went out of her like a punctured balloon. 'What happened?'

'Somebody left toast under the grill. Luckily, the postie saw smoke coming out of the kitchen and called it in. We found your dad sitting in front of the TV watching *Teletubbies*, oblivious to the smoke and the smell.'

'Is he okay?'

'From the fire? He's fine, but your kitchen needs a bit of work.' He stepped out of the way and she looked into the kitchen. A brown scorch mark crawled up the wall from the grill, and the ceiling was covered in an ebony-black soot. The metal of the hob and grill had melted from the heat. Everything was covered in a fine white powder from the extinguishers used to put out the fire.

'You're lucky the postie spotted it. Another ten minutes and you'd have lost the house… and your dad.' He wiped a small spot of soot off his face. 'Is he okay? Your dad, I mean.'

'Alzheimer's. Sometimes he forgets.'

'It's not my place to say, but shouldn't he be in a home?'

'He won't go, won't leave the house. He has a carer who comes in at nine and normally I'm around, but I had to work late last night.'

'I'll have to make a report on the Incident Recording System. Are you insured?'

Emma nodded absent-mindedly as she stared at the damage to the kitchen.

'The report will be sent to the police and the council. They'll decide if your father is a risk to himself and others.'

'I am police. He was too.'

The fire officer glanced back to her dad, still chatting away to the other members of the team. 'Sorry, still have to send it in. Can you give me your details? Are you the owner of the house?'

'No, my dad is.'

After answering all the officer's questions, Emma went to fetch her dad from amongst the firefighters.

'Come on inside, Dad, you'll catch your death of cold.'

Her father was wearing a thin white vest and his striped pyjama bottoms.

'Won't be a minute, lass, I'm just telling them about the time we arrested that bloke at the top of Snowdon for nicking a bike. Somehow, he had ridden to the top wearing nothing but his trainers…'

'Come away now, Dad. These lads have to go.'

She took his elbow, feeling the sharpness of the bone beneath the thin, paper-like skin, and nudged him towards the door.

'Thanks for coming, lads, see you again soon,' he shouted over his shoulder.

'I hope not, Dad.'

They stepped across the threshold through the open front door. As soon as she went in, she could smell the stark, acrid stench of smoke and burning.

'What happened here, love?' her dad asked.

'You tell me?'

He shrugged his shoulders. 'I was watching telly like I usually do. Suddenly the room was full of blokes telling me I had to get out. They were good blokes, though. Gave me a mug of tea, three sugars, just how I like it.'

'There was a fire in the kitchen, Dad.'

'Was there? I always said you needed to check the electrics, didn't I?'

Emma closed her eyes and took three deep breaths. There was no point in explaining to him what had happened; he wouldn't remember anyway. She took him inside, sat him down in his usual place on the couch, and switched on the telly.

'Good, it's time for *Good Morning Britain*.'

Despite forgetting everything else, including *her* sometimes, he still remembered the complete TV schedule.

'Any chance of a cup of tea and some toast? I'm starving.'

Chapter TEN

After saying goodbye to the fire officers, Emma sat with her dad watching *GMB*.

Most of the time, it was as if she wasn't there; his attention was totally focused on the television, like a drowning man clinging to a life jacket.

When Mrs Lockwood arrived, she took one look at the kitchen and said, 'He's been trying to cook again, hasn't he?'

'Forgot he left the grill on. We had the firemen round this morning.'

'How am I going to make his lunch?'

'Order a takeaway for both of you. He likes a curry now and then but nothing too hot or he'll be up all night complaining. I'll call the gas and electric people and get them to check the appliances. Don't use them till it's safe. The electrics in the rest of the house are okay, though, but I wouldn't use them in the kitchen.'

'Right. You want me to tidy up a bit?'

'If you could, I need to go back to work again at eleven to prep for the meeting at noon.'

Mrs Lockwood was a no-nonsense practical woman who lived on the next street. With a lifetime working in the NHS as a nurse, nothing fazed her, not even Ted's desire sometimes to take off all his clothes and wander around the house naked. 'I've seen them all, and his is nothing to write home about,' was how she put it.

Occasionally, Emma's father acknowledged Mrs Lockwood's presence, but most times he ignored her, accepting the lunches she served him as a God-given right.

Emma called the gas supplier and explained about the fire and the fact that a vulnerable adult lived on the premises. 'So when can you come round to check it?'

'As soon as we can,' said the disembodied voice with an unmistakable Indian accent from the call centre, presumably located somewhere on the sub-continent. 'I've logged the issue on the server and put a note about the presence of a vulnerable adult.'

'But when can you come round?'

'Just as soon as we can.'

'Is that today, tomorrow or some time in the next decade?'

'A gas engineer will call you with a time.'

'When will he call?'

'Just as soon as he can.'

Emma felt the conversation was going round in circles and could see no point continuing. She left her mobile number and rang off.

'They'll come when they can.'

Mrs Lockwood nodded. 'It might be better to get somebody private. Do you want me to find someone?'

Emma sighed. 'But I pay them over thirty quid a month insurance.'

Mrs Lockwood stared at her.

'Oh, go ahead. Try and get it done today. I'm going to take a shower and then head off to work.'

'Are you on that poor boy's case?'

Emma stopped. 'What have you heard?'

'Just that a young boy's body was found in the ruins near St John's Church with his eyes missing.'

It was amazing how nothing remained secret in a place like Chester. The concrete jungle drums had been incredibly quick at spreading the news this time.

'Anything else?'

'Not much,' replied Mrs Lockwood in her sing-song Welsh lilt, 'but he was strangled, apparently.'

'How do you know?'

'I can't remember. I think it was Mrs Evans in the bakery who mentioned it. Said not to go anywhere near the amphitheatre as the roads had been cordoned off.'

Shaking her head, Emma trudged upstairs to take her shower. Chester wasn't really a city, just a big village where everybody knew everything.

She took off her clothes in the bathroom, checking herself out in the mirror. 'Time to go on a diet again,' she said, grabbing a roll of fat from around her waist.

She hated diets, hated being on a diet, hated the thought of being on a diet, but it seemed that for the last three years she had been permanently watching all the food she ate. If she didn't, her weight rose like a hot-air balloon. And if she did, her weight still increased. She had only to look at food to feel the pounds attach themselves to her hips.

She remembered Colin used to love her curves. When she was with him was the only time she was comfortable with her body and, guess what, that was when she actually lost weight.

Go figure.

She switched on the water, sticking her fingers beneath it to check the temperature.

Freezing.

She brushed her teeth and checked again.

Still cold.

Damn. Dad must have buggered up the boiler too. Just what she didn't need. She stepped under the freezing water, feeling her skin shrivel with the cold.

As the water goose-pimpled her arms, she heard her mobile ringing. 'Who the bloody hell is it now?'

She stepped out of the cold shower and ran naked across the bathroom to answer the phone without looking at the caller's name. 'Yes, what is it?'

There was no reply for a couple of seconds before Emma heard DCI Davy Jones' dulcet tones. 'Have I caught you at an inopportune time, DI Christie?'

'Not at all, sir,' answered Emma, frantically searching around for a towel to cover her nakedness. 'How can I help you?'

'The investigation, how is it?'

'All good, sir. CSIs are still at the scene and we are canvassing witnesses and checking CCTV in the area.'

'Good. I hear you have closed the main road in front of the church.'

'We need to check it, sir.'

'It is a *main* road, DI Christie…'

'I am aware, sir, but the killer's car may have been parked there before the incident. I'd like the CSIs to check it thoroughly before opening it again.'

'Hmmm,' was the only response before the DCI changed the subject. 'It appears DI Riggs is still on his course in Warrington so you will be in charge of this inquiry for the foreseeable future. I don't need to emphasise to you the importance of this investigation for the reputation of the City of Chester Constabulary. The chief is watching our every move…'

'I do understand, sir.'

'I hope you do, DI Christie. Anyway, good luck.'

The phone went dead in her hand and the towel draped over her body fell to the floor.

Emma stood naked in the middle of the bathroom. 'Good luck to you too, you old weasel…'

Chapter ELEVEN

'Right, you lot, gather round.'

Emma was back in the Major Incident Room. John Simpson had arranged the chairs around a series of panels. He had also Blu-Tacked a map of the surrounding area on one of the boards next to a blown-up picture of the face of the dead boy, a full-length picture of him in the coffin on the wall and another close-up of the sign around his neck.

Emma felt that inevitable frisson of energy down her spine as she clapped her hands and shouted, 'Come on, hurry up – we haven't got all day.'

All the people from this morning were there, plus a woman taking notes on the far right and two detectives she knew by sight from Stewart Riggs' team.

'What are you two doing here?' she asked them.

'Assigned by Chief Inspector Jones, guvnor.'

'Does Riggs know?'

One of the two detectives answered. 'He's on a course in Warrington at the moment—'

'But you rang him anyway. My bet is he wasn't chuffed.'

The detective didn't answer, which confirmed her suspicions. 'Well, don't hang around – introduce yourself to the team.'

The older one spoke first. 'DC Robbie Dewar.' Followed by his younger, spottier colleague.

'DC Alan Holt. I'm just out of training, this is my first week on the job.'

Emma pointed to the woman scribbling in her notebook. 'You must be from Public Relations.'

The woman smiled the whitest smile Emma had ever seen. A perfect advertisement for the orthodontic skills of private dentists. Either that or the tooth fairy had never visited the woman's home. 'Penny Morgan, Force PR.' she announced.

'Hi there, Penny, we'll have to create a press release after this meeting. News of the boy's death has already reached the tom-toms of Chester.'

Penny held up a sheet of paper. 'I've already taken the trouble of crafting an announcement to the press. If you're okay with it, I'll release the news. We have to give the wolves something otherwise they'll start using their imaginations. Always a danger for any journalist.'

Emma took an immediate liking to the woman. She seemed efficient and was imbued with a professional cynicism which suggested she knew what she was doing.

'Welcome to the team. As you may or may not know, the body of an unknown male—' she tapped the picture of the boy '—was found in the ruins of the south-east chapel of St John's Church last night. His eyes had been removed and a notice hung round his neck. The pathologist stated the cause of death was strangulation but he will confirm at the post-mortem this afternoon.' She pointed to the constables sitting on the front row. 'You two were supposed to do a door-to-door. Anything?'

The PCs from this morning sat up straight. 'Not a lot, boss. Most of the area is offices and very few houses. All the people we did talk to heard nothing and saw less. But there are still a few offices we haven't been to yet.'

'You canvassed down to the Groves?'

'Yes, boss, nobody saw anything.'

'It doesn't surprise me. After six, when the tourists are no longer visiting the amphitheatre, this area is pretty quiet. Did you check the pubs and cafés at the Groves?'

One of the constables checked his notes. 'The cafés close between five and five thirty every night. The Boathouse was busy. We requested the CCTV from the bar area but the manager said it was just a normal night. He didn't notice anything different.'

'Any guests staying at the Boathouse?'

'Just two couples, both in their seventies, tourists from Wolverhampton. Apparently they went to bed at nine thirty, didn't hear or see anything.'

'Finish off the other offices and set up a table in the amphitheatre and along the river, asking if people saw anything suspicious yesterday.'

'I can help you with that. We have the materials back at police HQ,' piped up Penny.

'Good. And you...' She pointed at the fresh-faced constable in the front row. Why were all the coppers looking so young these days? Or was it her who was just getting old? 'You were supposed to check all the CCTV in the area.'

Gerry Rafferty stood up, unfolded a sheet of paper and began to Blu-Tack it on to one of the boards. 'I walked around the area, spotting the various sites of the cameras. I've marked them on this map, plus showed the angle they were pointing to. Of course, this doesn't include internal cameras or cameras in cars that may have been in the area.'

He stepped back to look at his handiwork. The map had seven round circles on it, each with an angle of view.

'The camera on the bus shelter may give us the best view of the road and the traffic passing along it. There are two cameras in the sunken amphitheatre but both are facing inwards and, as they are below the ground level, I'm not expecting anything from them. Two more here at the family law centre. I've checked them out. One is focused on the car park and the other wasn't working. Plus the two traffic cameras mounted above the traffic lights on Vicar's Lane. There could be others in the law offices, an architect firm and an auctioneers along the road, but I'm not too hopeful of anything. The foliage of the park hides the ruins from view. I've requested the footage from the traffic centre and the bus company.'

'Well done, Gerry, you achieved a lot in a couple of hours. As soon as that footage comes in, I want you to go through it starting from nine p.m. to eleven p.m. last night.'

'You don't want to go wider, boss?' asked Anna Williams.

'Not right now. Just check out those times, Gerry, and get back to me when you have it loaded up on a laptop. Talking of IT support, how are we doing, John?'

'The techies should have everything set up by this afternoon, Emma – phone lines, computers, the lot.'

Just as the civilian researcher had finished speaking, a burly sergeant knocked and entered to give Harry Fairweather a message.

He was about to hand it to the detective when he stopped and pointed to the picture of the boy on the board. 'What's he doing there?'

Chapter TWELVE

They were all dirt.

Defiling the city, spreading their disease, filling every nook and cranny with their filth, polluting the place he loved.

Nowhere was free.

Nowhere was clean.

It was all soiled, dirty, grimy, grubby.

Drugs sold openly on the streets. Pornography displayed so that even innocent children could see it. Lewd drunkenness staggering through the city's streets every evening. Immorality everywhere.

He remembered growing up in the city.

Nobody locked their doors.

Neighbours knew each other.

People said hello in the morning.

Life was clear and clean and Christian.

Not any more.

They had destroyed this beautiful place. This city he loved, with its long history.

Romans.

Saxons.

Normans.

Tudors.

Georgians.

Victorians.

Edwardians.

All had left their mark on the place, all leaving it better than they had found it.

Until today.

People these days thought only of themselves. Their television. Their holidays in Ibiza. Their designer clothes. Their curries. Their ugly tattoos. Their beer and wine. Their wanton women. Their fun and games.

Hatred everywhere, no love any more, no community.

The pandemic had been the beginning, but it had taken the wrong people; the old who had done no wrong. It had left those who had caused all the problems still in place.

They had despoiled the place and themselves.

It couldn't continue. He wouldn't let it.

The place had to be purged, cleansed of the evil that now pervaded it.

They were a boil that had to be lanced, and he was the steel that would do it.

It was his job, his God-given vocation.

His job and his alone.

Chapter THIRTEEN

Emma Christie stopped what she was doing and faced the sergeant. 'What did you say?'

'Him. What's he doing on the board?'

'He's our victim. You know him?'

'Not really, but I've seen him around.'

'Where?'

'Outside the clubs. We always thought he was dealing, probably coke and Es for the luvved-up clubbers. I searched him a couple of times but found nothing on him. Far too smart to be caught with the stuff.'

'Did you get a name? An address?'

'Nah, like I said, I never pulled him in, just moved him on. The desk sergeant down at the Town Hall nick might remember him though. Paul Tunney remembers everybody who's been through his doors, even if they only got a caution. I don't know if he's on duty now though.'

'Harry?'

'Yes, boss?'

'Get on to Paul Tunney. See if he remembers this lad.'

Harry Fairweather pulled out his mobile phone and began making a call. 'On it, boss.'

Emma turned back to the sergeant. 'Anything you remember about him? Was he from Chester?'

'I dunno. I'd see him outside the clubs for a couple of weeks, then he'd disappear for a month or so before coming back.'

'Anything, Harry?'

Harry held his hand up and listened to somebody speaking on the other end of the phone. 'We'll email you a picture of the vic, if you can check it out, Paul. Thanks for your help, mate.'

He switched off his phone.

'He thinks somebody with our vic's description was brought in about a year ago. Suspicion of dealing. He wasn't charged though, just let off with a caution. This young man stuck in Paul Tunney's head because even though he was only fifteen he somehow managed to get his own solicitor to come and get him out at two in the morning.'

'Did he get a name and an address?'

'Just let me send him a picture of our vic and he'll find the arrest report.'

'Good work. Get on it, Harry – the sooner we ID the vic, the better.'

For the first time, Emma felt they were making progress on the case. 'Right, where was I?' She pointed at the two young PCs. 'You two are going to finish the canvass of the area and Gerry is getting the CCTV. Anything from the CSIs, Jane?'

The crime scene manager stood up. 'We've nearly finished with the scene. No fingerprints or DNA on the sign board around the vic's neck. Nothing on his clothes either. It also looks like the hands and nails had been cleaned and scrubbed. The pathologist might find something but somehow I doubt it. Whoever did this is forensically savvy, Emma.'

'Isn't everybody these days?'

'Plus, the ruins have so many visitors each day, it's difficult knowing who left what behind. So far we've found three cigarette butts, two crisp packets, an old can of Fanta and a used condom, all in the area around the walls. I don't think any of them have a link to our perp though.'

'Check them out anyway, Jane.'

Anna Williams put her hand up. 'Are we going to search the park, boss?'

'Not yet. All we're going to get is more stuff like Jane found. If our perp is forensically smart, he won't have dropped anything at the scene.'

Anna checked her notes. 'What about the two other boys? Daniel said he was with two other boys in the park – Kev and Big Dave. Do you want me to go and interview them? Confirm Daniel's story?'

'I'd forgotten about those two. Yeah, go and see them asap, Anna. Plus, can you arrange for Daniel and his mother to come in to give a formal statement?'

'Will do, boss. Here or at HQ?'

'HQ would be better. It's closer to their home and I don't want the young lad to come here again if he can avoid it.'

'I'll arrange it, boss.'

'Right, anything else I've forgotten? Come on, speak up – we're a team and I can't remember everything.'

Penny waved her sheet of paper. 'The press release. I've already had three journalists ring me during this briefing; the pack can smell a juicy story.'

'I'll take a look.' Emma scanned the short press release. 'It's good, Penny, but can you make the contact person yourself or Chief Inspector Jones. I don't want to spend my life handling calls from the press.'

'Done, DI Christie.'

'One last thing, John – can you get on HOLMES and see if there are any other similar crimes on the Home Office computers?'

'What are the search parameters, boss?'

'Murders of children. Bodies on display. You'll think of a few others.'

'For the North or nationwide, boss?'

'Start with the North and then expand. And while you're at it, John, check the missing persons' files for any kids in the Chester area recently.'

'On it, boss.'

Harry rushed back into the room. 'We've got a name and an address for the vic.'

Chapter FOURTEEN

Gavin Newton checked his image in the shop window. A handsome man stared back at him.

Dressing that morning, he had aimed for a cross between Robert Redford playing Bob Woodward in *All the President's Men* and Mark Ruffalo in *Spotlight*.

Casual but professional. Stylish but responsive. Sharp but approachable. The look of an ace reporter without the five o'clock shadow and the hangover.

He thought he pulled it off rather well. The sandy corduroy jacket was a particularly nice touch. It didn't keep him warm though, and he began to shiver in the cool of an October day as the wind whistled down past Eastgate and rushed between the Rows.

This was his beat, the streets of Chester. He knew most of them like the back of his hand despite having only moved here just over a year ago. He'd gone to a red-brick university and acquired a very ordinary 2:2. Luckily, his mum knew the owner of the *Chester Daily* through her bridge club.

The pay was meagre, the prospects appalling, the hours horrendous but, for some reason, Gavin loved this job. And he knew, if he played his cards right, it could lead to bigger and much better things.

The point, as his mother had said so often when he was a child, was to play his cards right. She was a bridge player after all.

His phone rang. 'Gavin Newton, reporter on the *Chester Daily*, how can I help you?' He always answered the phone in this zealous tone. It made the punters think he was full of energy and vim. A go-getter on his way up, not a been-there-done-that man like the editor.

'I've got something for you, but it'll cost two hundred quid.'

It was his source in the police. 'The usual cost is fifty.'

'But this is special. A murder last night. A young boy. You could make your name with this one.'

Gavin's ears instantly pricked up. 'Go on...'

'The price is agreed?'

Gavin ummed and aahed. Would his editor cough up the money? Probably not. The man was ex-Fleet Street who had somehow ended up in Chester when he was too old to work the desks at one of the national newspapers. The last time this happened he had even been reluctant to give out fifty quid. He remembered their conversation in perfect detail.

'We're not made of money, you know. You may not have heard, Gavin me lad, but newspapers are suffering at the moment. Revenues down, costs up. And then we're being fucked daily by the internet. Anyone with a bloody phone is a reporter these days.'

'But you said yourself, boss, there are only three things that sell papers: sex, football and crime. And I've got a tip-off from an impeccable source. It's about the attacks on those pensioners.'

The editor sat forward. 'Pensioners are always good copy. They're the only people who actually still believe the crap we write.'

'It's an unimpeachable source, boss, right from the horse's mouth.'

'Right, Gavin. Fifty quid it is, but it had better be good.'

He'd finally coughed up the money and Gavin had his scoop with a byline on the front page.

The voice came through his mobile again.

'Well, do you want the tip or not? I'm sure another reporter would be interested, might even pay five hundred quid for it, the info is so good.'

Gavin had to make a decision.

Front up the money himself, write the story and then invoice the paper, or let it go by, with somebody else getting the glory?

He made one last attempt to bargain. 'How about a hundred quid? The rest after the story is published.'

He held his breath, waiting for the reply.

Silence at the other end of the phone before he heard, 'You're in luck, Gavin, I need the money. Meet at the usual place?'

Gavin breathed out. 'Yeah, what time?'

'Let's say three o'clock. There'll be a news conference at six tonight. You'll want to be up-to-date before then. This one's a biggie, young Gavin, it could make your name.'

The phone went dead in his hand.

'A hundred quid,' he whispered to himself. Where was he going to find that sort of money before this afternoon?

His credit cards were already maxed out. His bank account covered in minus numbers. Even his overdraft was overdrawn.

He thought of his erstwhile girlfriend. She had money saved, didn't she?

The woman bored the arse off him, but she was occasionally useful for a shag on a quiet Sunday afternoon when he hadn't picked up anything on the Saturday night before.

'Justine, it's Gavin here, how are you, love? Hey, I'd love you to do me a tiny favour, are you free for a coffee right now…?'

He used his little boy voice. She always fell for the voice.

'Great, see you in twenty minutes. Love you.'

Gavin felt pleased with himself. There was something in this story, he could feel it in his water. He took one last look in the shop window.

Robert Redford, eat your heart out.

Chapter FIFTEEN

'Mark Sinton was arrested but not charged with dealing coke and ecstasy in April this year. He gave his age as fifteen.'

'And the address?'

'23 Bolton Road, near the university.'

'Why wasn't he charged?'

'Dunno, boss. The desk sergeant at Central Nick, Paul Tunney, thought there was a good case for dealing, or at least possession, but then the order came down from above to let him go with a caution. A brief had turned up pretty quickly and there were some problems with the search, so maybe it was more trouble than it was worth. He remembers the lad well because of the small scar on his hairline. Said he was cocky all the time, like he knew he was going to get off easily, he was joking and laughing like it was no big deal.'

'Right, grab your coat, Harry – we're off to check out this place. Everybody else, you know what you're doing?'

There was a mumble of grunts and yesses.

'That's what I like to see; enthusiasm from the troops,' she said with heavy sarcasm. 'Listen up, bonny people – I want more energy from you lot. At the moment, I've seen more enthusiasm in a busload of zombies on a school trip to Rhyl. Got it?'

This time the responses were quicker and louder.

'We're back here at six tonight for a quick debrief. I want to see progress by then, understand?'

'Yes, boss,' came the quick response.

'Better. See you at six.'

She turned to her detective constable. 'There you go, Harry. All they needed was a bit of gentle encouragement. You can wipe the smile off your face and bring round the car, I'm not walking all the way there – the legs wouldn't take me that far.'

Harry drove quickly down St Oswalds Way, lights flashing, but in deference to his boss, the siren silent as a thief in the night.

The university had been carved out of an old Victorian area and, like all such districts the length and breadth of Britain, had now been invaded by bed-sits and rentals, populated with a dishevelled cohort of students, druggies and ne'er-do-wells.

'This used to be my patch, boss.'

'What's Bolton Road like?'

'The same as the rest of the area. Full of transients. Most of the old houses have been sub-divided and let. Not the most pleasant place on earth. You want to me to arrange a squad car to stand by?'

'Better have one, just in case. But, Harry, we'll play this softly, softly. Did the arrest sheet say who he was living with?'

'Not a lot, boss, just gave the address.'

'No parental names? He was only fifteen, a minor.'

'The solicitor signed in as *in loco parentis*, boss.'

'Strange. And we didn't get any details from Mark Sinton himself?'

'According to Paul Tunney, he refused to answer any questions till his brief turned up.'

Harry spoke on the radio, requesting backup at 23 Bolton Road. When he finished, he turned the car right at a fried chicken takeaway, on to a long street with Victorian terraced houses on either side, many with a small blue sign announcing that they were to let.

'It's up on the left, boss. You want to wait for backup?'

'Nah, let's have a chat first.'

They stopped outside one of the houses, smaller than the rest. In the tiny front garden, a rusting pram held an old bag of rubbish, while two overflowing bins stood guard like errant sentries on either side of the entrance.

'Not a great place for any child to grow up, is it, Harry?'

In the absence of a door-bell or a knocker, Emma banged on the unpainted door with her bare fist. 'Open up, police. Anybody at home?'

The post flap of the door squeaked open and a pair of disembodied children's eyes looked out. 'Mam and Dad are sleeping.'

'It's the police, son. Can you open up? We'd like to ask your mam and dad some questions.'

The flap in the door closed and Emma heard the sound of little feet running upstairs.

A squad car coasted to a stop behind their vehicle.

'Hi, Harry, you called for backup,' an old, well-built copper shouted through the open window.

'Hi, Darren, that's us. You been here before?'

'A couple of times. Neighbours complaining about noise. Usual stuff.'

'Can you check round the back in the alley? I have a feeling this one is going to do a runner,' answered Harry.

The squad car reversed back down the street, the noise of its engine echoing off the brick walls.

As it did, a dishevelled woman opened the door slightly, popping her head around the edge.

'What you want?'

A small child hung on to his mother's housecoat. Obviously the same small child who had peeped through the letterbox earlier.

'DI Emma Christie of City of Chester Constabulary.'
She flashed her warrant card. 'And this is DC Harry
Fairweather.'

Before she could say any more, the woman barked at the
small child, 'I told you never to answer the door to nobody.'
The small child flinched as she raised her hand, retreating
back inside out of sight.

'Can we come in? We'd like to ask you a few questions.'

The door opened slightly wider and the woman pulled
her housecoat around her thin body. 'What's it about?'

'Can we come in? It's a bit cold standing out here.'

'No, what's it about?'

Emma rolled her eyes. It was going to be one of those
interviews. 'It's about Mark Sinton.'

'Never heard of him,' the woman answered quickly, a
little too quickly.

'Are you sure? You see, he gave this address as his home
only six months ago.'

'Never heard of him.'

'So the name Mark Sinton means nothing to you?'

The woman crossed her arms in front of her chest. 'Like
I said, never heard of him.'

From the back of the house came a few shouts and the
sound of a short struggle.

'You need any help, Darren?' shouted Harry
Fairweather.

After a few seconds, a thin, unkempt man dressed in a
white vest and shorts appeared in the hallway being pushed
in the back by the burly copper.

'You were right, Harry, this one tried to nip over the
back wall. Had a bag full of this with him.' The copper held
out a small plastic bag with about twenty blue vials in it.

'You idiot,' the woman shouted. 'Why didn't you leave
it?'

The man looked sheepish but didn't say a word.

'Looks like crack, Darren,' said Harry.

'I'd say so too. Enough for a dealing charge.'

'Now, can we come in and ask a few questions, or do I have to take you and your... partner... down to the nick and we'll ask there?'

The woman stood aside, still scowling at the man, shaking her head.

They stepped inside, avoiding the bike parked in the hallway. The house was suffused with cigarette smoke, full ashtrays lay on every available surface alongside empty cans of lager.

The woman led them into the kitchen, sitting down at a table still covered with the detritus of last night's meal; a host of plastic trays covered in half-eaten curry and rice. The child was nowhere to be seen.

Emma took out her foolscap notebook and cleared a small area on the table. She wrote the date, time, and location at the top in neat block letters, before looking up. 'Your name?'

'Tracy Cummings.'

'And your partner?'

The man was still being held tightly by the copper. He remained standing in the doorway like an errant child reluctant to see a headmaster.

'Ian McNicol.'

'And the child?'

'He's mine, but Ian's not the father. He's from a previous relationship,' she added, brushing her hair away from her eyes and pulling the housecoat more tightly across her chest.

'Where is he?'

'My kid or my ex-partner?'

Emma rolled her eyes.

'The boy is in his bedroom on his PlayStation. My ex-partner, I haven't a clue, but good riddance is all I'll say about him.'

Emma motioned with her eyes to Harry to check on the child. 'I'll ask you one more time, do you know a Mark Sinton?'

This time the woman nodded. 'He stays here occasionally.'

'How often?'

'About once a month, he comes here and stays for a week before going off again.'

Emma frowned. Was this a fifteen-year-old boy they were talking about? 'Where does he go when he's not here?'

The woman shrugged her shoulders. 'I dunno.'

'You never asked him?'

'Why should I? None of my business where he goes.'

'He doesn't go to school?'

She laughed roughly. 'You're joking, ain't you? That one don't need no school.'

'What do you mean?'

'He's smart, that one. Sharp as a nail.' She looked around at the assembled coppers. 'Why are you asking me all these questions about Mark? What's he done?'

Emma was deliberately blunt. 'He's dead.'

'What?'

'We found his body last night. He'd been strangled.'

The woman nodded, trying to take it all in. Harry returned to the kitchen, giving the thumbs-up sign. 'The child's in his room, boss, on his PlayStation. Nice kid's room. And he could beat me easily on Gran Turismo.'

'The way you drive, I'm not surprised, Harry.'

'I look after Mattie, make sure he gets everything he wants,' Tracy interjected.

Emma focused back on the woman in front of her, sensing a weakness. 'If you love your child, how could you let him live in a place like this?'

The woman glanced up quickly at Ian McNicol. For a second the hardness in her eyes was gone and, in its place, fear.

'You can answer that later. How did you get to know Mark Sinton?'

'Like I said, he used to stay here.'

'But how did he arrange that?'

'He just used to turn up.'

'And you'd let him stay, just like that? Did he pay you rent?'

The woman stayed silent, quickly looking to her partner and at the bag of drugs in the burly copper's large paw.

Emma followed the eyes. 'He paid you in drugs, that's why you let him stay?'

'Don't say any more, Tracy.' McNicol spoke for the first time in a high, squeaky voice.

'I asked you if he paid you in drugs to let him stay here?'

The woman looked away extravagantly, refusing to speak.

Emma sighed slowly. 'Caution them both, will you, Harry.'

'What's the charge, boss?'

'Possession with intent to supply.'

'Tracy Cummings and Ian McNicol, you are both being charged with the possession and intent to supply Class A drugs. You do not have to say anything. But it may harm your defence if you do not mention when questioned something which you later rely on in court. Anything you do say may be given in evidence against you. Cuff them, Darren.'

'And, Harry, get on to child services – somebody has to look after the boy.'

'No, you can't take my child away, I won't let you,' Tracy said.

'Listen, there is drug dealing and probable drug use going on in this house. It's not a safe environment for a child.'

'Drugs are not taken here, I don't allow it,' Tracy uttered.

Emma noticed she didn't deny drug dealing. 'So I'll ask one more time. Does Mark Sinton pay you in drugs?'

'Don't tell the fat witch anything, Tracy,' shouted McNicol.

Emma shook her head. 'Stick him in the back of your car, Darren, and caution him again.'

Darren manhandled the thin man out of the room. All the time he was shouting, 'Don't say a word, Tracy.'

The noises continued down the hallway as he was taken to the squad car.

When it had all quietened down, Emma asked again in a quiet voice, 'Tell me all about it, love.'

All the fight had left the woman now; her head was down and her fingers played with the button of her housecoat.

'He'll batter me if I say anything.'

'He's hit you before?'

Tracy nodded.

'It's time to get out. Do you want me to ring the women's shelter? This is not the right place for a young kid. And don't worry, he won't be going anywhere for the next couple of days.' A slight pause. 'Tell me about Mark Sinton?'

'Not much to tell, he kept himself to himself when he stayed here.'

'He paid Ian in drugs?'

The woman nodded her head. 'He needed somewhere to stay.'

'Where did he go when he wasn't here?'

'I really dunno, he never said.'

'Where do you think he went?'

'To Liverpool, I think. He'd be here for a week, maybe ten days, then he vanished, turning up again about three weeks later...'

'With a fresh supply of drugs?'

'Coke, Es, crack, whatever people wanted, Mark could get.'

'Who was his supplier?'

'I dunno. Somebody in Liverpool, I think.'

'Do you have any pictures of him?'

The woman shook her head vigorously. 'Mark didn't like having his picture taken, wouldn't allow it.'

'How old was he?'

'Fifteen, I think.'

'How long had he been coming here?'

'At least a year. He came and stayed for a couple of months the first time.'

'He knew Ian before?'

'I don't think so.'

'So how was the stay arranged?'

The woman shrugged her shoulders. 'I dunno.'

'You didn't ask?'

'Didn't want to get belted.'

'When was the last time you saw Mark?'

She thought for a moment. 'A couple of days ago.'

'You didn't see him more recently?'

She shook her head. 'Him and Ian had a falling out.'

'Let me guess – Ian wanted to increase the rent?'

'How did you know?'

'There's nothing so greedy as a junkie with a bad habit. Exactly when was the last time you saw him?'

'Sunday at four p.m., I remember the time because I had to take Mattie to the shops, he wanted a new game for his PlayStation. Mark gave me some money for the game, he was good like that was Mark, generous.'

'So he left at four p.m.?'

'Give or take five minutes. Had his clothes with him. Said he had a meeting and then he was going home and wouldn't be back.'

'Did he say who he was meeting?'

She shook her head.

'Or where was home?'

'Like I said, Mark didn't talk much about himself.'

'How did he get around the city?'

'He used his bike most of the time, or the bus.'

'It's his bike in the hallway?'

'Yeah, that's Mark's.'

'So, if he left his bike here, he must have been coming back despite the row with your partner.'

She shrugged her shoulders. 'I guess so, I never thought about it.'

Throughout this time, Emma had been writing notes in her large black ledger. She closed it and stood up. 'You'd better pack your kiddie's things, I'll ring the women's shelter and see if they have a place.'

'He won't know where I am?'

'I'll make sure he stays away from you. And from the amount of crack he had on him, he won't be coming back here for a long, long time.'

She nodded uncertainly.

'One last thing, did Mark Sinton have a phone?'

'Yeah, one of those throwaway ones.'

'A burner?'

'He bought them from the local petrol stations.'

'Which one?'

'He didn't say, just bought them from there. Like I said, he didn't talk much, Mark, kept himself to himself most of the time.'

'Do you have the number of his phone?'

She shook her head. 'He changed it all the time.'

'How did people order drugs from him?'

'Snapchat. People sent him a message and he delivered whatever they wanted. He also used to hang around the clubs. Deal with the punters direct.'

'And you haven't seen him for two days?'

She shook her head.

'What was his handle on Snapchat?'

'Danny Ds, I think.'

Emma opened her ledger again and wrote it all down. 'Right then, start packing your stuff. I'll arrange the woman's shelter and somebody will pick you up this afternoon.'

'Ian won't know where we are?'

'He won't know. But a word of advice, love – the Ians of this world are users. They'll stay as long as there's a warm bed to sleep in and a woman to wait on them. If you really care about your kid, you'll make sure you never see Ian again.'

The woman nodded. 'I know, but he's not always bad. When he's not using, he can be really lovely, caring.'

'Take it from me, love. I've seen thousands of Ians in my time. If they are not using drugs, they are using you. For your kid's sake, you'd best give him up.'

The woman nodded but didn't say anything.

Emma knew then that Ian would be back with her within the next few days, and she'd be back with bruises within the week.

Sometimes, people just didn't want to be helped.

It wouldn't stop her though. She'd keep trying until Tracy realised the truth.

Never give up. It was another thing her dad had taught her.

Chapter SIXTEEN

After briefing Darren to book Ian McNicol with possession with intent to supply, Harry drove Emma back to the Incident Room.

'You're quiet, boss.'

'Thinking, Harry.'

'A penny for them.'

'That's all my thoughts are worth? What about inflation?'

'Okay, a couple of quid then. Can't go any higher though , the missus has set her heart on going to Spain for Christmas.'

'Costa del Sol?'

'Costa del Loadsamoney. Looks like everybody wants to go on holiday this year.'

'Not surprising, after being cooped up during the pandemic and England being like it is, everybody wants to get away.'

Emma thought back to her own time with her father. She had worked throughout the pandemic, all the police had. With the news of the number of deaths of vulnerable old people in nursing homes, she had been so glad she had decided to keep him at home. Seeing the news on television of families unable to say goodbye to their loved ones was heart-breaking. She couldn't imagine how painful the whole experience must have been.

Luckily, Mrs Lockwood had kept coming in every day she was at work, looking after her dad and making sure he was well fed. But her days off were stressful. Looking after her dad wasn't easy.

'I was thinking,' she finally answered. 'A young lad, probably going to Liverpool every couple of weeks, could only be one thing.'

'County lines trafficking. The drug gangs expanding their territories to smaller cities and towns using young people as their couriers and mules.'

'Got it in one, Harry.'

'But why kill him?'

'That's the question, Harry. Did he double-cross his gang? Did he nick some drugs and had to be made an example of?'

'Or was another gang pissed off, and he was collateral in a drugs turf war?'

'What was on the sign around his neck? "Not in my city".'

'Doesn't sound like a gang, boss.'

'You're right, Harry.'

Emma stared out of the window. Outside, the road was approaching the Fountains Roundabout.

'Why do these roads always look so ugly? Here we are in one of the prettiest towns in England and all we can see are prefab warehouses, charity shops, tattoo parlours and seventies offices that look like they were built with Lego.'

'It's progress, boss.'

'But we're going backwards, not forward, Harry – how can that be progress? How can people approve such buildings? How can they even design them in the first place?'

'You ask me and I ask who, boss?'

Emma didn't answer. 'Where has Mark Sinton been for the last two days?' she said quietly, almost to herself. 'Tracy Cummings said she last saw him at four o'clock on Sunday. Was he in Liverpool? Another town? Or was he staying somewhere else in Chester?' She then turned back to Harry. 'We need to find out if he'd been seen hanging round the clubs recently. Tracy said he used to meet his punters at the clubs.'

'And he was arrested six months ago outside one.'

'Where was it, Harry?'

'Checkers, a student place on Sealand Road.'

'Can you pay them a visit, see if he's been recently?'

'Will do, boss.'

Emma glanced at the clock. 'I've changed my mind. Let's go to the post-mortem, then go back and brief the team on Mark Sinton. Can you check with the drugs squad in Liverpool, see if he's on their radar and find out which gangs are looking to expand their operations?'

'Will do, boss. You want me to come to the post-mortem too?'

'You don't fancy seeing a dead body?'

'I've seen lots of those. It's just the missus has promised me a treat for my tea this evening; liver and bacon.'

'Liver and bacon is a treat? Remind me never to come to your house for my tea, Harry. No wonder you don't want to go to the post-mortem. But, sorry, I need you there, mate.'

Harry sighed. 'At least the missus isn't cooking ribs tonight.'

Emma stared at him. 'Sometimes I worry about you, Harry.'

'You and the missus, boss.'

'I'll debrief everybody back at the Major Incident Room when the post-mortem is finished.' Emma went silent, changing the mood. 'I've got a bad feeling about this one, Harry.'

He saw her scratching the inside of her wrist. 'Your eczema playing up?'

She nodded. 'This time, it's bad.'

Chapter SEVENTEEN

He watched the house from across the street. The garden was overgrown and heavy curtains covered the windows. The place looked empty and unloved. But he knew they were inside.

He'd followed one of the dealers back here one night. They'd been standing outside the den of iniquity in the centre of town, selling their poison, polluting the blood of the innocent and the guilty.

The police did nothing, of course. Sitting in their warm vans in a side street, reading their racing papers and watching their phones. While out on the streets, citizens were being preyed upon and perverted by the purveyors of poison.

It had to be stopped.

He had to stop it.

Only he could send the signal they needed to see.

'Not in my city.'

He'd watched the house for a week. Working out the rhythms and habits of the place. A young boy was inside, his soul already corrupted by the evil he produced.

It was the young he had to save. He understood. God understood. Soon everybody would understand.

A car had driven up at nine and a single man had gone inside. That was thirty minutes ago. Would the man spend the night?

He hoped not. Two people were too many for him to handle. He would have to postpone the operation. He didn't like to postpone his work. The time was now. He was ready, the world was ready. It needed to be done today.

The front door opened and he ducked behind the wall. A man stood in the doorway smoking something, the long tendrils of smoke floating up into the night air.

'I'll be back tomorrow evening with the van,' the man shouted. 'Make sure the crop is ready and harvested.'

From inside the boy answered, saying something unintelligible.

'Make sure it's ready,' the man repeated, before closing the door and walking down the pathway to his car. He sat inside fiddling with the car radio before putting the car in gear and driving off towards the centre of Chester.

Should he act now? The boy would think the man had forgotten something. He made the decision to move immediately. It was an impulsive decision. Not like him at all. Usually everything was planned down to the smallest detail but now the moment seemed too opportune not to act…

Checking that the houses on either side were quiet, he silently crossed the road, opening the garden gate.

A loud squeak.

He stopped, listening for any movement in the house.

Nothing, not even the twitch of a curtain.

He strode up the path and knocked loudly on the door, using exactly the same three firm raps as the man had used when he arrived.

He heard loud steps on uncarpeted floorboards.

The door opened slowly. 'Why, back again, work done like you—'

The boy's eyes opened wide and he stopped speaking as he saw the glint of the blade in the moonlight.

'I'm sorry but this has to end now. Your time is up. You must be ready to meet your maker.'

Chapter EIGHTEEN

'This heart weighs in at 290 grams. No sign of any ventricular degradation. A perfectly normal heart for a young man.'

Emma Christie made a note in her ledger. She and Harry Fairweather had already struggled into their Tyvek lab suits earlier.

'I think they are making these things smaller,' Harry had moaned, as he'd zipped up the front over his stomach.

'It's all the bacon sandwiches.'

'Nothing wrong with a bacon sarnie. Did you know brown sauce is one of your five-a-day?'

'Rubbish.'

'I swear it's true. I read it in an old *Reader's Digest* when I went to see the doctor.'

'What were you there for?' Emma had said, as she'd tucked her hair behind her ears and slipped a hairnet over her head.

'Blood pressure too high.'

'Goes with the job… and the bacon sarnies.'

They had finished and had strolled into the examination room. Emma always felt strangely comfortable there. She thought it was the precision and cleanliness of the place. The stainless-steel tables were always polished to a glimmering shine, while the white-tiled walls reflected her image back like a pottery mirror.

David Anstey was talking into a microphone above his head with an assistant taking pictures and reacting to the doctor's orders. In front of him, the young man's body was stretched out on one of the tables with the chest cut open and the skin peeled back off the face. He no longer looked human; more a slab of meat on a butcher's block.

The doctor noticed them out of the corner of his eye. 'Come in, come in, don't hang around near the exit. I can't show you what's going on from back there. I started early, no time like the present.'

'Anything yet?'

'I confirmed my suspicion of death by strangulation. See the bruising on the back of the neck? One can even make out the places where the fingers pressed into the skin.'

'Any fingerprints?'

'None, I'm afraid. Must have been wearing gloves is my bet, not dissimilar to these.' With the scalpel between his forefinger and thumb, he held up a bloody hand clad in blue nitrile gloves.

'A medical man?'

'Not necessarily. Any chemist stocks them. And looking at the way the optic nerves were butchered when the eyes were removed, I'd say the murderer has never seen the inside of an anatomy lecture. This wasn't done with any medical training.' The doctor sniffed in condemnation of the killer's lack of medical finesse. 'One other indicator of strangulation is present.' He pointed the scalpel towards the victim's throat. 'The hyoid bone has been crushed. Whoever did it was quite powerful, a lot of force was used.'

'Any more on the time of death?'

'Still can't be too precise. It was a relatively warm night for October, plus I can't be certain of the conditions the body was held in prior to being placed in the coffin on the wall.'

'He definitely wasn't killed at the scene?'

'I think not.' He gestured for his assistant to turn over the body. 'See, there is lividity all along the back, buttocks and the rear of the thighs.'

'Why does that show he wasn't killed at the church?' asked Harry.

'For such lividity to occur, the blood needs to drain downwards. This young man was lying flat on his back, not upright in a coffin. Such lividity would take at least ten hours.'

'So he was killed at another location at least ten hours before being moved to the ruins.'

'Precisely, Detective Inspector. I would say the body had lain on its back for at least that time before being moved, probably longer.'

Emma noted the doctor's words down in her notebook. Tracy Cummings said she had last seen the boy two days ago. What had happened in the meantime? Where did he go?

She looked up slowly. 'Anything else, Doctor? Age of the victim?'

'Difficult to tell. Puberty has begun but the body is not yet fully developed. The first puberty change is the enlargement of the scrotum and testes, but I'm seeing no significant enlargement of the penis. Plus there is very little pubic hair development. Unfortunately, the X-rays we took are inconclusive too.'

He pointed to a light box at the rear of the examination room. On it were X-rays of various angles of the boy's skull, his spine and a hand.

'The first and second molars are present but not the third molar, suggesting the boy was at least thirteen years of age. In addition, on the skull the sutures have not fused yet and if you notice the basilar suture…'

'It's something I'm always noticing,' said Harry.

The doctor ignored the interruption. '…on the base of the skull is still open. Normally, it would start to fuse between the ages of eighteen and twenty-four.'

The doctor scratched his nose.

'Moving along to the C-rays of the left hand, the carpals, metacarpals and phalanges on the X-ray image still show growth plates at both ends; these are the darker areas on the X-ray. Comparing the length and width of these growth plates with the data on a standard atlas of bone development, we get an age range of between thirteen years five months and fifteen years four months.' He pointed to a data-filled chart o this iPad. 'Finally, the last section of X-rays show the base of the spine, the sacrum. These bones are still unfused. Normally fusion occurs at between sixteen and twenty-three years of age.'

'What does all that mean, Doctor?'

'The boy is possibly aged between thirteen and fifteen years old. But I would caution you that our findings in this post-mortem reveal only skeletal age, not chronological age.'

'Meaning?'

'All people develop differently. Growth is not a linear process but happens in fits and starts.'

'A bit like police careers then,' added Harry.

'You could say that, DC Fairweather, I couldn't possibly comment.'

'Anything else, Doctor?' asked Emma.

David Anstey shook his head. 'Everything seems to indicate this young man was a fairly normal teenager. Average height, average weight, fully functioning heart and lungs. I've yet to weigh the brain but that looks within the usual parameters too. No major distinguishing marks or tattoos except for a small mark on the hairline probably caused less than a week ago, but I can't be certain exactly when.'

'How did he get it?'

'I don't know.'

'Any ideas?'

'A fight? Banged his head? Walked into a lamppost? Your guess is as good as mine, Detective Inspector Christie.'

Emma wrote a note in her ledger. 'Nothing else?'

'Everything seems completely normal. An extremely average young man…'

'Except he's lying on a stainless-steel table with his face peeled off, his heart on a tray beside his head, and he's missing his eyes.'

'Did you find them, Inspector?'

The question suddenly sparked something in Emma. 'No, we didn't. We haven't searched the park or the area near the river though.'

She wrote in her notebook.

Where are the eyes? Why did the killer take them?

Looking from her notebook to the small, undeveloped body lying on the table, a wave of sadness washed over Emma.

Why had this young man's life been ended so cruelly? It was up to her to find the answer to the question, she owed it to him.

The sadness was replaced with fear. What if she wasn't good enough?

What if she screwed it up?

What if she made another mistake?

Her dad never made any mistakes. In his twenty years as a detective, he had a one hundred per cent success rate at solving murders. It was one of the reasons he was so revered in the City of Chester force.

She had a lot to live up to. Perhaps too much.

Was she as good?

She snapped out of her thoughts, closing her notebook. 'Right, thanks, Doctor.'

'My pleasure. We're still waiting on the lab reports but you should have my post-mortem findings in a couple of days. One last thing, do you have a name for him yet?'

'We think it's a Mark Sinton, but we're still waiting for confirmation. I'll let you know as soon as we're sure.'

'Thank you, Emma, I'll wait for your call.'

She began to take off her plastic gloves. 'I look forward to reading the final report, but call me if anything unusual comes up before then.'

'Will do.'

Dr Anstey stopped what he was doing for a moment and stared at the body lying on his slab. 'Like I said before, I have a feeling this won't be the last of these killings. In fact, I believe our killer has only just begun.'

Chapter NINETEEN

'A pathologist with feelings, now there's a world's first.'

They were both walking back to where they had parked the car. Emma stopped suddenly and turned to face Harry.

'Sometimes your cynicism goes too far, Harry. Let me tell you about Dr Anstey. One day, I arrived early for one of these post-mortems. I forget who it was. An old lady we'd found in a house in Broughton who'd been dead for three weeks. Even though this body no longer looked or smelt like a human being, I still watched Dr Anstey say a prayer before starting his work. I asked one of his assistants afterwards if it happened every time. He told me that Anstey believes that inside every body is a human being who needs to be treated with care, kindness and humanity. I also asked him what religion Dr Anstey was, expecting the usual answer of Church of England or Roman Catholic. Instead, the man said he was an atheist. The prayer was to the human being, not to a god. He was asking the dead person to help him find out what had happened to them.'

'Whoa, that's weird, boss.'

'Is it? Put yourself in his shoes. How many post-mortems do you think he performs each year?'

'I dunno. Fifty? A hundred?'

'Most days, the good doctor does three a day, six days a week. That's eighteen a week, seventy-two each month, eight hundred and sixty-four a year, and that's when it's quiet. He's been working as a pathologist for twenty-two years, you do the maths.'

'Arithmetic was never my strong point at school.'

'I worked it out one day. The good doctor has performed over nineteen thousand post-mortems in his career. Can you imagine what that does to a man?'

Harry Fairweather whistled softly. 'How the hell does he sleep at night?'

'How does he carry on doing what he does, day in and day out, still retaining his desire to discover the truth? And let me tell you something, Harry, David Anstey never gives up, never stops working. He's constantly thinking about his work and his reports. I've had him ring me at ten o'clock at night, because he'd thought of something that might be important in a case.'

'Rather you than me, boss.'

'One last thing – why do you think he asked me the young lad's name just before we left?'

'I dunno. For his report?'

'His assistant told me he keeps a book with the name of every person he has ever examined in it; their age, date of birth and circumstances of death. Apparently, it is so he can remember every single one of them as a person, not a body, and definitely not a corpse. Sermon over, Harry.'

She continued walking back to where their car was parked.

'Sorry, boss, I didn't know.'

'Well, now you do.'

There was a silence between them for a moment before Harry said, 'Still a bit weird though, hey.'

Emma shook her head. 'Sometimes, Harry, I give up with you, I really do.' Then she stopped. 'I had an idea while we were in the post-mortem. We need to check up on that Snapchat page Tracy gave us. The one Mark Sinton used when he was dealing. Is it still active?'

Harry tapped on his phone like a woodpecker after a beetle.

'Unless we find his original burner phone, we're not going to be able to access the messages or track his movements.'

As Harry fiddled with his mobile, he spoke out of the corner of his mouth. 'I could go to all the nearby petrol stations, from memory there are just four, and collect all the numbers of burner phones they've sold in the last month or so.'

'Could be a lot of numbers?'

'But worth doing if we want to track his movements.'

'Do it, Harry.'

The detective constable then whistled loudly. 'That Snapchat page they told us about, Danny Ds, is now inactive. I just sent it a message and it's come back as no longer valid.'

'Strange. Did Mark Sinton deactivate it before he died? Or his gang?'

'Perhaps it wasn't him or his gang, maybe it was the killer, boss.'

'A lot of Chester's druggies are going to be terribly unhappy.'

'Somebody else will already be supplying them. It's like whack-a-mole; you arrest one and three others pop up in his place.'

Emma sighed. 'Who'd be in the drug squad? It never stops.'

'There are benefits though. It means there's always work. And plenty of overtime. When I was in drugs, the work paid for a trip to Mexico one year.'

'The missus must have been pleased.'

'Aye, she was, boss. She was planning a round-the-world cruise until I got transferred to your team.'

Emma shook her head laughing . 'I bet she was disappointed.'

'Not half, we went from a luxurious Cunard round-the-world cruise to a not-so-cheap package holiday in the Costa del Loadsamoney.'

Emma reached the car, still shaking her head.

'Now all she has is a murder and a couple of burglaries, boss.'

'She's definitely missing the drugs, Harry.'

'Aren't we all.'

Chapter TWENTY

'Right, everybody.' Emma Christie clapped her hands, getting a quick frisson of déjà vu as she did. The people in the Major Incident Room stopped what they were doing and made their way to the seats placed in front of the boards. Emma still hadn't changed the layout, so everybody sat in exactly the same place as last time.

'This is now officially a murder investigation. The pathologist confirmed the young man died through manual strangulation. We even have a name for our vic.' She tapped the picture. 'Mark Sinton, a thirteen- to fifteen-year-old, possibly from Liverpool. Harry, anything from Merseyside?'

'They've come back saying the name's not on their records, boss.'

'That's disappointing. Can you send them his picture? It might jog somebody's memory. John, can you put his prints on IDENT1 and look for a match? Try the dabs from his arrest and the ones taken by the CSIs before he was taken to the mortuary.'

'Will do, boss.'

'Batman and Robin—' she pointed to the two young PCs '—did you finish your house-to-house enquiries?'

The elder one, Richard Gleason, spoke for both of them, looking at his notes continually as if reading from a script. 'Nothing, boss, nobody saw anything. Not surprising really, given the area is mostly comprised of offices.'

'And the houses along the river?'

'Not a sausage. I think you could drive a tank through this area and nobody would notice.'

'Right, thanks anyway. Had to be done. Make sure you file your report with John.'

They both nodded.

'Gerry, Mr CCTV, anything?'

'I'm going through them one by one but it takes time. It's a shame the cameras on the church were broken...'

'The caretaker said it was done deliberately. Some guy in a balaclava smashed them.'

'I checked them both out. They had their power supply cables cut too. According to the caretaker it was done two nights ago. Looks like whoever did it really wanted to disable them.'

'Could the perp have done it? If he did, it suggests he planned to dump the body at the ruins and didn't want his face or car to be picked up by CCTV.'

'Or somebody was planning to rob the church?' suggested Harry Fairweather.

'Aye, there is that, but the coincidence of the CCTV cameras being smashed and two days later a body turning up is too much for me.'

'Could there be a link between the attack on the CCTV and the missing eyes?' said Gerry.

'I don't understand, son.'

'Well, they're both about sight and seeing, aren't they? It's as if the perp didn't want to be seen.'

'You've been watching far too many *Wire in the Blood* episodes, Gerry. Fancy yourself as one of these highfalutin psychological profilers, do you?' laughed Harry Fairweather.

'Hang on, Harry, the young lad might have a point.' Emma wrote **BLINDNESS, NOT SEEING WITH CCTV AND EYES**? on the empty board to the right. 'What happened to the eyes? Does the killer still have them? Or did he throw them away? Anna?'

'Yes, boss?'

'Can you organise a team for a fingertip search of the park first thing tomorrow? It'll probably turn up nothing more than a few used condoms and empty pop bottles, but we have to do it.'

'Right, boss.'

'Anything else on CCTV, Gerry?'

'We've downloaded the images from the traffic cameras at the lights but they're not great. Apparently, maintenance is due this week.'

'Typical. Do the images give us anything?'

'Not a lot. Some blurry cars with a suggestion of colour but no clear images of numberplates or drivers.'

Emma shook her head. 'See if the techies can clear them up, Gerry.'

'Already sent the footage to them, boss.'

'And the other cameras you found?'

'One was a dummy and the other has some footage, but it wasn't pointed directly at the ruins. I'm just going through it as we speak.'

'I want stills of every car that's in the area from nine p.m. to ten thirty p.m. last night. You two, Riggs's detectives?' They both sat up straight. 'Help young Gerry here to find more footage, widen the area to Souter's Lane, up to Eastgate and then across to Love Street.'

'Could be hundreds of CCTV cameras, boss.'

'If there is, I want you to check them all. I want footage of the roads, cars and pedestrians. While you're at it, check the bridges across the Dee: Queen's Park and Old Dee Bridge.'

'What time period, boss?'

'For now, look at nine p.m. to ten thirty p.m. last night. But make sure you get footage from the last week. I think it's far too much of a coincidence that the church CCTV was smashed two nights ago. If you can get CCTV that doesn't need maintenance, run a numberplate recognition cross-check for cars that were in the area yesterday and two nights ago.'

Both of their faces fell. 'Could give us hundreds of responses,' the officer on the left grumbled.

'Well, you'd better get started right away, bonny lads. How were your interviews with Dan's gang, Anna?'

'They both confirm his story about the initiation ceremony and the timings. After they heard his scream they did a runner, thought he'd been attacked by a ghost. They were still shitting themselves when I spoke to them.'

'Good. And the caretaker's story?'

'The wife confirmed he arrived home at eight thirty on the dot. Apparently, he arrives home at exactly the same time every evening.'

'An exciting life. Anything on HOLMES, John?'

'Nothing so far, boss. I've used a lot of parameters and nothing is coming up either locally or in the North.'

Emma made a moue with her mouth. 'Shame. Missing persons?'

John pulled a printout towards him. 'Nobody matching the description of the vic has been reported missing in Chester or Cheshire.'

'Expand the misper search to Liverpool, Manchester and North Wales, John. Somebody has got to care that this young man has gone missing.'

'Will do, boss.'

'Finally, Harry, anything from the petrol stations?'

'I haven't got to them yet, boss. I'm going right after this meeting.'

'Get a move on, Harry, we haven't got till next year. What about the student club where Tracy Cummings said our vic used to deal?'

'I went there and showed the photo. One of the bouncers recognised him, said he hung around the club but they never allowed him in. Underage.'

'Did they see him dealing?'

'To quote them, "Outside the club, we don't see nobody doing nothing."'

Emma shook her head. 'Typical.' She rubbed her eyes. A wave of tiredness swept over her. Suddenly, she was conscious that the first twenty-four hours after the discovery of the body were nearly over and they hadn't made as much progress as she'd hoped.

She couldn't let the troops see her disappointment. She forced a smile on to her face. 'Right, you all know what to do. Let's get cracking.'

One of the two young coppers, Richard Gleason, put his hand up. 'What do you want us to do?'

'Help Gerry and the others go through the CCTV. We need to view it all much quicker.'

Just as she spoke, Anna Williams' phone rang loudly. She answered it and spoke softly before handing it over to Emma. 'It's Chief Inspector Jones, boss. Apparently you're not answering your phone.'

Chapter TWENTY-ONE

Emma put the phone to her ear and began to slowly walk out of the Major Incident Room. 'Hello, DCI Jones.'

Before she could hear his answer, she covered the mouthpiece and said to the others, 'Carry on, this briefing is finished. If anybody is unclear on what they should be doing, have a chat with me later.'

Jones was speaking on the phone.

'Sorry, sir, I missed that?'

There was an exasperated grunt on the other end of the line. 'I just said, I am about to go into a meeting with the press but I haven't received an update from you on the progress of the investigation yet. I've been ringing you for the last hour but you never answered your phone.'

'I'm sorry, sir, I was—'

'In the future, DI Christie,' he interrupted, 'I will expect daily briefings in the morning at nine a.m., starting from tomorrow. Is that clear?'

He was trying to micromanage her. She thought about protesting and rejected the idea. Now was not the time. She simply answered, 'Yes, sir.'

'Well?'

'Well what, sir?'

'Your update. I have to brief the press in five minutes.'

'The pathologist has confirmed the death of the young man was caused by strangulation. We have a murder inquiry on our hands.'

'Do we have a name for the victim?'

Emma licked her lips. It was far too early to be releasing names to the press. 'I...'

'Well?'

'We have been given a possible name. A Mark Sinton, a thirteen- to fifteen-year-old, possibly from Liverpool, but it still has not been confirmed yet. Merseyside have no record of the name.'

'I won't mention it until it's been confirmed. Anything I can tell the leeches of the press?'

'Not a lot, sir. You could ask anybody who saw any suspicious activity in and around St John's Church and its ruins last night to come forward.'

'That's all?'

'That's it, sir.'

'Nothing else I need to know about? What about the witness who discovered the body?'

'A young boy, sir. Daniel Sangster. I don't want his name revealed to the press yet either. They'll be hanging round his house if we do.'

'Not a lot to tell them anyway. Not a lot you've actually told *me*.'

'It's early days, sir. We've only been going for less than a day.'

'Still… I need to give them something.'

'Sorry, sir, like I said, it's early days.'

Another exasperated grunt on the end of the phone. 'I need you to move more quickly, DI Christie, the Chief Constable wants this solved, and solved swiftly. The killing of young men is like red meat to the press. It gives them permission to moralise endlessly about the decline in civil standards and the lack of coppers on the beat. More than that, it sells newspapers. And there is nothing more sanctimonious or moralistic than an editor desperate to sell newspapers. We need this murder taken off the books as quickly as possible, understood?'

'Yes, sir.'

'DI Riggs will be back from his course tomorrow. He's already rung me, offering his help. Do you need any more resources, DI Christie?'

The idea of Riggs getting involved in her investigation sent a shiver of fear down Emma's spine. If it was later solved, it would be down to his help, and if it wasn't, he would have been brought in too late. She could already see his game.

'Well, DI Christie?'

'We're good, sir, I don't need anybody else.'

'On your own head be it. I'm being called by the PR person now. I wish there was more we could tell the press. If we don't give them something, they'll just make things up. The newspapers of England love a vacuum, DI Christie, it gives them the freedom to say exactly what they want.'

'Aren't they going to do that anyway?'

'True, but without anything to say we can't put our spin on the facts.'

'We could give them some alternative facts, sir.'

'What was that, DI Christie?'

'Nothing, sir, just a joke.'

'I don't like jokes, DI Christie, not when I'm going into a press conference like Daniel entering the lion's den. Are you sure you don't need DI Riggs' help?'

'Positive, sir.'

'Well, like I said, on your own head be it.'

With those ominous words, the line was cut off and a buzzing sound was left in Emma's ear.

Before she had switched off her phone, John had run out to see her. 'Boss, we've got a hit on IDENT1.'

Chapter TWENTY-TWO

Chief Inspector David Jones adjusted his tie as he sat at the table facing the assembled press. Next to him, Penny Morgan shuffled the stack of press releases nervously.

Behind both of them a large sign read *City of Chester Constabulary* with the shield of the city prominently displayed. The sign was beginning to fray at the edges, having been used for at least twenty years in press conferences. Penny had put in a requisition for a new one but it had yet to be signed off by the powers-that-be.

The conference was being held at police headquarters in a particularly dingy room that was always used for this purpose.

Penny clapped her hands. 'Right, people, if you can sit down we'll begin this briefing.'

Dutifully, the press began to take their seats. There were only nine people there, all men. There was just a single camera from one of the regional news programmes and, of course, cameras from the public relations department itself. The footage would be sent out to all local stations and used on their in-house monitors.

Penny breathed a sigh of relief. The biggies in London hadn't picked up the story yet. With a bit of luck the case would be solved before they did. But once the news got out after the press conference, they would be buzzing around it like flies on shit.

She crossed her fingers as she continued speaking. 'On my right is Detective Chief Inspector David Jones of City of Chester Constabulary. He will appraise you of an incident that occurred last night in the city. Over to you, Chief Inspector.'

Davy Jones cleared his throat and picked up his prepared statement. He coughed again, remembering to deepen his voice, to speak slowly and clearly.

The voice from the training at GMP's Sedgefield Park came back to him: 'Most of the press are still in the antediluvian age. They take notes by hand. A few will be recording you on their mobiles, but most will simply cobble together a story from the handout we give them and from their notes and memory. Memories that will definitely be dulled later by copious glasses of wine. Your job is to make it as easy as possible for them to follow your version of events. Don't give them too much information but do come across as calm, patient and in control. They are congenitally lazy so most won't follow up anything after the press conference. Always decide what the goals are from the briefing before you start. Never, repeat, *never* go into a press conference without goals. The role of a press conference is not to give information but to guide the press on your preferred course and with your preferred interpretation of events. Got it?'

The instructor was a former chief crime reporter for the *Daily Mirror*. A poacher turned gamekeeper, as he called himself.

Davy Jones cleared his throat for the third time, glancing up at the reporters, their pens and pencils poised over their notepads.

'Yesterday evening at approximately ten o'clock, we received a call regarding an incident at the south-east chapel of St John's Church,' he began hesitantly.

'Do you mean the old ruins?' asked one of the reporters.

He began to answer but found Penny's hand gripping his arm. 'DCI Jones will answer questions after his statement.

Please do not interrupt him until he has finished. Please continue, DCI Jones.'

Davy Jones glanced down at his statement and began reading again. 'At the chapel, the body of a young boy was found. We are treating this case as murder. We would like any members of the public who were in the area from nine p.m. to ten thirty p.m. to come forward, particularly if they saw anything suspicious at that time. The Crimestoppers number to contact is placed prominently behind me. The investigation is ongoing and further updates will be given to the press in the future.'

He finished and looked across to Penny. She nodded in approval before saying, 'DCI Jones will now take questions.' She pointed to a journalist on the front row. 'Tony, why don't you begin.'

'Tony Chalmers of the *Liverpool Echo*. DCI Jones, you said it was a young boy. Can you give us any more details?'

'I'm sorry, at the moment I can give no further details as we are just ascertaining his identity and have not told his next of kin yet.'

'Next question,' interrupted Penny Morgan before the reporter could ask a follow-up. 'Let's hear from Justin Green of *Granada Reports* next.'

'Hi, Penny. All the roads are closed around the crime scene; when do you expect them to open, DCI Jones?'

'As soon as possible, Mr Green. As you are no doubt aware, it is the job of the police to collect forensic and CCTV information from the area around the crime scene. I am absolutely clear this will be completed in the near future and the roads opened as soon as is humanly possible.'

Davy Jones was relaxed now. The media training had definitely helped. He had learnt the five ways to appear to answer a question without actually answering the question.

Penny pointed to a new reporter. 'Sorry, I don't know your name.'

'It's Gavin Newton of the *Chester Daily*. DCI Jones, is it correct to say the young boy was strangled and found in the coffin on the wall, a famous Chester landmark?'

DCI Jones frowned. How did the reporter know this? He glanced across to the PR officer but the reporter continued speaking.

'Around his neck was a plaque saying, "Not in my city". Isn't that true? Is there some sort of satanic rite happening in Chester? After all, the ruined church is still a consecrated site, is it not?'

All the reporters were now staring at Newton.

DCI Jones stuttered for a moment before remembering the words he had learnt when faced with an awkward question. 'I'm sorry, I am not at liberty at the moment to reveal the details of the crime. As you will appreciate, the relatives of the deceased haven't been informed yet.'

Penny stood up. 'I'm afraid, gentlemen, DCI Jones must end the press conference now. As you can appreciate, he is a busy man. Press releases have been prepared by my office and you can pick them up on your way out. Thank you for your attendance.'

Newton persisted with his line of questioning. 'Are there satanic rituals involving the murder of young boys being performed in Chester, DCI Jones?'

Penny Morgan grabbed the arm of the Chief Inspector and ushered him off the stage. 'The press conference is now over, gentlemen.

'

Chapter TWENTY-THREE

Emma stared at the IDENT1 results on the laptop.

'Who the hell is Roy Short? I thought our victim's name was Mark Sinton. That was the name he gave when he was arrested and Tracy Cummings knew him as Mark Sinton too.'

'It appears Roy Short is the real name of our vic, boss,' John replied, reading the details of the match that the fingerprint data had turned up. 'He was born in August 2009, which makes him fifteen years old and a couple of months. First arrest was for shoplifting in Liverpool in 2019, aged just ten, and again in 2023 for possession of crack cocaine. Neither time was he charged in court. The second time he was remanded to a children's home. He absconded from there and was re-arrested, but the Crown Prosecution Service decided not to press charges and he was released with a police caution. Not counting the time he was arrested in Chester, of course.'

'The lad is his own private crimewave,' said Harry Fairweather, looking over Emma's shoulder.

'He's certainly had a charmed life. Any addresses for him?'

'There's a children's home and before that a house in the Everton district of Liverpool. 22 Armitage Street.'

'His parents?'

John shook his head. 'Foster parents. A Mr and Mrs Wright. No biological parents listed. Looks like he'd been in care most of his life.'

'Harry, I need you to drive over to Liverpool tomorrow and interview them. Find out all you can.'

'Wouldn't it be quicker to do it over the phone, boss?'

'Quicker, but less effective and less personal. I want you to break the news of Roy Short's death directly to the foster parents, see their reactions and check out the house. Ask them if he had any friends, his history, how he was in their care, that sort of stuff.' She began to walk away before remembering something. 'And get a recent photograph and a brush with his hair on it. I want to check the DNA matches. Sniff around, see what else you can find out from them.'

'My nose will be sniffing like I've got Spanish, Asian and just a wee drop of Bird Flu, boss.'

'As it always is, Harry.' She turned back to John Simpson. Can you call Merseyside Police? Discover all you can about Mr Short. Known associates, criminal links and membership of any gangs. But do it on the quiet. ' She stopped for a moment. 'God, am I really talking about a fifteen-year-old boy?'

'Do I let them know I'm coming, boss?' asked Harry.

'Not yet, the fewer people know his real name the better at the moment. We can involve Merseyside after your visit.'

She stood up and walked over to the board. The single question was still there.

BLINDNESS. NOT SEEING WITH CCTV AND EYES?

She added one more.

WHAT WAS HE DOING IN CHESTER?

'I think we can answer that one, boss,' said Anna.

'Can we?'

'From his arrests and the information Tracy Cummings gave us, he was dealing drugs. County lines, probably a gang in Liverpool expanding their territory. He was their courier form Liverpool to the local dealers.'

'Maybe. Let's say it's true, we need to answer three more questions.' She wrote on the board:

WHERE DID HE GO WHEN HE WAS HERE?
WHO DID HE SEE?
WHY DID HE VANISH EVERY MONTH?

Harry put his hand up. 'I'd add a fourth one, boss. How did a fifteen-year-old child with no links in Chester manage to get a brief down to the nick to get him off in less than an hour?'

'A bit verbose, Harry, but a great question. Anna, can you go and see the brief, a Mr Sandway, if my memory serves me. Never heard of his company though.'

'I have,' said Anna. 'Big company based in the town centre, usually dealing in corporate law. I had dealings with them when I was working with the fraud squad.'

'It gets murkier and murkier. Go and visit him tomorrow and find out all you can. There's a lot about Mr Short's life that doesn't add up.'

Chapter TWENTY-FOUR

Liam Gilligan adjusted the gold chains around his neck and put on his latest Nike x Sacai VaporWaffles. 'Just going down the shops, d'ye want anything?'

This week's girlfriend, Patsy, looked up from her laptop. 'Can I come with you? I'm bored in the house.'

'Nah, this is business. Get yourself ready and we'll go out to Ronnie's this evening.'

'You won't be long?'

'Not too long.'

He hated it when they started questioning him. This one would have to go soon. A shame really, she didn't look half bad on his arm.

He closed the door without saying goodbye. Big Max, his driver, was waiting next to the Merc.

'Where we going, boss?'

'Dunno yet. Just drive around till we see a call box. One we haven't used before.'

He slipped into the back, enjoying the feel of the soft leather he had specially commissioned from the dealer. Big Max slipped the car into gear, pulled out of the driveway of the house near Formby and headed down the A565 towards Liverpool.

Gilligan hated leaving the bloody house just to make a phone call, but it had to be done. Ever since the police had cracked EncroChat, he couldn't ring from the house any more just in case the phones had been tapped.

He'd stopped using EncroChat well before the bizzies had started making arrests. There was something about the encryption service that worried him. How open it all seemed. You didn't have to use code, just send a message to order gear from the dealers in Amsterdam and Cali. He smelt a rat and his nose was never wrong.

Then his fears were confirmed by one of his inside sources. The French police had cracked the message service and fed all the details to the National Crime Office. Six months later the arrests started happening. Of course, he was well out of it by then. As the other gangs were put away, he expanded his territory and his profits. His suspicions were confirmed and the money spent on his source now paid back tenfold.

'Just because you're paranoid, doesn't mean they're not out to get you.'

'What was that, boss?'

'Nothing, Max, just thinking out loud. Find a phone box in Crosby if you can.'

'Not many left now, boss, nobody uses them any more.'

'Well, I do, so find one.'

Big Max shut up. He knew when it was best to keep his thoughts to himself.

Ten minutes later, Max spotted one on the left and pulled up beside it.

Gilligan stepped out of the warmth of the car, pulling his coat around his body. They were in the middle of a small estate, one of the areas that he controlled. The streets were empty, nobody was going out on a day like this.

He picked up the receiver and listened for the familiar ring tone. Thank God, it was working. He'd given out orders that none of the pay phones in his area were to be vandalised. It looked like the message had got through.

He pulled out a small book and checked one of the numbers pencilled inside it. These numbers changed every couple of weeks as his dealers dumped their burner phones and bought new ones. It was a pain writing them all down, but again, security was key. The book never left his side. Even when he was sleeping, it was in the top drawer of the bedside table. If the bizzies ever raided his house, he would have time to flush it down the toilet.

He dialled the number and put some coins in the slot. He didn't use his credit card; the bastard bizzies could track that too.

'Mickey, it's Liam. Any news?'

'Nothing, boss. The bastard's vanished, the gear and the money's gone too.'

'He's gone mad, stupid kid. Check out his gaff in Chester.'

'Already done that, boss. They haven't seen him since Sunday, don't know where he is.'

'You sure?'

'Definite, boss, they're junkies, they'd give up their mother for a fix.'

'You checked his usual places?'

'Not yet.'

'Whaddya waitin' for? Check them out and put a car outside his people's house in Liverpool.'

'You want us to turn their place over too?'

'Not yet. Concentrate on Chester first.'

'Right, boss.'

'I want my money and gear back. Nobody crosses me, understand?'

'Got it.'

'And when you find the little bastard, make sure I never see him again, Mickey?'

There was silence on the other end of the phone as the order sunk home.

'You understand, Mickey? I don't want to see him again. Not in Liverpool, not in Chester, not anywhere. And I don't want his body found. He vanishes, understand?'

'Understood, boss.'

Gilligan slammed the phone down. He opened the door of the phone box and stood there for a moment surveying his territory. A couple of kids on bikes were watching him from across the road. He nodded towards them and they waved back.

Respect.

That's what he had worked hard to get, and no little twat was going to steal it from him.

He lit a small Ritmeester cigar. He'd picked up the habit when he lived in Amsterdam and found they helped him think.

Why had Roy decided he could nick the gear now? Had somebody put him up to it?

Had Liam been too soft on his people recently, too generous? Was it time to cull the ranks, elevate some of the more aggressive youngsters before they got the same ideas and copied Roy?

As the cigar smoke rolled around his mouth, he decided he needed to talk to his brothers.

It was time to change the organisation.

Chapter TWENTY-FIVE

It had been a long day.

After the briefing had ended, Emma had watched Davy Jones on TV at the press conference with Penny Morgan at his side. He had been efficient and professional, giving nothing away to the assembled gentlemen of the press until one reporter had asked a question indicating that he knew details about the murder. How had he found them out? And what was all that guff about 'satanic rites'? A young man, probably a drug dealer, had been murdered, there was nothing satanic about it.

Jones looked like a rabbit in the headlights after that question. Luckily, Penny had finished the press conference immediately, before the DCI could be made to look even more stupid.

But the reporter worried her. How had he found out so much, so quickly? Was there a leak in their operation, somebody selling information to the press? Jones would not be a happy bunny if there was.

But then, even her father's carer had known about the death in the ruins. Once again, she remembered that Chester was a village pretending to be a city, where nothing was a secret for long.

To avoid thinking about this, she buried herself in the minutiae of any major investigation: making sure everything was accurately documented, all her decisions recorded with the correct justifications and checking she had forgotten nothing. She even had time to read through her extensive notes. It was something her father had always reminded her to do.

'Read them often, love, often there's stuff you note down at the time that later becomes important,' he used to say.

At ten, she'd driven home, leaving a message for John Simpson to ring her if anything came up.

Emma parked in the driveway, locked the car and walked slowly to the front door. 'Hi there, Hortensia,' she shouted as she entered the house.

The large woman, dressed in a bright blue lab coat over an impressively flowery dress, came rushing out of the kitchen. 'Shhhh, I've only just got him down.'

She beckoned for Emma to follow her into the kitchen. The nurse was obviously drying the bowls she had used to heat up Ted's dinner. The stench of smoke still filled the air as if it had impregnated the walls. A large scar of soot rose like Chinese calligraphy above the stove up to the ceiling.

'You had a problem after I left this morning,' the nurse whispered.

'He decided to make himself breakfast before Mrs Lockwood arrived at nine. Unfortunately, he also decided to watch TV…'

'And forgot about the cooker?'

Emma nodded.

'I deal with a lot of Alzheimer's patients. It doesn't get better.'

Emma let her head sink to her chest. This was the last thing she needed to hear right now. She was so busy at work that dealing with her father's problems was the last thing she needed to handle as well.

Instantly, she felt guilty.

Her father wasn't a problem. He was the man who had raised and loved her. Their mother hadn't been much good at the mothering part of life. Oh, she was great if a party needed to be planned or a birthday celebrated, but the day-to-day details of raising a kid were beyond her. Emma often wondered if that was why she was an only child – both her father and mother realising they could only take care of one kid and not any more.

'How did you cook his food?'

'Your neighbour offered the use of his microwave. Such a kind man, is Mr Davies.'

Emma would have to thank him tomorrow morning. Peter Davies was indeed a kind man, she had known him most of her life, but he was long-winded and verbose. She would have to put up with a long lecture from him about her father belonging in a home and being a danger to them all.

Well, sod him. Her dad had said he didn't want to go in a home and until he changed his mind, he was staying in the house they had bought all those years ago.

'Sorry, Hortensia, what did you say?'

'I said, Mrs Lockwood left me a note. The electrician is coming tomorrow to check the wiring plus a man from the gas board to look at the cooker. She will handle both of them.'

Great, that was one less thing to worry about.

'You can go home if you want, Hortensia, take an early night now I'm back.'

The care worker's face fell. 'You don't need me tonight?'

'No, I'm at home. But don't worry about it, I'll still pay. You can have a break this evening.'

A big smile erupted on Hortensia's face. 'I look forward to going home. It'll be nice to see the kids. Let me put together your dad's meds for you, Mrs Christie, then I'll pack my things.'

Hortensia always called Emma 'Mrs Christie'. She had told her quite a few times that she had never been married but it didn't seem to register with the night nurse. After a while, she had given up – and anyway, she quite liked the idea of being called Mrs Christie.

After Hortensia had gone, Emma poured herself a large – probably too large – glass of wine and was about to take her first sip when the phone rang.

'Harry, what is it?'

'Just thought you'd want to know. Merseyside have confirmed the identity of our vic. The copper who charged him remembered his face. And get this, our vic had ties to the Gilligan brothers.'

'What?'

Emma had heard about them. A ruthless Liverpool gang with links to the Mexican and Colombian cartels as well as the Amsterdam mobs. The brothers – Luke, Mark and Liam – were known for their aggression and their consistent unpredictability.

Had they expanded their operations to Chester? But if Roy Short was working for them, why was he killed? Did another gang want to muscle in on the Gilligans' operations? If they did, Chester could see an all-out gang war with all that entailed for security and safety. Or had Roy Short done something to the Gilligans and was being punished for his errors? They were famous for not tolerating mistakes of any kind. Either way, it wasn't good. She had to clear this up and clear it fast.

'Harry, be careful tomorrow when you go to Liverpool.'

'Today, I'm going today, boss.'

'Right, you'd better get some sleep, you'll have to leave early.'

'And what about you, boss?'

'What about me?'

'When are you going to sleep?'

'Soon, Harry, but first I have a bit of thinking to do.'

'One last thing, boss. I checked on the petrol stations where Roy Short might have bought mobile phones, and I have twenty-eight numbers.'

'Ask the service providers to track all of them for us, Harry.'

'Already done, boss, we should get the details tomorrow afternoon after I get back from Liverpool.'

'Great, take care, Harry.'

She put down the phone and took a sip of wine, enjoying the refreshing zing of the Sauvignon Blanc from New Zealand. She was just about to read her notes again when the door opened and her father walked in, dressed in his striped poplin pyjamas.

'You couldn't sleep, Dad?'

He shook his head vaguely, before discovering the remote and switching on the TV. It was an old film, *The African Queen*.

'You know your mum looked like Katharine Hepburn when she was younger?'

'Did she, Dad? I suppose you looked like Humphrey Bogart?'

He shook his head. 'I was Cary Grant. Everybody said I was Cary Grant.' He stared at the screen. 'Where is your mum, anyway?'

'She's dead, Dad. Mum passed away seven years ago, remember?'

A vague look passed over her father's face. 'Did she? I wondered what had happened to her.' He took Emma's hand in his own and held it tightly. 'But we're not, are we?'

'We're not what, Dad?'

'Dead.'

'Not yet, Dad.'

On screen, Humphrey Bogart was dragging the titular boat through a brown, muddy swamp of a river, a rope over his shoulder and the dark stains of sweat seeping through the brim of his cap.

'We're still alive, aren't we?'

'We are, Dad.'

'I'd love a cup of tea if you're making one,' he said, never taking his eyes off the flickering television.

'The kitchen is…' She stopped speaking. There was no point in explaining it to him. He had forgotten completely about this morning, it was as if it never existed. 'I'll make one, shall I?'

'That would be lovely.'

On screen, Katharine Hepburn was lounging in the rear of the boat, watching as Humphrey failed to repair the propeller.

'Did I ever tell you that people thought your mum looked like Katharine Hepburn? Same hair, same sparkle in her eyes.'

'Did she, Dad? You sure it wasn't Audrey Hepburn she looked like?'

Her father thought for a moment before turning back to the television without answering.

Emma sat up. 'I'll make that cup of tea, shall I?'

'Lovely, I'm parched,' he answered, never taking his eyes off Hepburn. 'She looks like your mother, you know. Where is your mother?'

Emma stood up and left the room, a tear forming in the corner of her eye.

Thursday, October 26th

Chapter TWENTY-SIX

As she promised, Emma Christie was waiting outside Detective Chief Inspector Davy Jones' office at 9 a.m.

'Where is he, Doreen?' she asked the secretary.

'On his way in, apparently, probably stuck in traffic. He lives out near the zoo.'

Emma's eyes rolled up to the ceiling. Just what she needed. To waste time in HQ briefing her boss when there was so much to be done at the Major Incident Room.

Eventually, Davy Jones rolled up at 9.20, clutching a fresh Starbucks coffee and a blueberry muffin.

'If I'd known you were coming in, I would have got you one.'

'We arranged a debrief at nine a.m., Chief Inspector.'

'Did we?' he said over his shoulder, unlocking the door to his office. 'Come in then, don't waste time.'

He hung his coat behind the door and sat down behind his desk, booting up his computer. Emma sat opposite him, smelling the aroma of the coffee and wanting – needing – a jolt of caffeine herself.

The computer came to life and Jones entered his password.

'Right, you can begin, but before you do, did you see the press conference last night?'

'Yes, sir. I thought you handled it very well.'

Despite herself, Emma found she was defaulting to her use of the word 'sir'. Years of training by both her father and grandfather had ingrained the habit deep inside her.

A brief smile crossed Jones' face. 'I thought I did well too. The police media training seems to have worked.

Fifteen different ways of saying exactly the same meaningless words, but being "absolutely clear" on everything I said.' He used his fingers to create quotation marks in the air.

'Politicians seem to use the same form of words when they are being deliberately unclear, sir.'

'That's the whole point, Emma. But I must admit I was thrown by the question about satanic rituals from that stupid local journalist.' He leant forward and dropped his voice. 'You haven't found any evidence of satanic practices, have you?'

'What the hell *are* they, sir?'

'You know – witches' covens, naked people dancing round graves, pentangles drawn on the floor.'

Emma shook her head. 'We've found nothing like that, sir.'

'Good.' Jones smiled. 'I can be absolutely clear at the next press conference that there is no evidence of satanic practices in relation to the murder.'

On the spur of the moment, Emma decided to push his buttons. 'But… it doesn't mean they don't exist, sir, simply that we have not found any evidence for them. At the moment, we are keeping all our options open regarding motives for the murder.'

His face fell. 'Right. You'd better brief me quickly and get back to work. The devil makes work for idle hands, Emma.'

Emma shook her head, trying to understand what that meant, then pressed on with the briefing. 'Anyway, satanism aside, we have discovered the real identity of the victim. It's Roy Short, a fifteen-year-old boy from Liverpool. Apparently, Mark Sinton was just a name he used in Chester. Harry Fairweather is on his way to see the foster parents as we speak.'

Jones wrote down the name. 'What was he doing here?'

'We're still trying to work that out, sir. Apparently, he came and went every month. He was arrested in the city and then released six months ago for possible dealing.'

'We released him?'

'With a caution, sir.'

'That won't look good for us. We need to keep that shtum, Emma. Understand?'

'We think he may have been a courier for a drug group in Liverpool. The only way we will be able to track his movements is by asking people what he was doing.'

'Was a mobile phone found on him? Couldn't we track him using his mobile signal?'

'We didn't find any phone. But if he was a courier then he must have had one. Harry has discovered the numbers of burner phones sold in petrol stations close to where he was living. John is checking the details and we should have the tracking reports later today.'

'You said he'd been strangled?'

'We're still waiting on the written post-mortem report, but that is correct.'

'Fingerprints?'

'None. Apparently the killer wore gloves.'

'Bloody television, bloody CSI – looks like killers know more about forensics than we do these days.'

Emma decided to remain quiet, deafeningly so.

'What about the sign we discovered around the victim's neck?'

'"Not in my city." No fingerprints on that either. Written with a common or garden felt pen on cardboard.'

'So what is this? A drugs war between two gangs? A courier war? Is a gang in Liverpool expanding its territory to Chester?'

'I would be surprised if they hadn't already done so, sir.'

Detective Chief Inspector Jones jerked his head back. 'We have received no intelligence about Liverpool drug gangs operating in Chester. To suggest they are is to state that we are somehow failing in our duty to the public. I really don't want the papers to pick up on this narrative regarding your investigation, Emma. That wouldn't be good for our reputation.'

Emma thought long and hard before answering. 'I haven't discovered what the motive for the murder of Roy Short is yet. I do not want to jump to conclusions.'

'And I would advise you that any conclusion that suggested that drugs gangs were active in Chester would not be the sort of positive image the force wants to portray to the public.'

Emma stayed silent.

Jones changed the subject. 'What else are you doing today?'

'Organising a search of Grosvenor Park, following up on CCTV in the town, and having a chat with the solicitor who represented Roy Short when he was arrested last April.'

'Good. Let Penny Morgan know about the search, it always provides good visuals to see coppers on their knees combing through the grass in a park. Looks like we are going the extra mile, looks good on TV.'

'But we *are* going the extra mile, sir.'

'Good. A quiet word, Emma. At the risk of repeating myself ad nauseam, the chief wants this wrapped up quickly and efficiently. The press have started sniffing around it looking for a story and we can't let it drag on. We don't want another Lancashire Constabulary nightmare, do we?'

Emma frowned. 'Sir?'

'The woman in the river. The case dragged on far too long and they had amateur detectives, the press, Uncle Tom

Cobley and all sticking their oar in. We can't have that in Chester.' A slight pause. 'Stew Riggs rang me from his course last night, offering his help if you need it. He's back tomorrow.'

'I think we'll be okay, sir.'

'Stewart could be a great help, Emma. He's just finished the same media course I attended. Very useful when it comes to handling the press.'

'I think we'll be fine, sir, I have enough people.' This time she said it more forcefully.

'So be it, your decision.' He stood up to indicate the meeting was over. 'How's your father?'

'He's fine, sir.'

'It's just that I heard there was a little trouble at your house yesterday…'

How did he know about that? Had the coppers or the fire service told him?

'It's just that we need you to focus on this case, Emma, I know you'll understand. If, however, your father requires your undivided attention at the moment…'

He left the rest of the sentence unfinished, but Emma understood the meaning.

'We'll be okay, sir,' she said.

Chapter TWENTY-SEVEN

Harry Fairweather had started out early that morning, leaving his wife, Barbara, asleep in bed. They had been married twenty-three years but had no children – not for want of trying though, both of them used to joke. They'd done a barrage of tests and finally discovered Harry's sperm lacked the required motility. They had ummed and aahed for a couple of years before trying IVF, only to discover after two attempts it didn't work either.

Instead of children, they had filled their house with a menagerie of dogs, cats, birds and rabbits, all of which got along somehow but gave them a problem each time they decided to go on holiday.

The dogs, cats and rabbits were relatively easy but the birds presented more of a difficulty. Luckily, Harry had found a fellow copper who was also a bird-fancier so the problem had been solved.

He'd fed and watered the animals, and taken Barbara her tea and toast in bed before setting out for the bright lights of Everton, one of the quieter suburbs of Liverpool.

The route took him along the M53 and under the Mersey using the Kingsway Tunnel. As City of Chester Constabulary were paying, he didn't mind the tolls or the traffic, arriving outside 22 Armitage Street at just after 9 a.m.

He sat there for a while, collecting his thoughts and reviewing the questions he had written last night. This was a tricky interview; he had to both inform the Wrights of the death of their foster child, Roy Short, and elicit as much information as he could from them.

The area itself was middling; not as rough as some but not as rich as others. By rights he should have informed Merseyside Police of his visit to their area, but the need for speed in contacting the foster family had worked against such a move. As the boss had pointed out, it was important to watch their reactions.

He got out of the car, taking the radio console with him, and making sure the vehicle was locked. A policeman couldn't be too careful in Liverpool.

Opening the garden gate, he advanced down the short path.

The front door opened when he was halfway down. A middle-aged, well-dressed woman stood in the doorway.

'It's about Roy, isn't it?' she said softly.

'How did you know?'

'When you have a bizzie sitting outside your front gate in his car for ten minutes, it has to be about one of the kids. I was pretty sure it was Roy this time. Do you want to come in?'

Harry hesitated for a moment, his rehearsed speech about bad news forgotten.

She stepped to one side. 'Well, do you want to come in or not?'

He stepped across the threshold.

'You'd better go into the front room. I'm just making a pot of tea, I suppose you'll be having a cup?'

Was there a hint of Ireland in the voice?

'I'd love a cuppa. Milk and two sugars,' he added before he was asked.

The front room was small, neat and tidy, with all the furniture facing an eighties gas fire set in a brick surround. Above the fire, a picture of a Chinese woman by Vladimir Tretchikoff was looking down on them with studied hauteur, the modern equivalent of the Mona Lisa.

Mrs Wright returned carrying a tray with a pot of tea, two mugs and a plate of Hobnobs. 'I always have a few in case the kids visit.'

'Haven't seen one of those in ages.' Harry pointed to the picture.

'I think it's been there since we bought the house. My husband isn't big on change.'

'Where is your husband?'

'Paul was called out this morning to take a leak.'

Harry looked at her quizzically.

'He's a plumber.'

'Oh, I was hoping to see the both of you.'

'You can wait if you want, but God knows when he'll be back. Could be five minutes or five hours, I never know.'

Harry listened for the sound of other children. There was nothing.

'We don't have any kids staying with us right now, if that's what you're wondering. We're both getting a bit old for the fostering. Roy was the last. Shall I be mother?' She indicated the pot with her hand.

Harry nodded his head. 'The reason I'm here is about Roy.'

'What's he done this time? He's not a bad lad, you know, just easily led. As Paul always says, Roy wants the good life, he just doesn't want to work for it.'

She finished pouring the tea, topping up the brew with a splash of milk and two sugars. 'You don't sound like a Liverpool bizzie.'

'I'm not. I'm from Chester. Detective Constable Fairweather.' Harry decided to take the plunge. 'I'm afraid I have some bad news, Mrs Wright. We found Roy's body the night before last.'

'He had an accident?'

'I'm afraid he was murdered.'

It had all come out far more bluntly than Harry had wanted. He wished Anna was here with him now. She would have handled it much better, knowing instinctively what to say.

The woman's hand flew to her mouth and the cup of tea fell back on to the saucer, spilling its contents across the tray. The noise seemed to startle her. 'Let me get a cloth, I...'

Harry leant forward and placed his large hand on hers. 'You've just had shocking news, take a few moments. I'll get a cloth. There's one in the kitchen?'

'Next to the sink,' she said absent-mindedly. 'My poor Roy. He was a lovely little lad when he came to us, bright as a button too.'

She drifted off into her memories, leaving Harry standing there. 'I'll get the cloth,' he said, but she didn't look his way, just stared out of the front room window.

Chapter TWENTY-EIGHT

At exactly the same time as Harry was wiping up Mrs Wright's spilled tea, DC Anna Williams was assembling a line of coppers in the lower field of Grosvenor Park.

She was conscious of the police PR woman, Penny Morgan, leading a gaggle of press and photographers towards her like the Pied Piper of Hamelin.

They all stood to one side, eyeing her warily as she began her briefing. She could hear the motor of a camera whirring and the occasional click of the photographers.

One even had the temerity to lie on the floor at her feet, pointing his camera directly upwards along her body to her face.

'It'll make you look heroic, silhouetted against the grey skies of Chester,' he said, clicking his camera again and again.

Anna ignored him, clapping her hands twice. 'We're here today searching for anything related to the murder of Roy Short in that building—' she pointed back towards the ruins of St John's '—the night before last.'

A big, burly copper put his hand up. Anna recognised him as being a member of a specialist search group. 'Could you be more precise? What exactly are we looking for?'

'Anything and everything that could possibly be related to the murder of the young man yesterday evening.'

'In other words, you have no idea what we're searching for but you'd like us to find it anyway.'

A ripple of laughter ran through the group.

Anna felt her face reddening, the heat slowly rising from beneath her roll-neck sweater to cover her ears and face.

Being a redhead didn't help, of course – even her freckles were blushing.

She heard the idiot photographer taking more pictures.

Her voice rose. 'May I remind you this is a murder investigation. A fifteen-year-old boy was killed and we need to find who did it.'

The assembled coppers went silent, the man who had asked the question suddenly finding the ground near his feet the most interesting place on the planet.

'We require you to search for anything and everything that may help us in our investigation.' She held up a small red flag attached to a pointed stick. 'But you are not to touch what you find, simply place one of these flags nearby. A CSI will evaluate and bag your find. Is that clear?'

She stared at the copper, daring him to ask another question. He had the sense to remain quiet.

Penny Morgan stepped forward. 'We will be taking some footage as you search, for the evening news. Please don't look at the camera, your eyes should be focused on the ground in front of you.'

'Thanks, Penny,' Anna said. 'Now, if you'd like to spread out in a line the width of this lower field, but not more than two metres apart.'

The men did as they were told while a camera operator ran around them, filming the proceedings.

'Please advance together and try to keep a straight line, making sure to place a flag near anything interesting.'

'What about the trees?'

'Just walk around them, but do check at the base of the trunk, it's one of the usual places where something may be deposited. On my signal, please begin.'

She dropped her arm and the line began to advance forward, occasionally stopping when a searcher placed a flag into the earth.

A half an hour later they had completed the first pass, having found four empty bottles of Grolsch, seven assorted soda cans, countless ring pulls, two used condoms, a rolled-up poster advertising one of Chester City's football games, and a pair of bicycle clips. All had been bagged and tagged by the CSIs.

Anna stared at the assorted rubbish lying in the clear plastic bags, realising that the chances of finding anything useful were extremely slim.

She gathered herself before announcing with all the energy she could muster, 'We'll now move to the upper field where we'll repeat the same procedure. Please keep your eyes peeled. The smallest clue may help us solve this murder.'

'Aye, and pigs might fly,' whispered an unknown Scouse voice behind her back.

Chapter TWENTY-NINE

After Harry had wiped up the mess, he poured Mrs Wright a fresh cup of tea and chatted with her about Roy.

'How was he as a child?'

'He didn't come to us until he was eight. A quiet child, didn't say much – just played with an old rabbit with a torn ear all the time. He'd been through a lot of foster homes.'

'Why was that?'

She shrugged her shoulders. 'They told us he had anger issues and was disruptive, but we never saw that. Just a quiet boy who didn't say very much. He had been put in care by the courts when he was two years old. The mother was a drug addict. By the time he came to us, she wasn't around any more.'

'What happened to her?'

'I don't know. Perhaps she died or remarried or simply moved away to another part of the country.'

'Roy didn't have any contact with her?'

'Not that we knew. At least, he never told us he did.'

'When was the last time you saw him?

'Five days ago, he came to see us. Brought the tea set you're using. He was always such a thoughtful boy.'

Harry checked his notes. 'Please let me understand, Mrs Wright, you and your husband were his foster parents but I thought one of your responsibilities was for the children in your care to remain in education?'

'He did stay at school until he was fourteen but he didn't really like it very much, even though he was extremely bright. One day, he decided he didn't want to go any more. Of course, we tried to make him but he would go for a few days and then vanish for a month before coming back to us for a couple of days. Last December, he was taken away from us and placed back in a care home, but he didn't stay there either.'

'You don't know where he went?'

She shook her head.

'But he still kept coming back to see you?'

'Every month or so, he'd come back for a couple of days, then he'd be off again.'

Harry checked his notebook. 'I thought he was just fifteen?'

'That's right, he was born on August 22, 2008.'

There was the sound of a key in the door.

'It's Paul, he must have finished his job.'

A small man appeared in the doorway, wearing blue overalls and carrying a heavy black bag. 'Who the hell are you?'

'He's a bizzie from Chester.'

The man hung his coat behind the door. 'Is Roy in trouble?'

'I'm afraid I have some bad news…' Harry began.

'Roy's dead, Paul,' Mrs Wright said bluntly.

The man's face was as inexpressive as a stone statue. 'Oh,' was the only word he spoke, followed shortly by, 'What's for lunch, Vi?'

'I haven't had time to make anything, not with Mr Fairweather being here.'

'I was just asking your wife about Roy and his life.'

'Not much to say, really,' Paul said. 'He was a quiet boy was Roy, not like some of the others we had. They were rascals, but Roy kept himself to himself.'

'When was the last time you saw him?'

'About five days ago. Just turned up and said hello. Didn't stay long, about an hour, and then went on his way.'

'Where did he go?'

'We didn't ask and he didn't tell us. As I said, Roy always kept himself to himself.'

Harry checked his notes again. 'When did he leave here?'

'Officially, last December. They put him back in a care home. Waste of time, really.'

'But when did he actually leave?'

'The summer before then.' Paul glanced at his wife. 'Must have been August, just after his birthday, when he first vanished.'

'Did you report it?'

Another glance at the wife. 'Not right away, we thought he was coming back.'

'But he didn't?'

The man shook his head.

'And you continued to be paid for him until December?'

The woman interrupted. 'That was our right. We always thought he was coming back.'

Harry made a note to contact Liverpool social services and ask for their files on Roy. He decided not to continue with this line of questioning; it wasn't his job to condemn these people for taking the money.

'Do you have any recent pictures of Roy?'

Mrs Wright pointed to the sideboard behind Harry's head. On top was a photo of herself and a young man who looked exactly like the body found in the church. He did look small for his age.

'We took that about six weeks ago. Had to really hassle him for a picture, didn't we, Paul? Roy never liked having his picture taken.'

'Could I take it with me? I'll let you have it back just as soon as I can.'

'I don't know…'

'It's important that we have a recent picture for our investigation into his murder.'

Mrs Wright stood up and walked over to the sideboard, looking at the picture for a long time before handing it over.

'I wonder, did Roy have a room when he lived here?'

'Of course he had a room. Where do you think he slept, on the floor or below the stairs?'

'Could I see it?'

'If you want to.' Mrs Wright moved to the door. 'It's upstairs.'

She led Harry up the narrow stairs to the next floor. Roy's room was on the left next to the bathroom. It was a typical boy's room; posters of cars and a map of the world above a desk. A single bed with, above it, a picture of Mo Salah. A Liverpool fan, despite living in Everton.

Harry took a pair of plastic gloves out of his pocket and put them on his hands. 'Has anybody stayed here since Roy?'

Mrs Wright shook her head. 'We're getting too old for the fostering these days. And the kids they send you, well, they're wild. Dad can't handle them any more.'

Harry walked around the room. A PlayStation and computer were on his left with a couple of books and Liverpool match programmes. The room looked tidy and clean.

'But you've been in here, right?' he said over his shoulder as he looked around.

'Just to tidy it up. Roy was a bit messy. All boys are, aren't they? But having said that, the girls we had, they were even messier. Must have been our luck, we were given the messy ones.'

Harry noticed a brush lying next to the computer with a few hairs still trapped in its bristles. 'Does that belong to Roy?'

'I think so. He loved combing his hair in front of the mirror, did Roy. He was always a bit vain.'

Harry took his phone out of his pocket and used it to take a picture of the brush. He then pulled out an evidence bag and gently placed the brush inside before sealing it, marking down the date and time and signing his name on the cover.

'I need to take this with me, if you don't mind.'

'Why?'

'So we can check the DNA of the victim with the hairs on the brush, to confirm his identity.'

'Oh, okay.'

Harry got down on his knees and looked under the bed; that was usually where teenage boys kept anything they didn't want people to see.

Underneath this bed was nothing but a few odd socks and a lot of dust. He stood back up and wiped the knees of his trousers.

'I'll need to send a CSI team to search the room and you'll need to come to Chester to formally identify the body.'

'I don't know if I…'

'It *is* necessary, Mrs Wright, we need to be certain we have the right person. You would like us to catch whoever murdered Roy, wouldn't you? We'll send a car for you tomorrow. They'll bring you back in the evening.'

She sighed.

'It would be great if your husband came too. We'd need to take a formal statement from the two of you.'

'Can you tell him? He's not going to be a happy camper. Time is money, he always says.'

'Plumbers always charge by the hour, don't they?' answered Harry, walking back down the stairs followed by Mrs Wright.

'One last thing,' he said over his shoulder. 'Did Roy give you anything last time he was here? Besides the tea set, I mean.'

'Funny you should ask…'

They went back into the front room. Mr Wright was sitting on the chair eating a cheese sandwich. Harry couldn't help but notice the dirt encrusted beneath his nails.

'Where'd you put the bag Roy asked us to look after, Dad?'

'In the cubbyhole under the stairs.'

Mrs Wright vanished for a second, returning with an old blue Adidas bag. 'He said he'd collect it later but he never came back.'

'You didn't look inside?'

A look of horror crossed Mrs Wright's face. 'It was Roy's stuff, why would we look at it?'

Still wearing his plastic gloves, Harry pulled back the zipper on the bag.

He let out an involuntary gasp at what he saw.

Chapter THIRTY

Gavin Newton tucked into his full English in the Greasy Joe's he liked just outside the Walls. When you had a hangover, there was nothing better than fried egg, bacon, black pudding, sausage, beans, hash browns and fried bread to sop up all the alcohol in the blood. Add in a couple of slices of white bloomer bread and a big mug of tea and he was in reporter heaven.

Last night had been fun. The other journalists had gathered around him at the wine bar, desperately trying to find out what he knew. He recalled the scene:

'You must have an inside source, Gavin,' asked the reporter from the *Liverpool Echo*.

'Might have and might not have. Let's just say, I know this patch better than most.'

'How'd you find out the victim had no eyes? From the pathologist's office? I always find slipping them a couple of quid for a drink always helps.'

'Might be. But as you well know, a good reporter never reveals their sources.'

A woman with a Welsh accent leant into him, pressing her breast against his left elbow. 'Come on, you can tell us. We're all journalists, right? Do you know more?'

He pretended to think about her request before answering. 'Let's just say what I revealed at the press conference is merely the tip of the iceberg, there's far more to come.'

'So all that malarkey about satanists and devil worship wasn't a load of old bollocks?' The Scouser was still digging for more info.

Gavin touched the side of his nose. 'You'll find out, mate, just read my byline.'

Even if he said it himself, the question about the satanists had been a stroke of genius. It had come to him as he was standing there, facing that stupid copper and his well-groomed PR woman. Somehow the words had slipped out of his mouth but, as soon as he had said them, he knew he had journalistic gold. The pot at the end of the proverbial rainbow. Here was a narrative that could run and run. Each new discovery about the case could easily be twisted to fit the idea of satanist rituals and witches' covens.

His belief was confirmed by the Welsh woman. 'It wouldn't surprise me if the nationals don't start to pick up on this story. The *Express*, the *Mail*, even a few of the qualities always love a good story about satanists and witchcraft, particularly when it comes from a place with such long history as Chester. When I filed my copy to Reuters on the wire earlier, the editor in London responded in a flash that he wanted more.'

So she was the local stringer for the wire service. He would have to get to know her better.

She lifted up the wine bottle from the bar, a cheeky little Tempranillo. 'This soldier seems to be empty, shall we get another? It's on Reuters.'

They had then proceeded to finish another four bottles as Gavin listened to their tales from the front lines of journalism. Tales that inevitably involved lots of feverish sex in unusual places and the consumption of copious amounts of alcohol.

He returned to the present and his breakfast, placing his knife and fork back on the plate. The full English had hit the spot and he already felt much better. As he sat back in the rickety chair, listening to the steam wheezing from the old boiler behind the counter, he thought about his next moves.

The satanist angle had to be pursued further. It was a great narrative moving forward, something that would interest the quality dailies. But he needed fuel to feed the fire. The hundred quid he had borrowed from his erstwhile girlfriend had already gone to his police narc.

Could he get more from him without fronting up the cash? He could only try. His editor wasn't going to give him any money, the tight bastard.

'Great story, Gavin. More like that if you can.'

'I'd love to, boss, but the source wants money before he gives me any more info.'

His editor's reaction was to pull out the pockets of his trousers to reveal they were empty. 'Nothing in the kitty, Gavin, you're gonna have to wing it.'

The man looked ridiculous, standing there looking like a baby elephant.

What was he going to do to get more money? Ask his girlfriend again? She'd already whinged and moaned last time. 'I think you only want two things from me, Gavin – money and sex.'

He'd totally denied it. The truth was he only wanted *one* thing from her and that was money. The sex he could take or leave.

Where was he going to get the money?

And then his phone rang. He glanced down at the screen. It was the source. Shit.

He pressed the answer button. 'Hi there, great to hear from you. Did you see the piece in the paper last night?'

Chapter THIRTY-ONE

After the meeting with Davy Jones, Emma went back to the Major Incident Room. She thought about going over to check on Anna and the fingertip search of the park but decided against it. Anna was more than capable of handling the whole process, plus she mustn't micromanage her subordinates.

The words of her last appraisal came back:

'You have a tendency to want to be in control of everything, Detective Inspector Christie, attending to every detail and not allowing your subordinates to implement your strategies and follow their instincts. By micromanaging everything, you end up managing nothing.'

She had tried to argue that the details in any case were important. A good copper had to be on top of the case.

As she spoke, she could hear her dad's voice in her head.

But the supervisor wasn't having it. 'Too many details and you obscure the bigger picture as well as de-motivate your colleagues. There is no "I" in team.'

She shook her head. Another one of those bloody silly sayings that irritated the hell out of her. There was no 'I' in arsehole either, but she didn't point it out to them. Management by aphorism, is that what they taught in Ryton these days?

But she did recognise it was one of her failings. Colin used to say exactly the same thing to her: 'You can't do everything yourself, Emma, you have to trust your people.'

She found it hard to let go. A function, perhaps, of her father's constant admonishments to her about being focused and knowing everything. Funny. With his Alzheimer's he was no longer in control of anything.

Perhaps there was a lesson for her.

She hung her coat on the hook at the entrance to the office, got herself a coffee and logged on to the computer set up by the techies. She was just about to check the investigation log created by John Simpson when the phone rang.

'Hiya, Harry, how is Liverpool?'

'Doing well, boss. Jürgen has them playing like superheroes again.'

She sighed. 'Now is not the time or the place for one of your jokes. I meant your visit to the Wrights. How's it going?'

'Oh, the investigation. I knew I was in Liverpool for a reason.'

'Harry, you're trying my patience.'

'The Wrights have confirmed that Roy left them about a year ago, but visited in the last five days. I have a recent photo plus probable DNA from a brush. We need to send a car for them tomorrow to make a formal ID.'

'Great. Well done, Harry.'

'There's more, boss.' Harry stayed silent, dragging out the moment.

'Go on…' Emma was finally forced to say.

'He left a bag with them when he visited.'

'And?'

'It's an old Adidas bag. There must be nearly sixty grand inside and two bags of white powder.'

'Coke?'

'I don't know, boss. Probably, but I haven't touched it.'

'Get it back here as soon as you can, and don't let it out of your sight. I don't want the chain of evidence broken.'

'Right, boss.'

'And we'll need a search and CSI team at the house. See if there is anything else there.'

'Already organised, boss.'

'Well done, Harry. Before I forget, get on to Liverpool CID and let them know what we've found, plus get all their intel on Roy Short and the Wrights.'

'Already done that too, boss. A DC Flanagan is sending everything they have asap. I had to promise a quid pro quo though.'

'What?'

'We'd keep them informed and, if there are arrests in Liverpool, they need to be involved.'

'Fair enough, I'd ask for the same in Chester. Well done, Harry. When are you due back?'

'On my way, boss, should be there in less than an hour depending on traffic.'

'I'll have Jane Eastham waiting to log the bag into forensics. See you soon.'

She switched off her phone. Finally, they seemed to making progress. Money and drugs. It looked like Roy Short may have done the dirty on his suppliers, stealing their gear.

Is that why they had him killed?

But why make it so open and hang a plaque round the boy's head? And why take out the eyes?

Emma turned to her computer, making a note of the phone call in the investigation log.

DC Harry Fairweather has discovered a bag belonging to Roy Short left at his foster parents' house. The bag contains a large amount of money and possible illegal substances, perhaps cocaine. He is returning with

the bag directly to the Major Incident Room from Liverpool. ETA 1.30 p.m.

She closed the file and sat back in her chair. They *were* making progress. She thought about grabbing something to eat but decided to pay a visit to Anna in Grosvenor Park before Harry returned.

She wasn't micromanaging, just checking progress. At least, that was what she told herself as she went to get her coat.

Chapter THIRTY-TWO

Altea Marku listened hard. Who was knocking at the door?

He'd just given the plants some feed before he would harvest the buds tomorrow morning, exactly as he had been told. He couldn't afford to piss them off, not again.

Was it Terry? What did he want?

He listened again. Three knocks, exactly the same as Terry. Had he changed his mind or simply forgotten to tell him something?

Marku ran downstairs and pulled open the door. A stranger was standing in front of him. 'Whaddya wan'?'

'Hello, I wonder if you could help me. My car has broken down and I wonder if I could use the phone in your house to call the AA?' He pointed to a jerry can at his feet.

'What?'

'I said my car has broken down…'

'I heard. No phone here.'

He went to close the door but found the man's foot stopped him. What was happening?

'Listen, you don' wan' here, next door better.'

He went to close the door again but the man's foot was still in the way.

He clenched his fist and opened the door again. He'd teach this stupid English bastard a lesson.

As soon as the door opened, the man rushed inside, turned Marku round and grabbed him round the neck, covering his nose and mouth with a damp cloth.

'Just take a few deep breaths, sonny. Relax and breathe deeply. That's it. A good, long sleep.'

Marku tried to struggle against the man's strong grip but couldn't move. He breathed in, feeling his legs begin to buckle under him.

What was happening? Why had this man come to the grow house?

'Another ten seconds and you'll be able to sleep for a long time.'

The sound of the man's voice was soothing.

For a moment, Marku drifted off to his days in Albania, guarding the goats with his grandfather Envar and the dog, Titi. Long nights spent in the mountains above his village, drinking sheep milk for breakfast and eating the rough cheese Grandfather carried in his sack. How he missed those days when there was no fear, no grow, no threats and no hate.

Just him, his grandfather, the dog, the goats and long, endless days in the high pastures above their village.

But that had all changed. They had come for him and told him he had to leave. Go to England, they said. You can make all the money you need there and then come back and buy up some land, marry a good girl and settle down with your family.

The journey began, saying goodbye to his grandfather. Long nights in the back of a van; no lights, no food, nothing.

And then the sea; crossing in a small boat under glowering grey skies, the waves threatening to capsize them every second. He didn't want to die in the sea, nobody wanted to die. The white cliffs of England beckoning him towards them. A cold welcome waiting, processing on a windswept airfield before being dumped in a dirty hotel with everybody else. The gang came for him there, threatening him to leave or his grandfather would be hurt. He owed them money, they said, so much money. They beat him until he agreed to work for them, anything to stop the beating.

He opened his eyes. The damp cloth was still over his mouth and nose, and the man's arms still held him tightly.

'Shhhh, little one, go to sleep.'

The last memory he had before his world went dark was of sitting around a camp fire on a cold night, throwing a roasted goat bone to the dog while his grandfather played the mournful notes of *Qaj Minus* on the fyell he carried everywhere he went.

A sad song, a plaintive song, but one full of hope for a better world and a better life.

Happy days.

And then there were no more memories.

Chapter THIRTY-THREE

Harry made sure the bag was firmly secured by the seat belt on the passenger side. He switched on the radio, tuning in to Heart FM, and Snow Patrol's 'Chasing Cars' belted out from the speakers. One of his favourite songs. He set the satnav for Grosvenor Park in Chester and waited while it calibrated the route and the time.

Forty-six minutes on the motorway or forty-three minutes via the A41. He chose the latter, glad that it was quicker but also happy not to spend too long driving on the motorway. He found nothing more boring than mile after mile of grey tarmac and even greyer skies.

He looked back at the Wrights. The woman was standing at the entrance to her semi-detached home, waiting for him to leave. The husband was nowhere to be seen.

Were they as straightforward as they seemed or was there something else going on in that home? Was that why Roy Short left so abruptly?

He was certain Mrs Wright hadn't told him everything about the departure. It was their lack of concern about Short that worried him. Surely foster parents still had a duty of care for their charges, even if social services had placed them back in a care home?

He made a mental note again to check with Liverpool social services. They could decide to give him the information voluntarily or withhold it. But this was a murder investigation, and he was sure he wouldn't need to serve them with a warrant.

He put the car in gear and drove away. In his rearview mirror, Mrs Wright waved goodbye. Probably glad to see him go. In this area of Liverpool a visit from the bizzies wasn't unknown and definitely not welcome.

At this time of day, the traffic wasn't too bad. He made good time down the A59 and through the Kingsway Tunnel under the Mersey. By sheer chance – or maybe it was programmed – the namesake song from Gerry and the Pacemakers began to play as he drove through the tunnel's open mouth.

'I'm not on a bloody ferry though, am I?'

Gerry's voice echoed through the car as he drove through the tunnel, only ending as he exited on the other side in Wallasey, Ed Sheeran's dulcet tones replacing the Liverpool whine.

'Thank God for that. I don't think I could have stood another verse.'

He accelerated the car to get on to the M53, making sure to keep to the speed limit of 70 mph as other cars raced past him.

What was it about motorways? People who were normally quiet and unassuming in their real lives suddenly becoming the Stig as they drove on the motorway.

'You won't get there any faster,' he shouted as they passed him on the outside. He realised, of course, they *would* get there faster – as long as there were no tailbacks in front – but he had to shout something at these idiots.

The motorway was relatively quiet and he made good time until the satnav indicated he should turn off at the next junction. He thought about staying on the M53 but a little man on the map indicated there were roadworks ahead.

He turned off, taking the A550 and then New Chester Road, checking in his mirror, remembering the adage of his driving instructor from twenty-five years ago. Mirror, manoeuvre, mirror.

Only a black BMW was behind him.

It was funny how these simple phrases stuck in the mind. 'Clunk click, every trip.' 'Go to work on an egg.' 'Hello Tosh, gotta Toshiba.' But he supposed that was the point. They were brainworms; phrases that were so memorable they stayed buried there for years, hotwired into the head.

Not long to go now. He checked the Adidas bag once again. Still nestled in the leather embrace of the front seat.

How had a fifteen-year-old boy accumulated so much money, and where had the drugs come from? Had he nicked them, and that's why he was killed?

A car pulled out from a side street directly in front, forcing him to brake sharply. He checked in his rearview mirror. The BMW had nearly run into his rear.

He pressed his horn, holding it down to form a loud squeal of outrage.

The car in front ignored him, pulling slowly away but not increasing speed greatly.

He beeped at it again, longer this time.

'Get a bloody move on, Sunday driver.'

The car still wasn't going any faster. Instead it seemed to be slowing to a stop. In his rearview mirror, the BMW was right behind him now, blocking him in.

Harry looked over his shoulder, and suddenly a shiver of fear ran down his spine.

The car in front stopped and two men, both in balaclavas, jumped out and strode towards his car, one on either side.

Harry couldn't help but notice the dull black object in the hand of one of the men. It came up and pointed straight at him, its dark circular mouth the entrance to hell.

'Get out of the car,' shouted a voice from behind the gun.

Chapter THIRTY-FOUR

Emma Christie strode over to the knot of people standing to one side of the upper paddock of the park. A line of coppers was still advancing across the field, eyes down, staring intently at the ground in front of them.

To one side a group of reporters, photographers and a film crew were following them, idly watching their progress.

'How's it going, Anna?'

'Nearly finished here, boss, just the far field to search and then we're done.'

'Found anything?'

'Quite a lot.' She pointed to the pile of evidence bags lying on a tray. 'But nothing related to the murder, as far as I can see. Lots of soda cans, ring pulls, cigarette packs, a few kids' toys. We even found a wedding ring belonging to some man called Tom who was married to Eileen on September 29, 2003.'

'She's not going to be happy he's lost it.'

'I got the feeling it had been thrown away, boss.'

'Another happy marriage.'

Emma scanned the field. The line of coppers was close to the far path that bisected the two sections of the park. A couple of CSIs, dressed in their white suits, were on their knees pulling something from the earth and placing it carefully inside an evidence bag. A few people were watching, fascinated by the sight of coppers actually working.

Off to one side a man in blue overalls, wearing a bright green high-vis jacket with 'City of Chester' stamped on the back, was standing next to a rubbish cart. He had stopped sweeping the paths and was staring at the coppers.

'You had a chat with him?' Emma nodded in the man's direction.

'He's here every day, sweeping the leaves off the paths and emptying the bins. Philip Jackson is his name. He didn't see anything unusual though.'

'Did he collect anything and put it in his cart over the last couple of days?'

'He told me there was nothing unusual. "Same old shit, different day, more leaves than usual" were his exact words.'

'Well, it's autumn, what does he expect?' She pointed to the reporters. 'Have they been any trouble?'

'No more than usual. One of them said I had the face of a model and would I come and do some pictures for him. Tasteful, he said.'

'We all know what "tasteful" means, don't we?'

'Yeah, he made it clear that clothes were optional but the uniform could spice up the shoot. I said I'd love to come and so would my boyfriend and all his mates from the police rugby club. He never asked again, strange that.'

Emma thought for a moment. 'But you don't have a boyfriend and there is no police rugby club.'

'But he doesn't know that, does he?'

Penny Morgan bounced up to them, smiling. 'Well, that was a successful search day.'

'We didn't find anything.'

'I meant a successful day visually. We'll definitely be on the evening news tonight. I added a segment with the usual message for anybody who saw anything to come forward and ring the number. I hope that was okay, Emma.'

'Fine, Penny. I would have preferred a weapon or at least a lovely fingerprint of the murderer. Successful visuals

I can take or leave.' Emma scratched her wrist. 'Where are all the reporters going?'

'I've arranged a liquid lunch with a few pork pies and sandwiches down the pub. You have to feed them or they won't come.'

'Right. I'm off back to the Major Incident Room. Can you both come to a briefing at two? Harry's found something in Liverpool, he's bringing it back as we speak.'

Chapter THIRTY-FIVE

Harry glanced from one balaclavaed man to another.
Both had guns pointing directly at him. In the rearview
mirror he could see two more men getting out of the BMW.

'I won't say this again, get out of the car.'

'You're making a big mistake, I'm a detective constable
with City of Chester Constabulary…'

'We know exactly who you are, copper, now get out of
the car.' The gun in the man's hand jerked twice to indicate
Harry should move. 'Hurry, get out.'

The detective's mind was racing. What should he do?
Put the car in gear and try to make a run for it? The men at
the rear were positioned on either side of the car. He could
reverse into them and pull away before the men in front had
time to react. He reached down to the gear stick—

The glass of the driver's side window shattered into a
thousand little pieces. A hand reached in and released the
door lock.

'You're not moving quickly enough, copper! Get out of
the car.'

The voice had a definite Scouse edge to it.

Harry released his seat belt and, holding his hands high,
stepped out of the car only to be thrown roughly across the
bonnet. His pockets were quickly searched, with his wallet
and warrant card opened. He glanced down at the car
parked in front, making a mental note of the numberplate.

'Detective Constable Harold Fairweather? It's not your
lucky day, Harry.'

The man on the far side opened the passenger door,
reached in and grabbed the Adidas bag.

'Got it, Mickey,' he shouted, before running back to the car in front.

'Your mobile?' the man holding Harry shouted.

'What?'

'Your mobile phone, dickhead.'

Harry reached into his trouser pocket and handed over his phone.

'Away from the car and down on your knees.'

Harry did what was ordered, feeling the rough concrete of the pavement bite through the thin fabric of his trousers.

The driver's side door of his car slammed shut and he heard the engine start up. The car was driven away.

'Sweet dreams,' said the Scouse voice behind him.

A second later he felt an immense blow to the back of his head, and suddenly the grey concrete of the pavement was rushing up to strike his face.

Chapter THIRTY-SIX

Emma Christie glanced at the clock. Where was Harry? He should have been back at least half an hour ago.

In the Major Incident Room, the officers were gathering for the 2 p.m. briefing. Anna was getting a coffee with John from the machine in the corner. The three young PCs were sitting in their usual seats at the front, while the crime scene manager, Jane Eastham, was in her seat at the back. The detectives from Stewart Riggs' team were whispering to each other, their hands covering their mouths. What were those two up to? If they'd been chatting with Riggs it was sure to be no good.

It always amused Emma that at these sorts of briefings people invariably sat in the same places every time, as if there was some unwritten hierarchy of seating or if each seat had their names invisibly written on the back. Next time, she would rearrange the chairs into a circle just to screw them up. It was another one of her dad's aphorisms: 'When investigations become predictable, change the way people look at the problem, make them see it from a different angle.'

Changing the seating might be a very literal interpretation of his words, but she had used it in the past and it had worked. Time to put it to work with this lot. Mess with their heads a little.

She glanced at the clock. Nearly 2 p.m. Where was Harry? She hoped he hadn't stopped off for something to eat on the way. But surely even Harry wouldn't be that stupid, not when he was carrying a bag containing sixty grand and a couple of kilos of coke?

'Can you ring him again, John?'

The civilian researcher picked up his mobile, pressed a speed-dial number and listened. 'Still no answer, boss. I've gone to voicemail for the fourth time.'

'What's the bloody idiot up to? Why's he not responding?' she said quietly, shaking her head. She'd kill Harry when he got back. He said it would only take him an hour from Liverpool and that was over two hours ago.

'Can we get on to the control centre, John, ask them to track his vehicle's location? If he's at a bloody chippy, I'll kill him.'

Her mobile vibrated on the desk in front of her. She looked at it but didn't recognise the number, answering it anyway.

'Is this DI Christie?'

'Speaking, who's this?'

'I'm Sergeant Trevoil of Cheshire Police. A Detective Constable Harold Fairweather was found at the side of the road just outside Backford, he's been attacked and badly beaten. We've taken him to the Countess of Chester Hospital to check for concussion.'

'What?'

The sergeant from Cheshire Police was about to repeat everything he'd just said even more slowly, before Emma interrupted him.

'What? Harry's been attacked?'

'That's what I just said. He seems to be okay, but we've taken him to the hospital to be checked over. Was he on a job?'

Emma spoke a quick, 'Thank you, Sergeant,' before clicking off the phone.

She clapped her hands. Everybody in the room stopped what they were doing and looked towards her.

'The briefing is cancelled, Harry's in hospital. Anna, you're with me.'

'I can't, boss, I've arranged an interview with the solicitor who bailed Roy Short when he was arrested for dealing, a Dominic Sandway.'

'That's more important, you go there. I'll get somebody else to drive me.' She turned back to the rest of the team. 'Now Harry's been attacked, it's become even more key we find out who's behind this murder. Work hard and work smart, people. Get whoever's behind the attacks.'

Chapter THIRTY-SEVEN

Harry was sitting in the corridor, looking pale and lost. Next to him was a tall, thin sergeant from Cheshire Police wearing the brightest fluorescent-green high-vis coat Emma had ever seen.

Emma had driven to the hospital as fast as she could, this time allowing both siren and flashing lights to clear the way. Normally she hated driving, but this time she knew it was necessary to race through the city's streets and out to the hospital.

'How are you, Harry?' she asked.

'A bit of a headache and a bruise the size of a golf ball on top of my noggin, but otherwise okay.' He touched the white bandage wrapped around his head. 'Won't be heading a football for a while though. Liverpool will be disappointed.'

'What happened?'

'It's all a bit fuzzy, boss. I was driving back from seeing the Wrights. All was going well, but then I was boxed in by two cars just outside Backford.'

For a second, Emma hated hearing that place name again. It brought back so many bad memories for her. *Don't think about it, not now, it was three years ago.*

She forced herself to focus back on Harry's voice.

'Four men got out of the cars. Two of them had guns, boss, pointed at me. They took the bag and the Vauxhall and left me on the pavement with a sore head.'

The local sergeant interrupted. 'He was found there by a member of the public who called it in. I went to the incident. He was awake and talking.' The sergeant paused.

'Actually, he was awake and swearing. We found out he was a copper on the job and called you. His car was discovered ten minutes ago not far from where he was attacked, somebody had set it on fire.'

'Probably the best thing that could have happened to it,' muttered Harry.

'Did you get a registration number for the car that hijacked you?'

Harry nodded.

'We already checked it out,' the sergeant interrupted. 'A false numberplate, not even issued yet, according to the DVLA.'

'And the bag?'

'Gone, boss, one of the men took it.' He stopped for a moment, staring straight ahead. 'It's just come back to me. The man who took it called out to the leader, he said, "Got it, Mickey." I remember that.'

'That narrows it down a bit,' said the sergeant. 'All we're looking for now is a Mickey from Liverpool. Can't be more than twenty thousand men with that name.'

Emma silenced him with a glare. She touched Harry on the shoulder. 'How're you feeling?'

'Okay, boss, just waiting on the all-clear from the doctors.'

As if on cue, an Asian woman wearing a stethoscope and white coat came out of the room opposite. 'You're free to go, Mr Fairweather, but remember, please rest for the next couple of days and avoid stress. If you have any periods of vomiting, change in behaviour, recurring headaches, problems with memory or any other unusual issues, please contact us again or go to your local GP.'

'But that's how I feel every day, Doctor.'

The woman stared at him, not knowing if he was joking or not. Finally she said, 'If you have any *unusual* periods of vomiting, change in behaviour, recurring headaches, problems with memory or any other unusual issues, please contact us again or go to your local GP.'

'Will do.'

'Remember – take it easy. You've just had a severe blow to the head.'

They all stood up and began to walk out of A&E.

'I'll drive you home, Harry. Your wife can look after you.'

'What? I thought you had a briefing this afternoon. If you think you're getting rid of me that easily, boss, think again. Besides, we have a team of Liverpool scallies to put away. Can't do that at home eating liver and bacon.'

Chapter THIRTY-EIGHT

'You got it?'

Liam Gilligan was in another phone box, this time on a main road in Speke. Big Max was standing on the street next to the car, checking for any trouble. This area wasn't Liam's, it was controlled by another gang. But he'd be okay as long as he was quick. It didn't hurt to check out the area anyway, it was time he expanded.

'No problem, boss. We took him in the same place we took that other copper three years ago. This one was easier. We left him making zeds on the pavement.'

'So our intel from the snout was kosher. Roy is dead. His body was found missing its eyes in Chester. You got the bag and the money?'

'Yeah, plus there was two keys of coke inside.'

How had Roy managed to get two kilos of coke? Had another gang given it to him? Or had he been thieving from the Gilligans for a long time and bought the gear himself? And who had killed him? Was it another gang? Had he stiffed them too?

Liam parked those thoughts for a while and concentrated on his conversation with his number two. 'Send the bag and money back to me. You keep the coke, Mickey, a reward for a job well done.'

'Thanks, boss.'

'What about the cop's car?'

'Melting in a parking lot next to the river. The bizzies do buy some cheap motors, this one had more plastic than metal.'

'He won't be able to ID you?'

'Nah, we were all wearing balaclavas, plus we used the false numberplates for the car. We swapped them in the car park. All they can look for are BMWs, and there are millions of those on the roads.'

'Good.' Gilligan thought for a moment. 'Listen, Mickey, I need you to go to Chester.'

'No problem, boss.'

'Find out what's happening with the operation there. Check out if Roy was a one-off or a symptom of a much bigger problem. I don't want our Cheshire, Staffordshire and North Wales operations compromised at the moment. Got it?'

'I'll go straight away, boss.'

'And Mickey, while you're there I want you to visit the grow houses. Check that security is really tight. I've got a big deal for some weed coming from Scotland in the next week or so, I'll need all the product I can get. Apparently, the crazy Jocks have decided they don't need our coke or crystal meth any more, they want some good smoke instead.'

'No worries, boss, I won't let you down.'

Gilligan let a little edge of menace creep into his voice. 'I know you won't, Mickey.'

He put the phone down and exited the call box. He stood outside as Big Max opened the rear door of the car. He was looking for the usual signs of dealing – boys hanging around doing nothing, other kids on bikes ready to deliver, still others checking out for the unwanted attentions of the bizzies.

There was nothing.

Had the Whitney Gang become slack? They didn't seem to be controlling their territory or building up their business. The mob had been around for such a long time, perhaps the hunger was no longer there.

Gangs were like sharks; once they stopped moving forward they died, to be eaten by the ones who were more aggressive.

It was the law of the concrete jungle; eat or be eaten. Kill or be killed.

He'd get Big Max to check them out later, see if they were ready to be taken.

He needed to expand and this area looked perfect.

He was still hungry and he would never stop till he got what he wanted:

Respect.

Chapter THIRTY-NINE

DC Anna Williams looked up at the large Georgian house overlooking the racecourse.

The whole place oozed old money and judicial prudence. The outside sash windows and doors were painted in a cream Farrow and Ball paint, beloved of interior and exterior designers to the rich and pretentious. Even the blinds behind the windows were embossed with the company's livery and a rather too ornate armorial shield.

This was Sandway and Company, Solicitors. She was almost tempted to kneel down and make abeyance before she crossed over the threshold.

She took a deep breath and pushed on the heavy, polished brass doorknob.

Inside, the sophisticated opulence continued with more pastel-coloured paint on the walls and a receptionist who was even more polished than the brass doorknob.

'Can I help you?' The voice cut glass like the chandelier hanging from the ceiling.

'I have an appointment with Mr Sandway.'

'You are…?'

'Detective Constable Williams, City of Chester Constabulary.'

She checked the list in front of her. 'Right, here you are. I'll see if Mr Sandway is available.'

She picked up the phone and spoke quietly into it.

'His secretary will be down in a few minutes to take you up to his office. In the meantime, here is your security pass. Please wear it at all times when you are in the building.'

Anna took the security pass, noticing for the first time a man in a grey suit standing to one side, the wire of an earpiece curling down to his pocket like a punk earring.

'If you would like to sit and wait.'

Anna glanced to where the receptionist was pointing. Three armchairs surrounded a long wooden table festooned with copies of *Cheshire Life*. Against the wall, a Georgian longcase clock by Robert Fletcher of Chester stood sentry. On the face, a painted moon was peeking out from behind the dial.

She walked to the area and sat down, being swallowed by the comfort and softness of the furnishings. The clock ticked loudly beside her.

She didn't bother reading any of the magazines. The Botoxed faces of Cheshire housewives had no charm for her.

After five minutes, an older woman in a twin set and a fabulous string of pearls appeared at the bottom of the stairs.

'Detective Constable Williams.'

Forgetting herself, Anna put her hand up.

'Mr Sandway will see you now.'

Anna stood and followed the woman up the stairs, turning right at the top. The woman didn't say a word as she used her pass to open the door, leading Anna past a large oak desk to another door.

She knocked, waited for the word 'Enter' before pushing the door open and, stepping back, allowed Anna to go in.

The room was immense, stretching the whole length of the building. Tall sash windows reached up to the ceiling. On the walls, a variety of Old Master paintings were individually lit by small spotlights. Intricately patterned Persian carpets covered a highly polished herringbone parquet floor. On the right, an informal meeting area with the more supremely soft furnishings lay at one end. At the other was a large walnut desk with a few papers on it and none of the usual equipment of the modern office.

No telephone. No laptop. No printer.

Anna decided they must be hidden behind the oak panelling somewhere.

The whole place reeked of intimidation. It shouted *we are wealthy, we are old money, we are powerful, we are connected.*

Out of nowhere, a man approached her with his hand held out. He was much younger than she expected, not older than thirty-five.

'DC Williams, I'm so pleased to meet you.'

She shook his hand, feeling the strength of the grip.

He led her towards the informal meeting area, adjusting his trousers slightly before sitting down and crossing his legs. Anna found herself staring at a pair of highly polished brogues in the softest leather.

'Why don't you sit down, DC Williams? Can I call you Anna?'

She sat down opposite him. She had never mentioned her first name when she'd arranged the appointment.

'How can I help our friends in the police? As I was saying to the chief constable only last week, our police in Chester command the respect and admiration of the city. It is our duty to help them in any way.'

In one sentence he had managed to flatter her force and remind her he was on friendly terms with her boss.

A good start.

She took out her notepad and notes from her briefcase, instantly aware of its shabbiness in these elegant surroundings. It wasn't even made from leather but some obscure form of plastic from China. She pushed it to the side of the armchair, out of sight.

'Thank you for seeing me, Mr Sandway, at such short notice.'

'Please, call me Dominic; everybody else does.'

She instantly knew that nobody else called this man Dominic in this office. *Sir* was probably his first name.

'I'd like to talk to you about one of your clients, if I may.'

He smiled and brought his manicured hands together to form a triangle. 'Much as I would like to aid the police, I'm afraid if it's about a client, all my conversations with them are covered by legal professional privilege.'

'Of course, I would not want to compromise any relationship with any of your clients. However, we believe one of them has been murdered and we are sure you would want to help the police with our enquiries.'

For the first time, Sandway looked apprehensive. 'Murdered?' The apprehension was immediately covered by a smile. 'We concentrate on commercial, not criminal law in our practice, DC Williams, I'm not sure we can help you with a murder.'

Anna Williams took a breath. 'Do you have a client called Roy Short, Mr Sandway?'

'I don't recall any of our clients with that name, DC Williams.'

'What about Mark Sinton?'

The man smiled and shook his head. 'As I said, we tend to represent large multinational companies and commercial clients, not individuals.'

Anna passed across Mark Sinton's detention report. 'This individual was arrested outside Checkers nightclub six months ago. If you look at the name of the solicitor representing him…' She tapped the box at the bottom. 'Is this you, Mr Sandway?'

Another smile. 'I think it is me, but I can't be certain.'

'We could check the station's CCTV for that evening, Mr Sandway, if that would help you remember.'

Anna was bluffing. Most police stations only kept CCTV for a month unless there was a complaint against the custody sergeant, but she hoped Sandway wouldn't know that.

'I remember now. I *did* get called out that night. The wife of our usual criminal solicitor was delivering a baby and I didn't want to disturb any other member of staff that late at night.'

'That's very kind of you,' Anna replied without a hint of irony. 'Mark Sinton's real name was Roy Short. Why was your company representing him?'

Another smile, this time obviously forced. 'I'm afraid that information is covered by client confidentiality, DC Williams.'

'Could you at least tell me how Mr Short, aka Mr Sinton, had your number?'

'I wouldn't know and I couldn't tell you even if I did.'

'Client confidentiality.'

'Correct, DC Williams.'

'I'm sure your services are not inexpensive, Mr Sandway.' Anna glanced around the large, opulent room. 'I was wondering how a fifteen-year-old boy could afford such an eminent solicitor as yourself?'

'Again, not information I could possibly tell you.'

'Client confidentiality?'

'You are a quick learner, DC Williams. I would ask the young man himself if I were you.' Sandway put his right hand in his pocket.

'That would be difficult, as he is dead, Mr Sandway.'

The solicitor shrugged his shoulders. 'What a pity.'

A knock at the door and the secretary appeared. 'Your next appointment is waiting, Mr Sandway.'

Anna was sure the secretary knew to interrupt them at that moment. Had Sandway signalled her somehow?

The solicitor stood up. 'I am terribly sorry, DC Williams, but as you can see I am an extremely busy man.' He put out his hand, indicating the interview was over.

Anna ignored it. 'One last question, Mr Sandway, before I go. When was the last time you saw Roy Short?'

'I'm sorry, but that information is also covered by client confidentiality.' The smile vanished. 'Mrs Harvey will now show you out.'

He walked down the office to his desk and began to shuffle some papers.

Anna found her elbow gently touched by the secretary. At the door, the security guard in the grey suit and earpiece waited.

She gathered her papers and put them in her plastic briefcase. 'Thank you for your time, Mr Sandway, I'm sure we will be meeting again.'

She held her head up high and strode out of the room.

As the door closed, Sandway opened a drawer and picked up the receiver of a phone concealed inside, before dialling a number.

'We have a problem,' he said.

Chapter FORTY

'Right, you lot, let's make this quick,' Emma began. 'As you may or may not know, although the dashing white bandage round Harry's head is a big clue, Harry was attacked on his way back from Liverpool this afternoon. Why don't you tell us what happened, Harry?'

'This morning I visited Roy Short's foster parents, the Wrights. They said they last saw Roy five days ago. He left a dark blue Adidas bag with them. I checked inside and my guess was that it contained about sixty grand in cash plus two large parcels containing a white powder, probably cocaine. I took the bag and was bringing it back here when I was hijacked by four armed men on the A41 just outside Backford. I got this for my troubles…' Harry gingerly touched the back of his skull.

'Doesn't seem to have done you much harm, Harry,' said one of the CSIs.

'Harry's head probably did more harm to the boomerang that hit him,' said John.

'Why do you think it was a boomerang that hit him?' asked Gerry.

'Because it's all coming back to him now. Boom, boom, tish.'

'Thank you, John. Anything else, Harry?'

'Only that they took my phone and the pool car. It was found a couple of miles away, burnt to a cinder.'

'Knowing our cars, it'll probably be back in use tomorrow,' joked Richard Gleason.

Laughter from the whole team echoed around the Major Incident Room..

'Okay, people, quieten down.' Emma raised her hands and paused for a moment. 'Thanks for the heads-up, Harry.' A collective groan went around the room. 'Anyway, we have to ask ourselves: how did the gang know Harry had the bag?'

Anna put her hand up. 'They were watching the Wrights and saw Harry leave with it.'

'Perhaps, Anna. If Roy Short stole the money and the drugs from his boss, they'd watch his old house to see if he went back there.'

'But surely they would have searched the house before now?' said Harry.

'Perhaps they were going to when you went there. Or maybe the Wrights rang the gang as soon as you left and said you had the bag.'

'But I talked with the foster mother and I can't believe she would have grassed me up. I was certain they didn't know what the bag contained.'

'Well, Harry,' Emma interrupted, 'however the gang found out, it ended up with them coshing you and stealing it back.' She paused for thought. 'It does give us a working hypothesis for the death of Roy Short: he stole the money and the drugs from his bosses and they dealt out retribution.'

'But why make it so public?' Anna asked. 'Usually these people end up encased in concrete in some building site or thrown into the sea and left for the fish.'

'I don't know, Anna. Perhaps they wanted to discourage anybody else from doing the same thing? It's just a working hypothesis at the moment, but we should keep all avenues of enquiry open until we gather more evidence. Lads, how was the CCTV?'

Richard Gleason stood up. 'As you suggested, we ran the ANPR for both nights – the night of the murder and the night when the cameras were destroyed on the church. After going through the results, it seems we have hits for ninety-three vehicles that were in the vicinity at the same time on both nights.'

'Great, can you start checking up on them?'

'What? All ninety-three?'

'That's right. You have the numberplates, get on to the DVLA and find the owners, and then contact them one by one to find out what they were doing in that area on those nights.'

'That could take years, boss.'

'You'd better start now then. Gerry, how are you doing with your local CCTV?'

'Not great, I'm afraid. The one on the building opposite hasn't been serviced for a couple of years. We've got a grainy photo of a white van in the area at the right time, 21.55 on the night of the murder, coming out of the lane beside the church. We can't see the driver or the numberplate. Like I said, the camera needs a good clean and a service.'

'Great. There's something for you, Richard. Start with all white vans on your list, but don't forget the others. Gerry, please liaise with him and share the footage. Let's see if we can track the white van's route after it leaves the area of the church.

'Anna, how was your search and your visit to the solicitor?'

'I'm thinking of becoming a scrap metal merchant. "Tin Cans R Us." Nothing approaching a weapon or anything similar. The CSIs are going through the finds as we speak, but I'm not hopeful, boss.'

'Not surprising, but it had to be done. According to Penny, your coppers are going to be on local TV tonight with their eyes to the ground. Can we make sure the phones are manned on the hotline, Penny? I'd hate to miss anything if, by some strange chance, somebody saw something.'

'Already done, boss.'

'The solicitor was about as forthcoming as a Welsh prop forward, citing legal privilege all the time. But he knows a lot more than he's saying. From the luxurious state of the office, his services are not cheap. No way a fifteen-year-old like Roy short could afford to get him out in the middle of the night.'

'Somebody else was paying.'

'That's my bet, boss.'

'Not one I'd like to take. But who could have been paying the solicitor's bill for him?'

The team looked at each other, but there was no answer from any of them.

'Let's park that question for the moment and add it to our list. Last but not least, young John.'

The sixty-year-old sat up straight. 'Nothing on HOLMES matching our killings. I've been on to Merseyside regarding known associates of Roy Short but they haven't got back to me yet. Should be soon.'

'Push them hard, John. If our hypothesis is correct and this was the murder of a county lines drug distributor, the murder was done by his gang or a rival. Either way, we need to know what's going on.'

'Right, boss.'

Anna put her hand up. 'Perhaps the gang paid for Sandway's services?'

Emma stared at the questions on the board. 'What if it's not a gangland murder?' she said under her breath.

'Why do you say that, boss?' asked Anna.

'It's just that gangs don't normally hang plaques around their victim's heads. What if it was something else?'

'Like?'

'It's the wording on the sign. The killer wrote "my city" as if he owns it or, at least, was possessive of it. What if this is a revenge killing or it was done by a vigilante?'

Emma paused for a moment, allowing her mind to examine all possibilities. 'Let's keep an open mind, people; a gangland killing is just one of the hypotheses we are following.'

She walked to a blackboard and wrote **POSSIBLE MOTIVES** at the top, heavily underlining the words.

She turned, looked back at her team, and then wrote beneath the headline:

Gangland retribution?
Gangland territory war?
A revenge killing?
A vigilante killing?

'Any possibilities I've missed?'

Harry put his hand up. 'There's one thing that's just occurred to me, boss.'

'It *was* a boomerang that hit him. See, it's all coming back to him now,' Richard said.

There was laughter around the room.

'It's not about the attack, Richard, it's the phone tracking reports for the burners bought from petrol stations in Roy Short's area. Weren't they supposed to be in by now?'

Emma stared at John Simpson.

'Nothing yet, boss.'

Emma continued staring until John looked away. 'I'll get on to them straight away.'

'Anything else?' There were no answers, so she continued. 'Does everybody know what they are doing?'

A chorus of yesses.

'Remember, people, these thugs have just attacked one of our own. Nobody, but nobody, does that to our people. *Nobody*. Clear?'

'Yes, boss,' was the chorused answer.

'Harry, get yourself back to your wife, you need to rest tonight.'

'I'll be back in tomorrow morning, boss.'

'If you're not feeling good, don't come in – you've just been hit over the head.'

'Don't worry, boss, I'll be back tomorrow. I've got a thick skull. It's one of the reasons I became a copper.'

Chapter FORTY-ONE

Emma spent the next couple of hours working closely with John Simpson to ensure the investigative log was fully up-to-date. With Jones breathing down her neck, the last thing she needed was for him to accuse her of unprofessionalism about the records of her decisions.

She checked that all her decisions and the reasons for them were well documented. She ensured that every detective had submitted their time sheets and case notes. She had even been through the spiralling cost of overtime with a fine-tooth comb.

All the usual details of the job of senior investigating officer that nobody, not even her father, had ever told her. Weirdly though, she found this sort of bureaucratic work mildly satisfying. It also meant she was across every inch of the investigation in case anybody asked. And she was pretty certain it would be Davy Jones who did the questioning.

Around eight o'clock, tiredness kicked in and she found herself yawning uncontrollably.

'You need to go home and get some sleep, gaffer,' said John.

'Don't worry about me, I'll be fine.' She yawned again. 'Has the post-mortem report from Dr Anstey come in yet?'

'Not yet, he's still waiting on toxicology.' John stared at her. 'Look, take it from me. I was a copper for thirty years, worked with your dad through thick and thin. A detective who's tired makes mistakes. Your dad did, we all did. Go home, get some sleep and you'll be better for it in the morning – and so will the investigation.'

Emma realised John was right. She had been working almost continuously since the discovery of the boy's body nearly forty-eight hours ago. Going home to a posse of firefighters in the kitchen hadn't helped, either. There was little left to do here. Her team had been briefed on their jobs and knew exactly what to do.

A tiny voice inside her head still encouraged her to stay on, to watch over everything. To be in control.

She stood up. 'You're right, John. I'll go home, get some rest. Can you tell everybody else to do the same? No point in them collapsing too.'

'Will do, boss. Say hello to your dad from me. He was a good man and a better copper.'

Emma didn't answer as she reached for her coat. Suddenly a wave of tiredness swept over her. She could hardly lift her arms above her head.

'Boss, are you okay?'

It was John standing beside her.

'I'm fine, but I do need sleep. More tired than I thought. Let's get everybody back at nine tomorrow morning and check where we are.' Then she remembered that Mrs Lockwood wouldn't arrive till nine a.m. and she had to brief Davy Jones at that time. 'Better make that ten thirty, give everybody time to wake up.'

'Right, boss. I'll get somebody to give you a lift, you're in no fit state to drive.'

'I'll be okay…' Another wave of tiredness swept over her and she felt like she was going to faint there and then in the middle of the Major Incident Room.

She steeled herself to fight against the feeling. She'd never live it down if gossip swept around City of Chester Constabulary that she had collapsed on the job.

'She's not up to it, you know.'

'Doesn't have the strength of her dad.'

'She was only promoted because of him.'

'Can't do the job.'

She could hear the bastards speaking now. She had worked hard to get where she was, and they weren't going to grind her down. But still the wee voice of the imposter syndrome wheedled away inside her head, prodding her brain, stirring up every single insecurity that may, or may not, have been there.

She straightened up and shook her head vigorously to rid herself of tiredness and the little demons.

'Shall I get a lift for you, boss?'

'Don't worry about me.' She smiled broadly. 'Get yourself off home as soon as you've finished, John. I'll see you tomorrow at ten thirty a.m.'

She strode out of the Major Incident Room, head up in the air, carrying her precious notepad close to her side.

Back at home, after a short drive with the window open, Hortensia greeted her as soon as she entered through the front door.

'I wasn't expecting you back so soon. I've given your dad something to eat and he's now in bed watching TV.'

'Great, Hortensia. Let me take a long bath, have a chat with Dad, and then I'll go to bed. You can go home. I'll stay with him tonight. Don't worry, I'll pay you for the full shift.'

'You can't keep paying me when I'm not working, Mrs Christie. Why don't I stay while you sleep in case your father wakes up in the middle of the night?'

'Would you?'

'Of course, that's what you pay me for.' Then Hortensia remembered something. 'Mrs Lockwood told me the electrics and the gas people came. The kitchen is safe to use. Still smells of smoke though.'

'Great. At least I can cook now.'

'Do you want me to run a bath for you?'

'No, I'll do it. But thanks for the offer.'

Emma hauled herself up the stairs, each step feeling like she was climbing Mount Everest. As she reached the top, she heard her dad's voice.

'Is that you, Hortensia? I'd love another cuppa.'

'It's me, Dad.'

She pushed open the door to his bedroom. He was sat on top of the sheets wearing his flannelette pyjamas and a dressing gown. The TV was on but the sound was low. Beside his right hand, the remote lay on the sheets.

The room itself hadn't changed since she was a kid, since her mother was alive. The same flock wallpaper, the same bedside table, the same pictures on the walls, the same dressing table still covered in her mother's oils, creams and perfumes. She had tried to get her father to re-decorate it after her mother died but he had refused: 'I like it how it is. Your mother wanted it like this.'

She had given up trying to change the rest of the house too. It was how it had always been when she was a child.

'You're back early.'

'I need to sleep, Dad.'

'How's it going?'

'What?'

'The investigation. I thought you said you were doing a murder. A child killed with his eyes removed.'

It was amazing what he remembered and what he forgot. 'I am, Dad. It's going slowly, too slowly. We think a Liverpool gang may be involved.'

He turned his eyes from the TV. 'The telly isn't what it used to be, you know. Look at this rubbish. Those coppers couldn't solve a bacon butty.'

On screen, the wild moors and even wilder seas of Shetland were displayed in all their glory. A female copper, blonde hair blowing in the breeze, was walking along the seafront, deep in thought.

'Change the channel then, Dad.'

'But I always watch the dramas at this time.'

'Right, I'm going to run a bath.'

'I'd love another cup of tea before you do.'

'You don't want to drink too much liquid before you go to sleep, you'll be up all night.'

His body stiffened on the bed and he turned back towards her, his face contorted with anger. 'Don't treat me like a fucking six-year-old! I was solving murders when you were still wearing nappies and sucking your fucking thumb. What are you doing back here when there's a case to be solved? Where is your commitment to the job?'

'Calm down, Dad.'

'Don't tell me to calm down, I'm not uncalm. What are you doing back here so early when there's a case to work?'

'I need to sleep, Dad.'

'Plenty of time to sleep when you're dead.'

And with that he turned back to watch the television.

She was used to these sudden outbursts of anger from him. They were a product of his disease, nothing more, nothing less. The words still hurt, though.

'I'll get you a cup of tea, Dad,' was all she said as she left the room.

He didn't answer.

Chapter FORTY-TWO

The bath water was warm and welcoming as she lowered herself into it, rising up above the overspill, making a gurgling sound as it did.

The scent of fresh pine from the bath salts relaxed and refreshed her, dissolving away the tensions of the day.

She looked down at her stomach. Still there after years of dieting. It didn't matter which diet she tried, and she had tried them all – Atkins, Paleolithic, intermittent fasting, steady fasting, total fasting, carb heavy, carb light, carb medium, the ice cream diet, and even a diet where she ate nothing but yogurt. Not surprisingly, she couldn't bear the smell of yogurt any more; even looking at a tub made her feel sick.

Perhaps she should give up all the dieting malarkey and just eat whatever she wanted. But it had become a way of life – getting on the scales in the morning, checking her weight, watching what she ate. It was a way of controlling herself, controlling her own body.

She ducked her head beneath the water, feeling her hair brush against her skin. For a moment, the problems with her dad and the case were forgotten.

There was something beautiful about a long, warm bath. A way to wash away the cares of the day, to forget about everything but the gentle waves of warm, soapy water across her skin, her body weightless.

She lay there for thirty more minutes, topping up the bath with hot water twice. The skin on her fingers was wrinkled and puckered by the time she got out, but she felt fresh and invigorated.

Time for a long sleep, and then she would be ready to attack the investigation tomorrow morning. Sod Davy Jones and his political games. She would crack the case, whatever he did.

She put on her dressing gown and went downstairs quietly, desperate not to disturb her dad.

Hortensia was sitting in the kitchen having a cup of tea. The brown scar from the fire still smeared the walls above her head, the smell of burnt toast and plastic lingering in the air.

'Do you want me to make fresh?'

Emma shook her head. 'I think I'll have a glass of wine, it'll help me sleep.'

'Drinking to help you sleep? It's never a good thing to do.'

'Just the one glass.' She walked over to the fridge and took out a fresh bottle of Sauvignon Blanc, pouring herself a large glass and then adding another slurp for the hell of it.

'Your dad has had his meds and is asleep. When is his next visit to the hospital?'

'A week on Thursday. They're assessing to see if his Alzheimer's has worsened.'

Hortensia looked down at her tea. 'It has. I only see him every three weeks when you're on the night shift, but I can see he's declined. You should be thinking of a nursing home for him.'

Emma shook her head. 'I couldn't. And besides, he'd never go.'

'I heard him earlier. The anger episodes are becoming more frequent. What was his last assessment?'

'I think they said it was Stage Five, moderately severe cognitive decline.'

'That was three months ago, right?'

Emma nodded.

'I'm no doctor, but I've been nursing patients like your dad for twenty years. His memory continues to get worse. He needs more help dressing and undressing, and those anger episodes seem to be becoming more frequent. Plus yesterday, the fire…' She left the rest of the sentence unsaid.

'I won't put him in a nursing home, I promised him.'

Emma glanced around the kitchen, finally letting her eyes rest on the brown scar. 'It needed repainting anyway. Hasn't been touched since Mum died. Dad doesn't like change.' Emma enjoyed painting; she found her mind slipped quietly into the rhythm of it and she loved the smell of fresh paint.

Hortensia laid her hands carefully on the table. 'Yesterday's fire was no accident. I blame myself. I should have stayed until you returned. So from now on, I stay until Mrs Lockwood comes, no extra charge. My kids are old enough to get their own breakfast.'

'That's not necessary, Hortensia.'

'It is. He can't be left on his own any more.'

'I know. But when I'm here, I can look after him.'

'So you go and get some sleep and I'll carry on reading Mr Russell.' Hortensia pointed to a Bertrand Russell paperback on the table before she stood up and began washing her cup in the sink. 'You can't look after him forever, you know.'

Before Emma could answer, her phone rang. She picked it up without looking at the number and listened.

'I'm on my way,' she finally answered.

Chapter FORTY-THREE

Gavin Newton was back in the same wine bar as last night, surrounded by the other journalists. They'd been joined by two new reporters – both from the red-top nationals in London.

His latest byline in the *Chester Daily* had created a stir and he was the new centre of attention. The picture of the crime scene had particularly interested them. The reporter from the *Mail* had been extremely pushy in asking Gavin for details about the case.

'Who discovered the body?'

'Were the eyes really removed?'

'What's the copper in charge like?'

'You wrote about a satanic angle to the story; that's just bollocks, right?'

'You've got a source in the coroner's office, haven't you?'

Gavin had avoided all the questions with a quiet smile and a shrug of the shoulders. His refusal to divulge any information only seemed to encourage the reporter from the *Mail* to ask even more questions.

The meeting with his source had been brief that afternoon. Gavin had managed to get them to wait for their money with a promise of a big payday as long as the tips kept coming. He knew he was only postponing the time when he had to finally cough up, but a week was a long time in journalism, anything could happen between now and then.

Gavin could only hope that it did.

'We havin' another?'

The London accent of the reporter from the *Mail* cut through the buzz in the wine bar.

'Why not? The night is still young.'

'A man after my own heart. Drink and be merry, for tomorrow we die. Or we get sacked, one way or the other.'

The reporter held up the empty bottle in one hand, his index finger outstretched, indicating to the waitress that he wanted one more. She smiled and reached for a corkscrew.

He leant into Gavin and whispered, 'Now, while we wait for the next bottle of Chateau Fleet Street, how about you help Uncle Quentin with this case. There's a monkey in it for you.'

Gavin shook his head. 'What's a monkey?'

The reporter smiled. 'You haven't been doing this long, have you? A monkey is five hundred quid. One of the most important units of currency in journalism. What about it? Anything for Uncle Quentin? I'd love to know who discovered the body.'

Gavin thought long and hard. Five hundred quid was a lot of money. It would go towards paying his source and leave a bit over for a few more bottles of wine.

'The body was found by a young kid.'

'Brilliant, but I already guessed that from your article. What's his name and address?'

Gavin held out his hand. 'Money first.'

'You learn quick, Gavin.'

He turned his back away from the other journalists and took out an envelope from inside his jacket, selecting ten fifty-pound notes from a large wad. Gavin gazed greedily at the remainder of the money.

The reporter went to hand over the money and then snatched it back. 'Name and address.'

'The body was discovered by a young boy called Daniel Sangster. He lives with his mother who's a single-parent nurse and works for the NHS. The address is Flat 4, 23 Salmon Street, Blacon.'

The reporter passed across the money, making sure the other journalists didn't see. 'There's plenty more where that came from.'

Gavin stuffed the notes in his pocket as the waitress delivered the new bottle of Chateau Fleet Street.

They turned back to the rest of the journalists. 'Who needs a top-up? Don't be shy, now. Viscount Rothermere is being extremely generous tonight. He's here with us in spirit, even though the rest of him remains in his tax haven of Monaco.'

Gavin's mobile rang as he brought his now full glass to his lips. He fumbled for the phone, trying not to spill any of the wine. 'Hello?'

A familiar voice was on the other end of the line. 'There's been another murder. You'd better get yourself down here.'

Chapter FORTY-FOUR

Emma was standing in front of one of the pedestals that lined the Roman Gardens. On it, the body of a young boy was slumped, his arms outstretched as if begging for mercy. The sightless sockets of the eyes stared upwards to the night sky above Chester, never to see the stars again.

Around his neck, a white placard had letters written on it in black marker:

NOT IN MY CITY

In front of the body, Dr David Anstey was making his checks.

'Who found it, Anna?' Emma asked her DC, pausing for a moment before correcting herself. 'Who found him?'

'A young copper. He was doing his rounds on the Walls and looked down into the Roman Gardens. He thought it was just another dosser sleeping it off. He shouted down but had no response, so he came round and checked him out. Called it in straight away.'

'What time was that?'

Anna checked her notes. '11.03.'

'Doesn't the place shut early?'

'The gate was open, according to PC Collins. I checked and it's pretty easy to get in anyway, boss.'

Anstey stood up and moved back towards the detectives. 'I'm calling this at 12.32. You can get the CSIs in now to take fingerprints before we move the body to the mortuary.'

'Is it linked to our young lad in St John's?'

'Similar MO. He's been strangled too, the marks around his neck are still livid. Eyes removed as well. I'll know more when I open him up back at the lab, but I'd say the deaths were similar. Both boys were roughly the same age.'

Emma stared into the face of the young man. His expression was strangely peaceful despite the dark sockets where the eyes had been, as if he no longer had any cares in the world.

'What ethnicity do you think he is?'

The doctor paused for a moment. 'Difficult to say. Could be southern European, North African, or Somali. Hard to tell.'

'And age?'

'Again, hard to know for sure. Fourteen, fifteen or sixteen, perhaps.'

A CSI was busy taking fingerprints as the pathologist's assistant waited impatiently to remove the body. A photographer wandered around the scene, his flash illuminating the tableau for a brief moment before it went back to normal.

'How far are we from St John's?'

'Can't be more than 150 metres over towards the east, boss.'

Emma scanned the whole scene. The gardens were long and thin with Roman remains discovered from all over the city placed here. The City Walls, with their path on top, dominated the right side of the gardens, overlooking everything. It was easy to see how the copper had spotted the body lying here. In summer, the area would have been full of people walking on the Walls or perhaps watching one of the movies shown in the outdoor theatre. But now, in the middle of autumn, fewer people were willing to brave the cool of the evening.

'Looks like the body has been dumped here just like the young lad at St John's. Anna, I want you to check his prints on IDENT1 as soon as possible.'

'Will do, boss.'

'Where's Harry?'

A voice came from the entrance to the gardens. 'Here, boss.'

'How are you feeling?'

'Fine, boss.'

'Go home if you want, but if you're going to stay here…' Emma pointed to the Walls. 'Make sure those are closed off. And check out the CCTV at the local car parks. Pepper Street, behind the Smokehouse and the Law Centre, plus I want the footage from all the local roads this evening. Get the numberplate recognition software to search for vehicles in this area tonight and two nights ago. If the body wasn't killed here, it must have been moved by vehicle.'

'Right, boss.'

'And, Anna, arrange for a search of the area first thing tomorrow morning. Use the men from the search in Grosvenor Park to help you.'

'Will do.'

'I'm going to be back at the Incident Room if you need me.'

Emma made a move to leave the gardens, still dressed in her PPE. As she did so, a man wearing a dishevelled suit approached her.

'Detective Inspector Christie?'

'Who's asking?'

'Gavin Newton, I'm a reporter with the *Chester Daily*. Is the body found in the gardens linked to the murder at St John's?'

'No comment, Mr…? I didn't hear you tell me your name.'

'Newton, Gavin Newton. This is the second young boy found murdered in three days. Do we have a serial killer in Chester?'

Emma moved past him but he jumped in front of her.

'No comment, and out of my way, Mr Newton.'

'Have the police been slow in responding to this threat?'

Emma manoeuvred around him. 'No comment.'

He ran after her as she got into the front seat of the car. 'Are satanists involved?' he shouted.

Emma slammed the door shut.

'Or is it drug related, Inspector Christie?'

She wound the window down. 'Why do you ask that, Mr Newton?'

'Because you raided a house near the university yesterday and a man was arrested and charged with dealing in drugs. Is it related, Inspector Christie?'

Emma tapped the driver on the arm. 'Let's go.'

The car pulled away from the kerb with the reporter still shouting his questions after it.

'Are these murders gangland killings?'

Chapter FORTY-FIVE

Back at the Major Incident Room, Emma opened a new case file for the murder.

'Get a witness statement from the copper who discovered the body, John, a PC Collins, I think. We need to move on this quickly.'

'Right, boss.'

'And why are you still here, anyway? I thought I told you to go home?'

Out of the corner of her eye, Emma noticed a camp bed had been set up in the corner of the room.

'No point, boss. Since the wife left I live on my own. May as well sleep here.'

For a second, Emma flashed back to a time when she was a small girl, being picked up and whirled about the garden by John. A younger version, with his breath redolent of alcohol and her father watching from the sidelines. He had worked as a copper for thirty years before retiring. His wife had left soon after, so he returned to the force as a civilian investigation officer. What he didn't know about City of Chester Constabulary wasn't worth knowing.

'What about the kids?'

'Married and live down south. I see them now and again.'

She glanced at the ruffled sheets of the bed, deciding to change the subject. 'Get on to HOLMES again. See if you can find any crimes linked to Liverpool gangs. Check out the MO – strangling and the removal of eyes.'

Around her the room was filling up with coppers, either working on laptops, collecting data or simply drinking coffee. All the people who were supposed to have gone home were still there.

The boards had new photographs now. The shot Harry had found at the foster parents' home had been blown up and placed next to the picture from the ruins. The contrast between the happy smiling boy in the former, and the corpse in the latter, was stark in the extreme.

Emma sighed. And now there was another one.

She glanced at the clock. 1.15 a.m.

Should she ring Davy Jones now or wait till the morning?

Sod it. If everybody else was working, so should he. She rang him on her mobile, the call ringing ten times before a sleepy female voice answered. 'Yes?'

'Is Inspector Jones there?'

'He's asleep,' the female voice answered curtly.

'It's DI Emma Christie from City of Chester Constabulary, I need to talk to him.'

'Is it really necessary?'

The woman was beginning to annoy her. 'It is.'

A long, exasperated sigh. 'I'll wake him.'

A few seconds later a drowsy voice came on the line. 'What is it?'

'It's DI Emma Christie, City of Chester Constabulary.' The words were already out of her mouth before Emma realised she didn't need to say them to Jones. 'There's been another murder.'

'What?'

'Another murder of a young man.'

Emma could hear the rustling of sheets as the chief inspector sat up, the voice suddenly awake. 'Where?'

'The Roman Gardens, sir.'

'What? The mayor isn't going to be pleased.'

'It's the same MO, sir.'

'Are you sure?'

'According to Dr Anstey, strangled and the eyes removed after death.' She waited a long time before adding, 'Sir.'

'Why are you telling me now, Christie? You could have waited till morning.'

'I thought you wanted to know, sir.'

'I'd prefer to sleep, particularly when there is nothing I can do.'

'Right… sir.'

'Brief me at nine a.m. when you have more information.'

'At HQ, sir?'

'Where else?' Jones said irritably. 'Are you sure the two deaths are linked?'

'I am, sir.'

'Shit. I'll brief the mayor myself. But we need to keep this out of the papers. We don't want everybody panicking.'

'I don't think that's possible, sir. A reporter was already questioning me. He seemed to know a lot about the investigation.'

'Shit, shit, shit. I want this sorted, Christie, asap. Understand? A-S-A-P. If you can't do it, I'll find somebody who can.'

The phone went dead in her hand. 'Yes, sir,' she said, before putting it back in her pocket.

A shiver went down her spine. This wasn't looking good for her. Or for the young men of Chester.

Friday, October 27th

Chapter FORTY-SIX

At 5 a.m., after completing all the bureaucracy required of a senior investigating officer in charge of a murder inquiry, Emma went back to the crime scene in the Roman Gardens.

She passed through the outer cordon, signing in, and then through another cordon placed in front of the entrance to the gardens.

The CSIs were still there, hovering around like ghosts in their white suits. Some were collecting material from the area while others were examining one of the plinths closely. The body had already been removed to the mortuary, its absence revealed by a chalk line drawn on the stone where it had rested.

Jane Eastham, the crime scene manager, spotted her and strode across the gardens.

'How's it going?' Emma asked.

'We've just completed the first pass and we'll do another once it gets light.'

'Anything?'

'Not a lot. As clean as the last scene at the ruins. Whoever committed these murders knows about forensics.'

'Not necessarily. They just have to watch any of the shows on TV and they know enough to wear gloves and not leave a trace.'

'But this scene is more than that. There's absolutely nothing, as if whoever did it spent time cleaning up after himself. The only thing we've noticed is a few spots of blood on the ground next to the plinth. My bet is he placed the body there before putting it upright on the stone.'

'So you agree with Dr Anstey – the boy wasn't killed here?'

'There's no sign of struggle. This is a dump site, not a murder scene.' A long pause. 'We haven't found the eyes either.'

Emma wrote in her notebook. 'The sign around his neck, anything on it?'

'Nothing. We're testing the ink from the last one but I think it will come back as common or garden marker pen, available at any WHSmith. We should be able to tell you the brand, though, from the composition of the ink, if that's a help.'

'It may be. Anything on the writing?'

'We'll get one of the graphologists to check, but the killer wrote in block capitals. When you find a suspect we may be able to make a comparison, but I wouldn't bet on it.'

Emma shook her head. 'Like you said, not a lot of forensics. Whoever did this knew what he was doing.'

'You think it's a man?'

'Not ruling out a woman, but if this is a dump site, the body would have had to have been carried from the car park to here.'

'Wouldn't somebody have noticed?'

'I'm hoping, but I'm not holding my breath. Anything you need from me, Jane?'

'We've got all we need, thanks. Maybe we can see something else in the full light of day.'

'We can hope.'

Anna walked over to join them. 'We've closed off the area but left the main road open, boss.'

'The Walls?'

'Blocked from the Groves to the Eastgate Clock. The local tourist board isn't going to be happy.'

'I don't care, Anna, the least of my worries. Pepper Street car park and all the local roads' CCTV?'

'All downloaded and sent to John, boss. The CCTV cameras behind the Smokehouse weren't working. Apparently somebody smashed them two days ago and they haven't been repaired yet.'

'Another coincidence. Any footage from Souter's Lane and the alley from the river to the Roman Gardens?'

'There aren't any CCTV cameras there, boss.'

'What?'

'They were supposed to have been installed two years ago, but local government cuts…'

Emma shook her head. 'Check everywhere else, just in case.'

'Okay, boss.'

Emma walked back towards the entrance on Pepper Street. As she stepped out past the cordon, she saw the reporter from before, Gavin Newton, staring straight at her, a broad smile plastered across his face.

Chapter FORTY-SEVEN

Liam Gilligan turned in his sleep, knocking his girlfriend's leg away with his knee. The phone beside his bed was ringing.

Instantly he was awake and aware, checking the clock. 6.15 a.m.

'I told you never to ring me on this phone, Mickey.'

'Sorry, boss, but I thought you'd want to know as soon as I heard.'

'What is it?'

'I just got a call from our snout. There's been another killing, boss.'

'Who? One of ours?'

'I dunno, but I thought I'd better ring you. The snout didn't have a name.'

Was it one of their boys? After Roy Short's death, was somebody going after their dealers? Another gang muscling in on his territory?

His girlfriend stirred, half-asleep. 'What is it, honey?'

'It's nothing, go back to sleep.'

He got up and walked into the bathroom. As he peed in the toilet, he spoke to Mickey. 'You need to find out asap. If it's another one of our boys, we need to know what's going on. Whatever happens, I want a crew in Chester, protecting all the grow houses and our dealers.'

'On it.'

'Anybody been giving us strife?'

'That's the weird thing, boss – all the lads tell me Chester is really quiet now. There's a new lot of students at the university, so business is great. The dope, speed and Es are selling better than ever. Nobody has seen new muscle from any of the Manchester mobs or the other Liverpool gangs. It's business as usual. In fact, it's business far better than usual.'

'Except one of our best dealers has just been murdered after vanishing with sixty grand of my money.'

'We got it back though, boss.'

'You should never have lost it in the first place. And where did Roy get two keys of coke? It wasn't from us. Somebody must have been supplying him.'

'I'll check it out, boss.'

'You're moving too slowly, I need this sorted out asap, Mickey. I want it done yesterday.'

'Will do, boss.'

Gilligan ended both the call and his pee, flushing the toilet.

'Come back to bed, it's cold without you,' his girlfriend called to him.

Stupid bitch. She really would have to go soon.

Gilligan hated not knowing what was going on. He'd built his career on always being in control and always in charge, at least three steps ahead of anybody else.

Now here he was, reacting to a death in a poxy little city like Chester when he should have been concentrating on his new deal with the Cali syndicate. Three tons of coke was at stake and he was worrying about some small-time dealer in a small-time city.

Shit.

Shit.

Shit.

If Mickey couldn't sort this, he'd have to go himself, or send one of his brothers. If that happened, all hell would be let loose. They didn't mess around, preferring to keep order through the gun and the knuckleduster.

It was one of the reasons he had taken over. The business had changed from the old days. Now it needed the leadership qualities of a businessman, not those of a thug.

If his brothers got involved again, it would be hard to keep them out of the business and then all his carefully crafted negotiations with Cali, Amsterdam, and all the other gangs would come crashing down.

All because of some poxy city at the arse-end of the world.

Shit.

Shit.

Shit.

He knew then he'd have to sort it out himself. It was getting far too big for Mickey.

Chapter FORTY-EIGHT

After checking that progress was being made on the investigation, Emma went over to police HQ, her mind ticking off all the steps a senior investigating officer should perform.

She was certain she hadn't missed any, but the same was true of Roy Short's murder and they hadn't moved very far on that.

One thing she wasn't particularly looking forward to was the usual morning briefing with Chief Inspector Davy Jones.

'Come in and sit down.'

As she sat down, he tapped away on his laptop like a happy little woodpecker. He continued for two more minutes as Emma sat watching him. Another little power game, she thought.

Finally, he looked up. 'How's Harry Fairweather?'

'Bandaged and sore, but he'll be okay. His ego was more bruised than his head.'

'What actually happened?'

'He was hijacked on his way back from Liverpool. The place was well chosen; there are no CCTV cameras on that stretch of road. Cheshire CID are checking the local houses to see if there is any footage from security cameras, but I'm not hopeful.'

'Didn't Harry get the numberplates of the attacker's cars?'

'One of them, but it was false. Plus the pool car was found burnt out a couple of miles away. Cheshire are looking into it, it's their patch.'

Jones ran his fingers through his thinning hair. 'Something else I'll have to pay for.' A long sigh. 'And the murder?'

Emma took out her notes. 'Another young man, similar in age to Roy Short, with the same placard around his neck. "Not in my city."'

'What does the pathologist say?'

'He thinks it was a similar MO to Roy Short's killing: manual strangulation. It all points to there being a serial killer on the loose.'

'Do we know who the victim is?'

'Not yet. We're waiting for an ID. One piece of good news, CCTV has given us a possible white van in the area on the night of the murder.'

'What are you waiting for? Get the driver.'

'Unfortunately, the footage is unclear; we don't have a clear picture of the numberplate or the driver.'

'Typical. How was the search of Grosvenor Park?'

'Found nothing of value. The CSIs are still trawling through the evidence bags.'

'Still no witnesses after my press conference?'

'Nobody has come forward with anything useful. But the search was only shown on local TV last night so we may get some responses today.'

Jones rolled his eyes. 'That was a PR exercise and nothing more, and you know it.' He sat back in his chair. 'Let me get this clear. After two days' work, you have no leads and no suspects, despite a callous murder being committed in one of Chester's busiest tourist areas? And now we have another killing?'

He reached beneath his desk and threw a newspaper towards Emma. 'Look at that.'

The massive headline was splashed across the front of the paper:

KILLER STALKS CHESTER

Accompanying the headline was a picture of the latest crime scene with the body lying on the ground being attended by Dr Anstey.

'How did they get these pictures so quickly?' Jones demanded.

'I don't know, sir.'

'Is one of your team selling stuff to the papers? If I find out who it is, they'll be out quicker than a Scouser with a benefit cheque.'

He took off his glasses and rubbed his eyes, making them bright red.

'This case is starting to go national. I've just had the bloody *Daily Mail* on the phone, asking what we are doing.'

He stared at Emma for a long time with his red eyes, trying to intimidate her. But she was used to it. And anyway, her father was far better at intimidation.

Correction. Her father *used* to be far better.

Eventually, Jones looked away. 'I want movement on this, Detective Inspector Christie, and I want arrests. Do I make myself clear?'

'Yes, sir. We'll get there, it's just a matter of time.'

'Time is something you don't have. The chief is breathing down my neck. This case is going national, and now we're in the news for all the wrong reasons. Get it sorted, DI Christie. If you don't, I'll find somebody else who will. Understand?'

'Perfectly, sir.'

He put his glasses back on, returned to his laptop and began typing. Emma understood that the meeting was over. She stood up and walked to the door.

'Oh, one more thing, DI Christie – an inspector from Merseyside will be joining you. With today's events and the likelihood of the involvement of Liverpool gangs, the chief and I thought it wise to involve their expertise.'

'Who is it?'

Jones checked his notes. 'An Inspector Mark Kennedy. Don't know him and never heard of him.'

'But it's still my case, we're not handing it over to Merseyside?'

'For now it is.'

He returned to his typing and Emma was left standing there. 'Thank you, sir,' she said before she left.

It sounded more like a snarl than an expression of gratitude.

Chapter FORTY-NINE

Back at the Major Incident Room, Emma immediately began to brief Sergeant Harris. Despite not having slept at all, she didn't feel tired. She had already rung home and Hortensia had agreed to stay until Mrs Lockwood took over at 9 a.m. These days, she couldn't leave her dad on his own for a second.

She was interrupted by a tall, thin man with a sharp, ascetic face. 'Are you Detective Inspector Christie?'

'I am. And you are?'

'Detective Inspector Mark Kennedy, Merseyside Serious and Organised Crime.'

A bony hand was thrust towards her. Emma shook it, expecting a cold, firm shake, and was surprised to discover warm, rather gentle fingers.

The man smiled at her through a bushy beard. 'I've been asked to brief you and your team on the latest intel we have on the Liverpool gangs.' There was a slight pause. 'And to be briefed by you on your investigation so far. We've heard there may be a Liverpool connection.'

Emma's eyes widened. 'I was only told you were coming this morning, I didn't expect to see you here so quickly. Give me a minute.'

'Take your time.'

Emma turned back towards the young sergeant she was briefing. 'I want you to set up a desk with your men, here and here, on the Walls themselves. PR are producing some flyers and publicity materials for you as we speak. I want you to hand them out and ask anybody if they were walking on the Walls last night after six p.m. in the vicinity of the

Roman Gardens. We're looking for anything out of the ordinary, or if they saw anybody in the area last night. Take pictures of anybody who comes forward. We want to eliminate them from our enquiries.'

'Are we the only ones doing it, Inspector?'

'No, there'll be three other teams, plus PR has organised articles in the local rags and a spot on lunchtime TV with a number to call in. Remember, we're trying to build up a picture of people in the area of the Roman Gardens from six p.m. and then eliminate them from our enquiries. The place is overlooked by the Walls, anybody walking there may have noticed something.'

'Got it. We'll start at two and stay until ten this evening.'

'Perfect, there must be people who walk on the Walls every night, just taking an evening stroll. Those are the people we want to hear from.'

'Will do.'

She turned back to face Inspector Mark Kennedy, who was standing patiently in front of her waiting for her to finish.

'Right then, Inspector Kennedy. Brief away.'

He looked around him, seeing the hustle and bustle of activity in the Major Incident Room. 'You want to do it here?'

She nodded. 'Actually, I've just had a thought. It might be helpful for you to brief everybody at the same time and then we can let you know what's been happening. Do you mind?'

Mark Kennedy looked around him once more. 'You look busy. I'll make it brief.'

He tapped the attaché case he was carrying.

'Do you have an IT guy who can help me set up? I've been using these things for twenty years but my eleven-year-old kid knows more about them than I do.'

'Tell me about it. John,' she shouted across at the civilian researcher. 'Can you help Inspector Kennedy set up?'

Simpson stopped what he was doing and strode across. 'Mac or Microsoft?'

'It's a Dell, actually.'

Simpson's eyes rolled towards the ceiling of the Incident Room. 'I'll set it up for you. You can project your slides against the wall over there.'

As they were setting up, Emma clapped her hands loudly. 'Gather round, everybody.' She pointed to the seats in front of her.

When the people had stopped what they were doing and assembled in front of her, she spoke again. 'I'm sure you're all aware of the attack on Harry yesterday.' She pointed across to her detective constable, who looked sheepishly at his feet. 'An armed gang robbed him of a bag he was bringing back from Liverpool. This bag contained a quantity of drugs and approximately sixty thousand pounds in cash. It had been left by Roy Short with his foster parents a few days earlier. Detective Inspector Kennedy of the Merseyside Serious and Organised Crime Squad is here to brief us on any criminal gangs Roy Short may or may not have been working with.'

Mark Kennedy stepped forward and pressed a key on his laptop. On the white wall opposite, a slide appeared which just stated baldly: 'The Gangs of Liverpool.'

'How much do people know about the gangs, or as we now call them, the organised crime groups, of my city?'

There was silence from Emma's team.

'Right. Well, here's a short, potted history. Firstly, there have always been gangs in Liverpool. Ever since the massive expansion of the city and port during the nineteenth century driven by the slave trade, gangs flourished amongst the recent immigrants from Ireland. In the 1850s, these were mainly warring Catholic and Protestant mobs, with names like the Hibernians, the Dead Rabbits, and the Cornermen. Later gangs emerged, preying on and providing for the thousands of sailors who thronged the city. The most notorious of all were the High Rip gang, based along the Scotland Road, who waged a vicious war against all rivals and controlled prostitution, gambling, theft and rackets around the docks. Later, there developed local juvenile gangs such as the Lemon Street Gang and the Housebreakers.'

'Sounds like a band from the nineties.'

'These were slightly more vicious; slit throats, stabbings, and localised gang warfare were common, all of them fighting over some patch of waste ground or a street. Throughout the early twentieth century, across both World Wars and into the sixties, the gangs still remained, still local, usually based in one street or small area, controlling criminal activity and fighting with rivals. All through the Merseyside Beat and the Beatles and the Swinging Sixties, the gangs remained...'

'Why were they so prevalent in Liverpool?'

'A great question. The majority of the Liverpool population are Irish, or of Irish descent, and the new arrivals brought the clannishness of their old country to the city. Plus, it's a port so there was a constant flow of transient individuals and sailors from all over the world. Inevitably, the city attracted a large number of outsiders or those people who lived on the edges of society. This sense of being isolated from normal society was exacerbated by levels of urban deprivation and poverty unknown in other cities, which contrasted with amazing wealth created by the slave trade, creating an "us against them" mentality which was the perfect breeding ground for gang activity.'

Harry put his hand up. 'Thanks for the history lesson, but what's happening today?'

'Drugs is what's happening today. Starting in the 1980s, the gangs became more organised and outward-looking. They had always been involved in the drugs trade, but mainly that of all seaports; opium and cannabis. The rise of the popularity of heroin and cocaine, followed by ecstasy and crack in the nineties, allowed a vast expansion of their activities, earning the city the unenviable title of "Smack City" or "Skag City". Connections were made overseas to South America, Turkey and Amsterdam, particularly the Cali Cartel and Pablo Escobar, and large distribution networks were developed. There were vast profits to be made in the trade. Underworld figures such as Colin "Smigger" Smith and Curtis Warren became supremely wealthy. The latter were even listed on the *Sunday Times* Rich List. But inevitably, the vast wealth attracted conflict and, like Manchester, Liverpool was rife with gun crime by the late 1990s. It all came to a head in 1996 when Merseyside Police were the first police force to be authorised to openly carry arms after there were six shootings in seven days.'

Harry put his hand up again. 'But what about the gang that attacked me?'

Mark Kennedy smiled.

'We prefer to call them Organised Crime Groups these days. Despite being localised to certain areas of Liverpool, in the eighties and nineties they spread their wings across multiple counties and jurisdictions, carving up the country amongst themselves. Liverpool OCGs even control drugs networks in countries like the Netherlands and in many of the Mediterranean resorts. And their crimes have now expanded to financial fraud, money laundering and people smuggling. Here's a list of the groups operating in the city.'

He pressed a key on his laptop and a long list of names appeared.

Manc Joey
The Deli Mob
Wavo 420
East Side Boys
The Strand Gang
The Croxteth Crew
The Whitney Gang
The Fernhill Gang
Kirkstone Riot Squad
Scottie Road Crew
The Laneheads
Linacre Young Guns
The Everton Mob
Hopgood Street Maniacs
The Nellies

A collective sigh came from the team. Anna asked, 'You're dealing with all these at the same time?'

Kennedy nodded. 'And more. They are constantly changing and re-forming as we arrest and put away the ringleaders. But it's like standing on the shore and telling the waves to stop coming in. You can work as hard as you can, but they won't stop.'

'How do you continue? It must be so frustrating.'

'It was hard until a couple of years ago.'

'What happened then?'

'I can explain in one word. EncroChat. The French police managed to decipher the messaging system used by the OCGs, which meant we could listen to their internal communications. We managed to put away the leaders of the first three groups before they realised we could read everything they were up to.'

Anna spoke again. 'I read about the Manc Joey OCG. They ran a county lines operation smuggling millions of pounds' worth of crack and heroin, to Devon of all places.'

'They used teenage boys for their operation as delivery boys. I'm sure that rings a bell with your case.'

Emma stared at him. She was about to speak when Harry piped up. 'But you still haven't answered my question. Which gang was Roy Short part of, and which gang attacked me?'

Mark Kennedy shrugged his thin shoulders. 'The answer is, we don't know. Roy Short came up on our radar only six months ago after his arrest in Chester but we don't know his affiliation. If I were a betting man, and based on the area he lived, he was a member of one of the last three.'

'The Everton Mob, the Hopgood Street Maniacs and the Nellies?'

'Right. We know most about the first one.'

'The Everton Mob?'

Kennedy pressed another key on his laptop. 'It's run by a man called Liam Gilligan, he took over from his elder brothers, Mark and Luke, a couple of years ago. Amazingly, he has a clean sheet. Never been arrested or charged with any offence. His brothers, on the other hand, have rap sheets longer than a Dickens novel, mostly for theft or violence. But those arrests stopped in 2015 and they've been clean ever since.'

'Anything from EncroChat on Liam Gilligan?'

'Not a sausage. It was almost as if he knew we could read their messages. He used it until 2017, but as soon as the French police cracked the code, he stopped using it.'

'A coincidence?' asked Anna.

'You might think that. I couldn't possibly say. But like most coppers, I don't believe in coincidences.'

Emma stepped forward. 'Thank you, Mark. Any questions?'

The room was silent.

'If you want to know anything, please come forward and ask me. I don't bite... much. I'll be here to help for the rest of your investigation into these murders.'

That was the first Emma had heard about him staying in Chester.

'Thank you once again, Inspector Kennedy. Please continue what you are doing, and please remember a gangland connection is just one of our theories regarding the murder of Roy Short. We now have the additional complication of another young man being found murdered last night.'

People stood up and there was a gentle murmur as they returned to their jobs.

'Inspector Kennedy, can I have a chat, please?' Emma said.

Chapter FIFTY

Emma pulled Mark Kennedy into a quiet area in the corridor just outside the Incident Room. 'What was that you just said? You're staying for the duration of the investigation?'

He looked straight at her. 'I've been seconded to City of Chester Constabulary.'

'First I've heard of it.'

He scratched his head. 'Sorry, I thought you knew. We got a phone call in Serious and Organised Crimes yesterday from our assistant chief and, as I was between jobs, they sent me here.'

'What time was this?'

'About six p.m. yesterday. I came this morning. Looks like your problems have escalated with another killing, though.'

'Why did nobody tell me?'

'I don't know. Ours not to reason why, and all that malarkey.'

Emma gritted her teeth. Stay calm, she told herself. 'I don't have to remind you, do I, Inspector Kennedy? You are here to assist. This is still City of Chester's case. We will run it—' she corrected herself '—I will run it as I see fit.'

Kennedy held his arms out wide. 'Please, call me Mark. It's your case, I'm here to assist you in any way you need. Use me like you would any other copper seconded to your team.'

'Just so we understand.'

John was hovering to one side, holding a sheet of paper. 'What is it?'

'Sorry to interrupt you, boss, but I thought you should hear this right away. IDENT1 has found a match for the fingerprints of the boy we found in the Roman Gardens.'

'Tell me,' she snapped. 'Don't hang around.'

Instantly, she regretted snapping at John. She was too tired and too stressed, plus the news of Mark Kennedy's advisory role had annoyed her more than she realised.

'He's Albanian, boss. Picked up in the Channel seven weeks ago and taken to a local authority hotel in Brighton used to house migrants claiming asylum. He was reported missing from there only a week after he arrived.'

'What?'

'His name is Altea Marku. At least, that's the name he gave the border force when he arrived here, but he didn't have any documents or ID. And there's more, boss.'

'More?'

'The CSIs swabbed his hands before he was taken away by the pathologist. There were traces of cannabis on them.'

'He'd been smoking dope?'

'More like handling the stuff. Lots of cannabis pollen too.'

'Can I add something?' interrupted Mark Kennedy.

'Go ahead.'

'The OCGs often use these children in their cannabis farms. It's slave labour, but who are the children going to complain to? They are here illegally.'

'But I thought John said he was staying at a migrants hotel in Brighton?'

'Look, they go missing all the time and there are no figures for how many abscond. They fall through the gaps in the net.'

'Doesn't anybody follow up and look for them?'

'Why should they? The company who's supposed to be caring for them only gets paid when they are in the hotel, not when they've left it. They don't get paid to look for them. They simply fill in a form and report the absence to the Home Office.'

'What about the border force?'

'Too stretched, and with no local intelligence to find them once they are taken by the OCGs.'

'You're telling me these kids just vanish?'

'Most are kidnapped or sold by the OCGs. Remember, they have paid money or borrowed it to cross the Channel. They have to pay off their debt somehow. The girls inevitably go into prostitution, the boys into working for the OCGs or running cannabis farms.'

'But how did this boy—'

'Altea Marku.'

'—get to Chester? And why was he killed?'

'That, Detective Inspector Christie, is the 64,000-dollar question.'

'Actually, it's two questions. And we are going to find out the answers to both of them.'

Chapter FIFTY-ONE

The boy hadn't struggled at all. Just stared up at him with those big, doleful eyes, almost welcoming death.

He'd strangled him, feeling the neck bones compress through his gloved fingers. The Rohypnol helped. The boy didn't know what was happening until it was too late.

He enjoyed the immense feeling of power as the boy gagged, his legs kicking out until they moved no longer and were still.

An easy death, a quiet death. Just like Roy Short.

Dumping him at the Roman Gardens had been planned two days in advance. The cameras had been taken care of and the route mapped out. He was sure nobody would notice. His disguise was one of the invisible people of their small city, those that went about their work but were never seen.

The Rohypnol was easy to acquire. A couple of the dealers had been selling it online. There had been a few cases where girls had woken up after a night at a club, not knowing who they were or where they were.

All they remembered was meeting somebody in the club and waking up the following morning, their bodies aching and abused.

He had to stop it.

He had to stop those dealers of filth.

If he didn't, it would only get worse; the drugs, the anti-social behaviour, the fights in the city centre at weekends, the young girls being abused.

It was already out of control.

Chaos ruled and nobody cared any more.

But he cared.

He was doing something about it.

It would have to get worse before it got better, but that was always the problem. Sometimes the cure was as bad as the disease.

So it goes.

The national papers were beginning to pick up on his work. Feeding the local reporter, Gavin Newton, had helped spread the word of his deeds. Chester Police couldn't keep it quiet any more. It was as it should be. The more publicity, the better.

He'd go back to Altea Marku's grow house. It was time to purify the area. They had to see his work, understand its power.

And then, one more should do it.

One more death and they would be swarming round the city like seagulls after a crust of bread, fighting over the news, scrapping to discover the latest titbit.

One more death and the gangs would be fighting each other. He couldn't do all the work, they had to do it for him.

But that was the beauty of his plan.

All he had to do was light the blue touch paper and stand back.

The explosion was going to happen anyway.

Chester had to be purified.

Sometimes you had to plunge to the bottom of the abyss before you could begin again.

Sometimes you had to kill to cleanse.

Chapter FIFTY-TWO

Gavin Newton finished his full English by scraping up the runny remains of his fried egg with a piece of white bread and washing everything down with a long slurp of tea.

The reporter from the *Mail* was sitting opposite him at an outside table. 'I don't know how you can eat all that first thing in the morning.'

'Easy. Sets me up for a hard day around the city.'

'A heart attack on a plate, that's what it is, mate.'

'Tastes good though. Best way to start the day.'

They were sat outside the café. The day was cold but clear. Quentin Forde was wrapped up in a jumper and two jackets; Gavin was just wearing a shirt and tie with a loose windjammer.

Gavin had called him at 9 a.m., when the police-work at the crime scene had begun to wind down. The man had answered his mobile sleepily: 'Whassup?'

'Hiya, it's Gavin, you should meet me at Greasy Joe's next to the Northgate. I've got some news for you.'

Now here he sat opposite him, desperate to find out what was going on.

Gavin dragged out the tension a bit longer, pushing his plate away and lighting a Marlboro Red. He liked a good cough after a full English.

'So you didn't call me at this unearthly hour of the morning to make me watch you eat.'

'Nah, like I said, I've got some news for you.'

'Where did you go to last night? One minute you were with us, the next you were gone.'

'I got called away.'

Forde leant forward. 'Something happened?'

'While you were enjoying yourself, I was working.'

'And?'

'What's it worth to you?'

'I don't know until you tell me what it is.'

Gavin took a long drag on his cigarette, followed by an even longer slurp of his tea. 'What about another murder?'

The *Mail* reporter's eyes opened wide. 'How? When?'

'Last night a body was discovered…' Gavin let his voice trail off.

'Where?'

'Near here. Police are keeping it quiet though.'

'Why didn't you tell me last night?'

Gavin shrugged his shoulders. 'What's it worth?'

'I'll have to talk to my editor. The usual rate is a monkey a day for local stringers.'

'This isn't a usual case…'

'I could see if he'd go to seven-fifty a day.'

'Plus expenses.'

'Agreed.'

'I get to carry on writing for my local newspaper.'

'Okay, no skin off my nose what the local rags print. But we get first dibs on everything you discover, plus it's exclusive. Agreed?'

'Done.'

'What have you got?'

Gavin took him through the details of the police discovery of a new body last night, with the eyes missing and a sign around the neck.

All the time, the reporter was scribbling in his notebook. 'This is fantastic. What's the name of the victim?'

'The police don't know yet. I'll give you a heads-up as soon as I find out.'

'Any pictures?'

'I took some of the crime scene but they're far away.'

'Any pictures of the body?'

'I can ask.'

'For pictures, we can cough up more. A lot more.'

'I'll see.'

Gavin took another long slurp of tea as the reporter checked his notes.

'Anything more on this satanism angle?'

'I just made that up.'

'It doesn't matter, it makes good copy. Are the police looking into it?'

'Perhaps, perhaps not.'

'You realise once I write this up and it goes on the website, all hell will be let loose. All the other nationals, the Beeb and the rest of the cockroaches are going to come out of the woodwork. We have an exclusive, right?'

'That's what we agreed.'

The reporter stuck his hand out. 'Welcome to Fleet Street, Mr Newton.'

Chapter FIFTY-THREE

Emma was back in the place she liked the least in the world. The second time in three days and she hoped it was going to be her last visit for a long, long time.

Dr David Anstey was bent over the open chest of the young boy known as Altea Marku. Emma could see the white of the rib bones where they had been peeled back to reveal the lungs and the heart.

'Interesting,' he muttered.

'What is it, Doctor?'

'This young man has three broken ribs and extensive bruising to his chest and body. The bones are beginning to repair themselves and the bruises seem quite old. I would estimate they were broken at least two weeks before he died.'

'So not at the same time as he died?'

'Definitely not. And if that is a subtle way of asking me for a time of death, Inspector, you may well have succeeded.'

The doctor continued to stare at the exposed ribs of Altea Marku.

'Well?'

He stood up straight. 'The body was discovered at eleven p.m. last night. From the temperature and the progress of the rigor mortis, I would say he'd already been dead for at least twelve hours prior.' He nodded as if confirming his own conclusions. 'Definitely twelve hours, maybe even a few hours more if he was kept somewhere cool and dry.'

'So a time of death of roughly noon yesterday?'

'Give or take a couple of hours.'

'So transported to the crime scene and dumped there?' said Harry Fairweather from behind his mask. Like Emma, he was dressed in full protective gear, looking like a slimmed -down version of the Michelin Man.

'I wouldn't say dumped exactly, more like *placed*. He was sitting upright with his back to one of the pillars. Very similar to the placement of the body in the ruins of St John's.'

'So you think it's possible the same man killed both of them?'

'I think that is a conclusion that you must reach on your own, Detective Inspector. What I will say is that both boys were manually strangled from behind, both were placed upright at the scene of the crime, and both were killed at least twelve hours before their bodies were found, transported to their final resting place, and placed in situ.'

'And the eyes?' asked Emma.

'Yes, the strangest part of this scene. Enucleation is very rare.'

'Enucleation?'

'The complete removal of the eyeball from the eye socket and the severing of the optic nerve. As opposed to evisceration, where the eye contents are removed, leaving the muscles and sclera, the white part of the eye, in place. Whoever did it has got better, more professional this time.' He pointed to the empty eye sockets on the young boy's face. 'See how there is little damage around the eyes from the knife? He's learnt that you don't need to use so much force to remove an eye. Simply insert a sharp object, a knife or screwdriver, into the exact place and out it pops like a jelly bean.'

'Thank you, Doctor,' Emma said distastefully. 'Anything else?'

She hoped there was nothing more, but of course there was.

'We have taken scrapings from under his fingernails. Now I'll wait for the full results from the lab, but cannabis sativa has an extremely distinctive smell.'

'You think he was working in a cannabis farm.'

'I don't know, Inspector, that is for you to discover. I do know he was certainly touching and working with cannabis plants. The lab will tell us more.'

'Thank you, Dr Anstey.' Emma turned to go, desperate to get out of the examination room and tear off her protective clothing.

'One last thing, Inspector…'

Emma turned back, the young man's cadaver lying on the stainless-steel table right in front of her. Somebody's son who was now just some body on a pathologist's slab.

'The toxicology results have come back for Roy Short. There is the strong presence of flunitrazepam in the blood.'

'Flunitrazepam? That's a bit of a mouthful.'

'The trade name for it is Rohypnol. It's a central nervous system depressant that belongs to a class of drugs known as benzodiazepines.'

'Roofies. The kid was given a roofie?' said Harry.

'From the concentration of the drug, more than one. I checked the body of Roy Short again and I found an injection mark in the crook of his right elbow. I don't know how I missed it last time. But I've just looked at this young man, and the same injection mark is here too.'

'Rohypnol was used on him as well?'

'The toxicology lab will confirm the findings, but I'd put my mortgage on flunitrazepam being present in his blood too.'

Chapter FIFTY-FOUR

'Right, Harry, we've got a lot of work to do.'

'You're telling me, boss.'

They were standing outside the mortuary, waiting to get into the car. For the first time, there was a slight tang of coldness in the air and the wind was freshening as it blew through the lime trees.

Autumn was coming.

Emma pulled her jacket tightly across her body. 'I think whoever is doing this is going to strike again.'

'Another dead kid?'

'If it's a gang fight over a county lines drugs operation, it could be anybody next time; a dealer, a distributor or even a small-time user. We just don't know.'

'It could even be one of the gang leaders.'

'Get on to intelligence. See if there any records of Organised Crime Groups operating in Chester. HOLMES has given us nothing so far. While you are there, check on any local cannabis farms, confirmed or just suspected. If our latest victim had been working in one, perhaps we can at least find out the place. There can't be many in Chester.'

'I'll do it, boss.'

Emma stared into mid-air, thinking.

'A penny for them, boss?'

'It'll have to be a quid.'

Harry turned out his pockets, revealing they were empty. 'The wife watches my spending; one of her major jobs when she's got time off from planning her next holiday.'

Emma sighed. 'I was just wondering if we are *assuming* an OCG is involved.'

'The people who hijacked my car weren't the Salvation Army.'

'True, but if we hadn't heard about Roy Short's involvement with drug dealing, how would we have treated this investigation?'

'What do you mean, boss?'

She closed her eyes, trying to put her thoughts into words. 'My dad always used to tell me that making assumptions was the copper's worst nightmare. Look at the Yorkshire Ripper case. West Yorks Police assumed he was killing prostitutes, when in fact he wasn't so choosy, he was killing any woman he could find. They hardly changed their tune even when he began killing "respectable" women.'

'And after the tape arrived, they assumed he had a Geordie accent and came from the north-east, while Peter Sutcliffe was actually living less than a couple of miles from the police HQ in Heaton. They even interviewed him a few times but discounted the possibility he could be the Ripper because he was a local lad.'

'That's it. I wonder if we are making the same assumptions in this case, that this involves organised criminal gangs when we might actually have a serial killer at large…'

'Who's just targeting drug dealers because they are easy prey?'

'Or because they represent something to him. I can't get the notice he puts round their necks every time.'

'Not in my city.'

Her forehead creased in a frown. 'Those are the words of a vigilante, not—'

Before Emma could finish her sentence the radio inside the car squawked. Harry opened the door and answered it. 'DC Fairweather.'

'Hi, Harry, it's John Simpson. Is the boss around?'

'I'll put her on, John.'

He handed over the mic to Emma. 'Hi, John, what's up?'

'I don't know if it's useful, boss, but I've just heard over the network there is a major fire in a house over in Christleton.'

'And?'

'It may not be relevant, boss, but a local copper has just reported the strong smell of dope from the fire. Apparently, half the local druggies are standing downwind getting a free sample.'

'We're on our way, John.'

Chapter FIFTY-FIVE

'I want an update, now, Mickey.'

Liam Gilligan was back in the telephone box he'd used a couple of days ago in Crosby. Not the smartest move if the police were tracking him, but he didn't have time for the extra security.

'What I've heard is one of their lads has been taken and killed.'

'Their lads? Whose lads?'

'The word on the street is that it was one of the Cheetham Hill mob from Manchester.'

'What was he doing in our area? We had an agreement with them. Chester and North Wales is ours, they are not allowed to sell there.'

'Apparently he wasn't a dealer, boss, but ran a grow house for them. A young Albanian lad, just arrived in the country, fresh off one of the boats.'

'What was he doing in our area?' Liam emphasised. 'It's off limits.'

'Nobody knew he was even there, boss. Like I said, he wasn't dealing, just running a dope farm for Cheetham Hill.'

'Right, get on to— to…'

'What was that? Just a minute, boss.'

Liam Gilligan was fuming. He could hear somebody else talking to Mickey while he was waiting.

Bastards. What were Manchester doing on his patch?

They had an agreement. He wouldn't deal in Stoke and Staffordshire, and they wouldn't go anywhere near Chester and North Wales. He wasn't surprised the Cheetham Hill

mob were using Albanians though; he got half his women
from them, smuggled across the Channel.

'What is it, Mickey?' he shouted down the phone.

Silence for a few seconds followed by, 'There's a fire
over in Christleton, boss, one of the dealers thinks it's a
grow house. Not one of ours.'

A sigh of relief from Gilligan, followed shortly
afterwards by the realisation that this was a problem.

'Did we have anything to do with the fire, Mickey?'

Again he could hear Mickey speaking to his associates.
'Nothing to do with us, we didn't even know the farm
existed.'

'Make sure you make an example of whoever runs that
area. For him not to know a farm is operating on his patch
is a disgrace.'

'Right, boss.'

'And, Mickey, set up a meet with Manchester asap, one
of the usual places. If we're not careful, this could get out
of control, with them hitting our farms in retaliation. The
last thing we need is war right now. Are you sure we had
nothing to do with it?'

'Positive, boss.'

'Set up the meet, Mickey.'

'On it.'

'And one more thing, Mickey – break both his arms. I
want our people to be hands-on in their patch, not keep it at
arm's length. Do you understand, Mickey?'

'Got it, boss.'

Gilligan slammed the phone down. This was the last
thing he needed right now; a turf war with Cheetham Hill.
The deal with the Cali Cartel was just about to go through.
After he brought the coke into the country, he could do
what he wanted. Until then, he would have to be Mr Nicey-

Nicey. He could deal with the Cheetham Hill mob afterwards.

It was just a question of timing. He needed the Glasgow deal and the coke, then he'd be flush with money. Nobody would question him any more.

Not his brothers.

Not the other Liverpool gangs.

Nobody.

He'd have the respect he wanted like his druggies needing their daily fix.

Afterwards, Cheetham Hill and all the other Manchester mobs wouldn't know what hit them. He'd have so much dosh he could do exactly what he wanted. Then he'd get his own back for the years of humiliation and of eating humble pie.

It would make Manchester gang wars of the nineties look like a children's tea party.

It would be time for Gunchester again.

Chapter FIFTY-SIX

The fire was almost extinguished before Emma and
Harry arrived at the scene. They badged their way through
the police cordon set up to keep the onlookers from getting
too close.

The house was still intact but all the windows were
broken, and soot marks rose from the upstairs windows
towards the roof. Through the open front door, Emma could
see water still pouring down the stairs.

The smell reminded Emma of her own kitchen and the
fire created by her dad. She realised how lucky she had
been that the postman had seen the smoke.

The fire brigade were already rolling up their hoses and
one of the two fire engines called to the scene was loading
up its men ready for departure.

Emma looked for the chief fire officer, spotting his
distinctive white helmet to the left of the front gate. It was
the same man she'd seen at her dad's house.

'We meet again, DI Christie. You going to be
investigating this?'

'Should I?'

'Definitely, it's a death trap. Whoever wired this place
up deserves to be shot.'

'Hang on. Start from the beginning. We heard this was a
possible cannabis farm.'

'You heard right. All the rooms in the top floor and the
downstairs at the back were rigged to grow plants;
hydroponics cabling, water sprinklers, ventilation systems
and high-intensity lamps. The only room not affected was
the front living room. Somebody had been sleeping there.

The electrics of these houses were not built for this sort of use.'

Emma pointed to the front room. 'Anybody inside?'

'We haven't found anybody, but somebody was definitely living there. I found this in the room.' The chief fire officer indicated a small pile of belongings placed roughly to one side of the gate.

Emma bent down to check them out. A pair of white Nike trainers, an old t-shirt, an orange shell suit and three magazines. She took out a pair of bright purple gloves from her pocket and put them on. She picked up the magazine and leafed through it. Pictures of pop stars she did not recognise, striking ridiculous poses against walls and in assorted studios, dominated the pages. She couldn't read any of the text, it was in a foreign language she had never seen before.

Harry leant over her shoulder. 'I think it's in Albanian, boss.'

'How do you know?'

'Me and the missus went to Croatia for a holiday one year. We saw magazines like this over there.'

'You never cease to amaze me, Harry.'

'Travel, boss, you should do it more. Broadens the mind and narrows the arteries.'

For a second, a thought raced through Emma's mind. She couldn't travel because of her father. What would he do without her? She dismissed it quickly, focusing on the job in hand.

She picked up the t-shirt and examined the label. It was in the same language as the magazines but somebody had written in blue ballpoint on the bottom:

ALTEA M.

Harry whistled as she showed him the label. 'Our victim?'

'Could be.'

The chief fire officer spoke again. 'Whoever was looking after these plants probably did a runner as soon as the fire started. Could have burnt down the whole street. Lucky we got here quickly.'

'How did you hear about it?'

'You'll have to check with fire control. Somebody must have called it in.'

Emma walked a couple of steps to see inside the open windows of the front room. 'So what caused it?'

'Probably a short on one of the lamps. The plants they were growing acted as material to feed the blaze. From the size of the ones inside, they were pretty close to harvest time.'

'Can we take a look inside?'

'Not yet, I need to check it out first. The fire and our water may have damaged internal walls and floors.'

Another fire officer stood at the corner of the house. 'Robin, you need to take a look at this.'

Emma and Harry followed the chief fire officer through the gate at the side to the patio doors of the back room.

Emma could see all the walls were scorched and damp from the fire hoses. Burnt-out and blackened lamp fittings, steel racks and melted plastic plant pots lay strewn around the floor, all mixed with the ash from the burnt plants.

Over everything, the strong aroma of cannabis lay like a shroud on a decomposing body.

Robin, the chief fire officer, was staring at the right-hand side wall where a large, circular scorch mark rose from the corner to the ceiling and trailed back to the patio door. This mark was deeper, blacker than the rest.

'That's interesting,' he said.

'What?' asked Emma.

'I think we've found the source of the blaze. I was mistaken, it didn't come from a short in one of the lamps. Somebody used an accelerant to start the blaze.'

'What?'

'In layman's terms, somebody laid a trail of paraffin or petrol from that corner to the door then set it alight. This fire was started deliberately, it wasn't an accident.'

Emma shook her head. 'Right, thanks for that, Robin. We need to get back to the Incident Room, Harry, we've got work to do.'

On their way back, they were both silent for a long time before Harry spoke.

'Do we have a full-on gang war on our patch, boss?'

'What are you thinking, Harry?'

'The OCG that employed Roy Short was pissed off at his death and decided to kill our Albanian and burn out the farm as revenge. Tit for tat, boss.'

'Could be, Harry, but there's another way of looking at it.'

'Go on...'

'What if... it's not a revenge attack at all, but something else?'

'Why do you think that?'

'I don't know, it's just a feeling.' Emma tried to put it into words. 'I know I sound like a record stuck in a groove, but I can't get over the words on the signs around their necks.'

'Not in my city.'

'Right, it doesn't sound like the revenge attack of an OCG, it sounds far more personal. "*My* city."'

'Could be them just claiming the territory, boss. Like Mark Kennedy said, the gangs have carved up the country amongst themselves. Chester is one OCG patch. Our

Albanian was working for them and he's collateral damage in some turf war.'

'But why remove the eyes? We now have two murders with the same MO.'

'It's a signature, boss. The gang's way of saying "we did this".'

'But there are no similar killings on HOLMES. If it was a signature, they would have used it elsewhere. These murders only happened in Chester, *our* city.' She thought for a moment. 'But first things first, we need to show that the person operating the farm and the body in the Roman Gardens are the same person.'

'That's why you decided to bag up all the gear before we left. You're going to check it for fingerprints and DNA, aren't you?'

'I'm hoping we'll get a match with our victim.'

'Altea M could be a common name in Albania, boss, like John Smith in England.'

'It's a long shot but worth the effort.'

'I'll get the stuff down to the lab as soon as we get back to the Major Incident Room.'

Emma was staring out through the windscreen, a deep furrow of thought etched between her eyes. 'If his death was the work of an OCG, why destroy the cannabis farm too? I bet it's not even on our list of possible farm locations.'

'To destroy any evidence that he'd been there?'

'But the fire officer found all his things still in the front room, apparently untouched.'

'We don't know for certain they were his.'

'We'll know pretty quickly. If you were trying to destroy all evidence that our victim had been in the house, wouldn't you start the fire in the front room?'

Harry didn't answer.

'And if it was the OCG who did it, why not harvest the crop first? It must be worth nigh-on fifty grand. And why not take away all the equipment? All those lights and sprinklers are valuable. Those guys are used to setting up in new locations all the time. It doesn't make sense, Harry.'

'We're not dealing with the brightest tools in the box, boss, they're gang members.'

'But you heard Mark Kennedy's presentation – these are not your common or garden criminals. They are clever, ruthless, internationally connected and professional.'

'Still gang bangers, boss.'

Emma shook her head. 'It doesn't make sense, Harry, none of it makes sense.'

Chapter FIFTY-SEVEN

Gavin Newton was surprised.

He'd seen the copper leading the murder investigation go inside the cannabis farm with the fire officers. What was she doing here? Were the constabulary so short-staffed they were taking officers from a murder inquiry to look into a fire, or was something else at play?

He'd heard the call on the police channels when he was sitting in his car.

'Officers to Christleton, major fire reported.'

For a second, he'd thought about telling Quentin but decided not to. After all, this was just a local issue and it would keep his editor at the *Chester Daily* happy while Gavin was moonlighting for the *Mail*.

He'd driven over and was surprised to see DI Christie already there with her hulking detective constable. The smell of dope was strong in the air. A crowd of young, and not so young, locals had gathered downwind, all breathing deeply

He'd asked a firefighter what was going on and they had been extremely forthcoming.

'A fire at a cannabis farm. Could have destroyed the whole street, except we got here quickly and put it out.'

'Who called it in?'

'Didn't leave a name, just somebody who spotted the fire on the ground floor.'

'How did it start?'

'It looked like it was deliberate.'

'Arson?'

The fire officer nodded.

'Why? Why would somebody start a fire in a house full of dope plants?'

'I don't know. It's a question you should be asking her.'

The office pointed to DI Christie, now standing in the entrance of the burnt-out house, talking animatedly with her detective constable.

'But between you and me, it looks like the work of another gang. The lad who was guarding the farm has gone missing too.'

'Do you know who it was?'

'Some Albanian boy, apparently.'

An Albanian? Wasn't the body found in the Roman Gardens Albanian too? Was that the link, and the reason why DI Christie was here?

He'd ducked down when she emerged from the house. Her oppo was carrying some clothes in evidence bags and a local CSI team had just arrived.

Why were they putting so many resources into a fire at a cannabis farm? He'd have to quiz his source for the details. It would probably cost him another 100 quid but he didn't care any more. The *Mail* was funding him and so his old worries about money had vanished like the aroma of dope on a breeze.

He would enjoy it while it lasted and, perhaps with a bit of luck, he could turn it into something more permanent and infinitely more lucrative.

For now, though, the day job called. He picked up his mobile and called the duty sub-editor. He wouldn't mention the link to the fire at the cannabis farm; he'd save that for Quentin and the *Mail*. He was a sure a tale of a gang war in sleepy Chester would be a great story for them.

'I'm at a fire in Christleton, Dennis. Are you ready for the copy?'

'Fire away, Gavin.'

'Headline: Cannabis Farm Fire. Copy reads: Today, in the Chester suburb of Christleton, a fire broke out in a cannabis farm on the outskirts of the village. New paragraph: Mrs Doreen Pugsley, a local resident, described the scene to this reporter. "Flames were gushing through the downstairs and upstairs windows as the fire officers arrived. The smell over the village was terrible."'

He'd made up Mrs Pugsley. The editor always liked a bit of local colour and direct quotes from witnesses always helped add immediacy to his reports. The fact that these people didn't exist was neither here nor there. They *could* have existed and that was all that mattered to Gavin.

He continued with his report. 'Fire officers arrived on the scene within minutes after an anonymous tip-off.'

The last part was a bit too close to the truth and he wanted to save that for Quentin. 'Sorry, scrub that last sentence, Dennis. It should read: Fire officers arrived on the scene within minutes after a call from a concerned neighbour.'

That was better. Added a bit of local colour and flattered the yokels. His editor would be pleased.

The truth he would save for later, after a bit more digging.

Chapter FIFTY-EIGHT

'Gather round, all of you, it's five o'clock briefing time.'

The team members stopped what they were doing and assembled on the chairs place in front of Emma in neat rows.

Once again, they all sat in exactly the same places they had used last time. She really would have to change the layout.

The boards behind her had been updated with the latest pictures of the second victim, plus images from the Roman Gardens where he had been found.

'Right, we now have two murders with a similar MO,' Emma began. 'Our first victim is Roy Short, and we have a name for our second victim. He has been tentatively identified as Altea Marku, an Albanian national, who arrived illegally in this country only seven weeks ago. This may or may not be his real identity. He was taken to a migrants' hotel where he was last seen. John, did you contact Brighton?'

'I did, boss. They confirmed that he was a resident having been brought there from Dover by the border force. They said he left sometime around the beginning of September.'

'They're not certain when he left the place after arriving here illegally?' asked Anna. 'What sort of place are they running?'

'I don't know.' John checked his notes. 'But they reported seventy-seven other children have vanished from the hotel in the last three months.'

'These were kids?'

'Their records show that they were. All of them were between the ages of eleven to sixteen.'

'Where did the seventy-seven children go?'

'I asked the same question, Anna. Their answer was that it was the border force and the police's job to apprehend any people who absconded from the hotel. Their concern was for the existing residents.'

'What the hell are they doing?'

Emma clapped her hands. 'Focus, people.' She scanned everybody. 'We need to concentrate on the job in hand, not – I repeat, not – on the policy of the government with regards to child refugees.'

Mark Kennedy put his hand up. 'I think I can answer Anna's question.'

Emma nodded for him to continue.

'These children vanish into the hands of criminal gangs involved in drug smuggling, prostitution, counterfeiting, and running protection rackets. Once they are taken by the OCGs, it's virtually impossible to trace them.'

'Why don't they run away from the gangs?'

'Because if they go to the police, we are obliged to report them to the border force and they go back in detention with possible deportation. They simply swap one prison for another.'

'Thank you, Mark. Have you asked for information on Altea Marku from Interpol, John?'

'Already done, boss. Plus I sent an email to the Albanian police, but no responses from either organisation at the moment.'

'Great. Dr Anstey believes both our victims were killed using the same MO; strangulation from behind followed by the removal of the eyes. Both had probably been drugged with Rohypnol before they were killed, but we are still waiting on the lab for the toxicology report on the second victim. Finally, neither was killed at the place they were found. They were transported and placed there.'

'Why?' asked Gerry.

'If we knew that, Gerry, we could probably solve this whole case. But what we can be certain of is that the same person or persons killed both victims and then placed them at the ruins of the church and in the Roman Gardens. It leads us to add two new questions to our list. She turned to the board and wrote in large letters:

WHERE WERE THEY KILLED?
HOW WERE THEY TRANSPORTED TO THEIR SITES?

'But let's not get ahead of ourselves.' Emma opened her large notebook. 'There are a few things left we need to follow up. Richard, how about the checking of ANPR and CCTV?'

'We've contacted the owners of the ninety-three vehicles, only eleven have not replied. All have reasons for being in the area on both occasions, most going home from work.'

'Have you added last night between nine and eleven p.m. to the list?'

'Done, boss. There are just twenty-three vehicles who appear all three times.'

'Contact them. The body must have been transported to the Roman Gardens.'

'But we don't know when,' said Anna. 'Should we widen the search times?'

'Good idea, go from six to eleven a.m., Richard.'

'But that will take in rush hour, could be thousands of vehicles.'

Emma was beginning to get annoyed with his continuous whining. 'Just do it,' she said abruptly. 'All the local CCTV downloaded, Anna?'

'Gerry's going through it.'

The young constable shook his head. 'Nothing so far.'

'Right, keep going, Gerry. Harry, did you get the information we wanted on Roy Short from Liverpool social services?'

'They're playing silly buggers but it should be in tomorrow. The Wrights confirmed the body we found is that of Roy Short. It wasn't an easy ID, the lack of eyes...' Harry didn't need to say any more.

Anna shook her head. 'I still don't get it. If this is a gangland killing, why place the bodies in such visible locations? Why not bury them in a landfill or underneath the foundations of a building? We wouldn't find them for twenty years, if we ever found them at all. And why take out the eyes?'

'Great questions, Anna, and it's been puzzling me too. Perhaps it was to send a message to another gang? Or frighten them into leaving Chester?'

Anna nodded. 'The sign around their necks would then make sense.'

'But does it? "Not in my city" sounds more like a vigilante group than an OCG. And if it was an OCG, all they've done is attract police attention to themselves. Mark said these gangs are business organisations. I'm sorry, Harry, but I can understand them stopping you to get their money and drugs back, but dumping bodies in prominent places in Chester just doesn't make good business sense.'

Emma recognised the echo of her own words just half an hour earlier.

'Anna's right. That these killings are the work of an OCG is just one hypothesis we are following. Don't make any assumptions about this case unless they are proven with evidence, is that clear?'

There was a chorus of yesses from the assembled coppers.

Finally, she turned back to John. 'Anything else to report?'

'Still waiting for most stuff, but the tracking details of the twenty-eight burner phones bought from local petrol stations have come in from the service providers. I passed the logs to Harry.'

'There's over three thousand pages but I'm going through them, boss, we've been a bit busy today.'

'Good, keep at it, Harry. We still need to work out Roy Short's movements in his final hours.'

'Will do, boss, but working out which phone, if any, belonged to Roy is proving harder than I thought.'

Emma checked her notes. 'One last thing. Dr Anstey found traces of cannabis pollen on our second victim's hands. Coincidentally, we received a call from the local plod that a possible cannabis farm was on fire in Christleton. Harry and I went to the scene and we found clothing items and magazines that may have belonged to our victim.'

'I've already sent the stuff to the lab.'

'Good man, Harry.'

'Our victim may have been in charge of a cannabis farm?'

'As Mark said, children trafficked by the OCGs are often used to run these farms.'

John stuck his hand up. 'I got on to force intelligence. Officially, there are zero cannabis farms in the Chester area.'

'Zero?'

'Nada. Zilch. Nothing. Not a one.'

'So what was that we saw this afternoon? Chopped liver?'

'To quote them, "We opened a new file with your intelligence."'

'Brilliant. One other thing, the fire at the non-existent cannabis farm was started deliberately, it wasn't an accident.'

'By who? Why?'

'We don't know, Anna.'

'But this man thinks he does.' John Simpson held up the *Chester Daily*. On the front in lurid type was a headline: CANNABIS FARM FIRE. 'Hot off the press, boss.'

'At least he hasn't made the connection to Marku.'

'Not yet,' said Emma, 'but he's getting his info from somewhere. Let me warn you all, if it's anybody on this team, you'll be out of the force before your feet touch the floor. It's gross misconduct, so no pension and you'll be banned for working for any other police force for life. Clear?'

'Davy Jones isn't going to be a happy bunny,' said John.

Emma hadn't thought about their boss since that morning. 'Before I forget, anything from the flyers and the lunchtime TV appeal?'

'Nothing but the usual cranks, guv,' said Sergeant Harris. 'The weirdos of Chester seem to be coming out of the woodwork. One woman is convinced the murders were committed by the ghosts of Roman legionnaires seeking retribution against the druids. Apparently, she's going to Anglesey to pray for us all this weekend.'

Laughter erupted from the team.

'They all come out of the woodwork in a murder investigation.' Emma paused, composed herself and changed the tone of her voice as her dad had taught her. 'But remember, be careful out there. Whoever is committing these murders is vicious and deranged. Please be careful. Go over your notes once again, see if you've forgotten something or missed a clue we should have followed up. Check once, twice, and then check again. This person, or persons, will kill again. I feel it in my water. We need to stop them before they do. Understand?'

'Yes, boss,' they all chorused.

'And what do you have to do?'

'Check the notes again.'

Emma smiled. 'Good lads and lasses. Anything else that I've forgotten?'

They all shook their heads.

'Right, back to work. We need to crack this case, the sooner the better.'

With that final reminder, she took out her phone and pressed speed dial for Chief Inspector Jones. It wasn't a call she was looking forward to making.

Chapter FIFTY-NINE

'Aaah, Detective Inspector Christie, good to finally hear from you. I'm happy you remember that I actually do exist.'

Her boss's sarcasm was dripping like a melting ice cream on a hot day.

'Sorry, sir, I've been busy.'

'So I heard. Is it normal for a senior investigating officer to be attending fire incidents in the middle of an investigation?'

'No, sir…'

'In my day, we were always too busy doing our work – in your case, investigating the brutal murders of two young men – to go swanning off to watch our esteemed colleagues in the fire brigade put out a house fire. But perhaps you have a certain attraction for firefighters these days…'

Was he referring to the fire started by her dad? Or was he just being sarcastic?

'Let me explain, sir.'

'I'm all ears, DI Christie, particularly as I seem to get most of my information from the newspaper these days rather than from my officers.'

'Dr Anstey swabbed the hands and under the nails of our last victim from the Roman Gardens, Altea Marku.'

'What sort of name is that?'

'It's Albanian, sir. He arrived just over seven weeks ago in the UK, was detained at Dover and placed in a migrant hotel.'

'From which he escaped by simply walking out of the front door.'

'You know about the places, sir?' Emma couldn't prevent a note of incredulity creeping into her voice.

'I do read the papers, DI Christie. Remember, it's where I find out about investigations on my own patch.'

Emma decided to get back to the case. 'Anyway, Dr Anstey found traces of cannabis and cannabis pollen on the hands of our victim.'

'So for some obscure reason, you hot-footed it over to a fire. What did you find?'

'It was a cannabis farm, sir, one we knew nothing about. There was nobody there but we did discover the fire had been started deliberately, and we found possessions that may have belonged to Altea Marku.'

There was a long silence at the end of the phone.

'Sir?'

'You say the fire was started deliberately?'

'Yes, sir, confirmed by the senior fire officer.'

Another long silence. Emma was about to say something when her boss finally spoke.

'Do we have a gang war beginning in Chester?'

'I don't know, sir.'

'You don't know? I'm asking you about the possibility of more killings, even perhaps the shooting of innocent bystanders, and your answer is "you don't know"? What does Mark Kennedy say?'

'He's given us a background to the gangs of Liverpool already, and he's checking which gang Roy Short may have belonged to.'

'What about the other victim? The Albanian?'

Emma found herself internally wincing at his question. The memory of the thin, frail white body lying on the pathologist's stainless-steel table flashed through her mind. These were people, young men, whose lives had been taken away from them brutally. He wasn't just 'the Albanian'.

'Altea Marku may have been kidnapped and forced to work at the cannabis farm.'

'Who kidnapped him?'

'I don't know, sir.'

'How did he escape from the gang?'

'I don't know that either, sir.'

'How did his body get to be at the Roman Gardens?'

Emma was silent.

'You don't know that either, do you, DI Christie?'

'We know he wasn't killed at the Roman Gardens, but his body was placed there.'

'So where was he killed?'

Emma didn't answer.

'I take it from your silence, you don't know.' A long sigh down the phone. 'I want this cleared and cleared quickly, DI Christie. You have two more days. Unless I see progress in that time, you're off the case. Stewart Riggs is itching to get his teeth into this and I'm tempted to let him have a go. Two more days, understand, DI Christie?'

Emma closed her eyes. 'Yes, sir,' she said slowly.

'One more thing. These articles in the *Chester Daily* have got people up in arms. Even worse, I've received notice of a new article in a national newspaper tomorrow morning. We haven't seen it yet, but we've heard it could be critical of our investigation. This has got the chief constable very worried, and when he becomes anxious, the force trembles. Do I make myself clear, DI Christie?'

'Yes, sir.'

'Because of the possibility that this may be the start of a gang war, I'm putting the whole of the City of Chester Constabulary on high alert; more street patrols, more coppers on the beat and on standby in local nicks. We will not have the streets of Chester running with blood.'

'Sir, I don't think such emotive language—'

'I don't care what you think, DI Christie!' he shouted. 'I do care that you solve these murders. One more day. Understand?'

Emma pulled the microphone away from her ear. When she put it back, the line was dead; he'd already rung off.

One more day. Could she solve it in time?

Chapter SIXTY

At precisely 6.00 p.m., Liam Gilligan turned off the M6 into the southbound side of Knutsford Services.

The sun was beginning to set over the Cheshire countryside and the sky had the wonderful orange glow of an autumn twilight.

This venue was chosen as it was neutral ground between Manchester and Liverpool. The other option had been Buttonwood on the M62, but he preferred it here as it was more private.

The meeting had been set up quickly by Mickey. A little too quickly for Gilligan. How had his number two managed to contact the Cheetham Hill mob in such a short time and get them to agree to come?

It was a question that troubled him as he drove around the car park, checking all the vehicles. His nerves were on edge, his antennae anticipating, expecting, trouble.

He relaxed a little as he drove around a second time. At this time of the evening, the place was pretty empty. The tell-tale signs of an ambush were missing. No people were watching. No cars with a couple of people inside apparently doing nothing. No vans with blacked-out windows.

Big Max had stayed in Liverpool while Gilligan drove himself. Before he left home, he had left clear instructions with his brothers. If anything happened to him, they were to hit Cheetham Hill quick and hard. There were three teams of men, all sat waiting and armed. If he didn't call them before 6.30, they would act.

He parked up next to the charging station. Within seconds another vehicle entered the car park. A black BMW

M5, a classic Manchester gang car. They never did have any style.

As he had done, the BMW circled the car park, checking out the environment. After going round three times, it slowly came to a stop so that both drivers' windows were next to each other.

The blacked-out window of the BMW slowly wound down.

'Hiya, Linton.'

The man inside the car made no response. Around his neck, the gold chains glittered in the twilight. As if on cue, the lights in the car park went on.

'No hello? I thought this was a friendly meeting?'

'We've just lost a grow house, burnt down, and one of our slaves is dead.'

'Nothing to do with us. But you shouldn't have been operating in our territory, you know that.'

The man's arm appeared out of the window, gesticulating wildly, the tattooed initials 'C.H.G.' clear to see. 'Nowt to do with us either. One of our young dealers went rogue you know how they are. He's been punished already.'

'You won't be in our area again?'

He shook his head. 'Like I said, the dealer's been punished. He won't be out of hospital for a couple of weeks. Needs facial reconstruction.'

'Sounds like he had a bad accident.'

'It happens to those who break arrangements.' The implied threat hung over the meeting like a decayed shroud. 'But his "accident" doesn't hide the fact we lost a grow house, a lot of money and a lot of weed today. When I find who was responsible, it ain't gonna be pretty.'

'Like I said, nothing to do with us.'

'How can I be sure it wasn't your mob?'

Gilligan shrugged. 'You can't, Linton, but it makes no sense for us to kill your boy and then burn out your grow house without nicking the weed and the gear. We're not stupid.'

'Wha? Our boy is dead?'

'Your man was found dead in the centre of Chester last night. You didn't know?'

The man in the other car stared out of the windscreen, his fingers tapping the steering wheel.

'We lost one of our dealers a couple of days ago too. A young lad from Liverpool, Roy Short. I had you in the frame for it, Linton, but after last night and the fire today, I'm not so sure any more.'

A long silence.

'It wasn't us who killed your boy. Not good business. You think Moss Side are at it again?'

Gilligan shook his head. 'Mickey is there. He can't see any other gang in the city. No muscle. No activity. Nothing.'

'Wha's going on?'

'That's why we're meeting. It's all mad. If you lot have nothing to do with it, then we'll sort it. Our territory, our problem. The weed's gone though, Linton—' he touched his fingers to his mouth '—up in smoke.'

'Shame, a new variety we were trying.'

Gilligan didn't ask how Linton knew they were cultivating a new variety of dope in a grow house operated by a rogue dealer. But he filed the information in the back of his mind.

'The death of the boy and the burning of your grow house was nothing to do with us. We cool, Linton?'

A tattooed hand came out of the car and they bumped fists.

'Like ice, Liam. You gonna make the call now?'

Gilligan played it cool. 'What call?'

'To those soldiers you got armed and ready in Liverpool. We got a team watching them.'

Gilligan smiled. Delroy Linton was getting up himself. He would have to take him and his gang out soon.

'I'll make the call.'

'Good. And we'd like a taste of the coke you got coming in soon.'

He was well-informed. How? Was Mickey shooting his mouth off?

'You'll get a taste when it gets here.'

'When's that?'

'Soon, Linton, soon.'

'Don't wait too long, man.'

With that, the window of the BMW wound up and the throbbing engine slowly pulled the car away from the charging station.

Gilligan picked up his phone and called his brother. 'Luke, you can stand down. It wasn't the Cheetham Hill mob who killed Roy.'

'What were they doing in our city?'

'A rogue dealer, he's been punished.'

'You believe them?'

'Nah, but right now we've got a problem in Chester we need to sort out. Mickey needs backup.'

'You want me to go?'

'Not yet, just send more soldiers.'

'I'll send them tonight.'

'And, Luke, double the protection on the gear at the docks.'

'You smell trouble?'

'Just because you're paranoid…'

'…doesn't mean they're not out to get you.'

'I'm going to Chester myself.'

'Is that wise?'

'No, but it's necessary. Look after the gear, I'll look after Chester.'

Chapter SIXTY-ONE

Emma was just finishing the update of the case log with John Simpson when Sergeant Harris came rushing into the Major Incident Room.

'I think we've got something,' he said, loud enough to make everyone turn and stare at him.

An old man wearing an even older anorak was standing beside him, held firmly in the sergeant's grip.

'We set up the desks on the Walls and handed out the leaflets. Nobody came forward until ten minutes ago, when Mr Hopkins here approached us at Eastgate.'

'I saw the leaflets, see.'

The sergeant gestured towards the old man. 'Apparently, he walks the Walls at the same time every night. Last night, he was making his usual rounds when—'

Emma held up her hand. 'Why don't you let the man tell his story, Tom?'

The sergeant looked dubious but stopped talking, pushing the man forward towards Emma.

'Your name is?'

'Harold Hopkins.' The voice was like rich tobacco; old, leathery and coming from a chest that had inhaled far too many Capstans. 'Lived in Chester all my life, I have. 'Cept for the war. I was sent out to Wales with me brother then. Couldn't stand the Welsh, mean bastards.'

Anna visibly bristled at the old man's words. Sergeant Harris, however, was smiling broadly.

'Thank you, Mr Hopkins. Could you tell us what happened last night?'

The man seemed to be thinking but didn't answer.

'You told me you saw something, Harold, remember?'

'Don't prompt him, Tom.'

The old man's eyes suddenly lit up. 'That's right, I saw something from the top of the Walls, near the Roman Gardens. I've walked there every night for the last twenty years, you see. One complete circuit around Chester, that's what I do, before I go down the pub. Keeps me active, it does. Better a good walk than all that yoga and pirates malarkey the young people go in for. Load of old tosh, if you ask me, sticking your bum in the air for no reason.'

'I think he means Pilates,' said the sergeant.

'I'd worked that out, Tom. So, Harold, what did you see last night?'

'Well, it must have been about nine thirty. You see, I always start my walk at five to nine and finish it at nine forty close to Eastgate. Best pint in Chester at the Boot Inn. That landlord knows how to keep his ale, he does, and they don't like having mobile phones and all that modern stuff in there. My sort of place with a decent pint. And I should know, having drunk barrels of the stuff in my time. Four pints a night, every night, never more, never less, since I were a nipper.' He leant closer to Emma. 'I'll let you into a secret; never drink in odd numbers, they always gives you a hangover, them odd numbers. Me, I stick to four pints a night. Once or twice, I might have six, but only if the throat is feeling a bit parched. Keeps me regular, it does, and did you know a good drop of ale has enough vitamins and iron to feed a family? A doctor told me that down the pub.'

'Yes, Harold. But what did you see last night?' asked Emma, a note of frustration creeping into her voice.

'That's it, didn't see much at all. The Walls were pretty quiet that night, it's the weather, you know. Even Touchy Tony who hangs around Bridgegate, waiting for the tourists to put a few bob in his hat, had gone home early. He always tells them he's homeless, but he's got a lovely flat over in Handbridge. It's a job, he always tells me.'

Emma was about to ask him again when he carried on speaking.

'Anyway, the Walls were quiet but towards the end, where they overlook the Roman Gardens, I saw something.'

He stopped speaking, a broad, toothless smile plastered across his face.

Emma waited for a few seconds, hoping he would continue speaking. When he didn't, she asked, 'Well, what was it? What did you see?'

'I saw a man in the gardens.'

Emma whistled. They were finally getting somewhere. 'Can you describe him?'

'Not really. It was dark and the moon wasn't very bright.'

'Can you remember anything about him? His face? His hair colour? His height? Was he as tall as the sergeant or as short as me?'

The man thought for a long time; Emma could almost see the cogs whirring in his beer-fogged brain.

Finally he answered. 'Hard to say, really. You see, I was up above him looking down and there was nobody to compare him with.'

So he wasn't as stupid as he looked, thought Emma.

'But I would say he was about average height with average build and hair.'

'Average hair?' asked Harry.

'Exactly,' said the old man. 'Average brown hair.'

'At least we know the hair was brown,' said Harry, noting it down in his book.

The ends of the old man's nicotine-stained fingers touched his lips. 'Then again, it could have been dirty blond. It just looked brown because of the light.'

Emma's eyes rolled up in her head, staring up at the ceiling of the Incident Room.

'Thank you, Mr Hopkins, you've been very helpful. The sergeant will give you a lift home or down the pub if you want.'

'Just wait a minute,' Tom said. 'Ask him what the man was wearing.'

'I don't know if that will help, Tom.'

'Trust me, guv.'

She made a moue with her mouth. 'Okay, Mr Hopkins, what was the man wearing?'

The man pretended to think. 'He was wearing one of those bright greeny-yellow jackets with "City of Chester" on the back.'

'A high-vis jacket?'

'Is that what they're called, the ones that help you be seen at night? I think that's why I noticed him.'

'Because of the jacket?'

'No, because it had "City of Chester" on the back.'

Emma frowned. 'I don't understand.'

'It was because he was working for the council, see. Nobody works for the council sweeping roads at nine thirty at night. I know because I worked for them for thirty-five years, man and boy. They won't pay the overtime, see.'

'Hang on a minute, Mr Hopkins, how do you know he swept the roads?'

'Because he had his cart with him. Call me suspicious if you want, but nobody sweeps the gardens then. The council just won't pay them.'

Anna stepped forward. 'Boss, I talked with a road sweeper yesterday when we did the search of the park. Philip Jackson, he said his name was. He said the gardens were also his patch.'

'Find him, Anna, find him now.'

The detective constable rushed out of the Incident Room.

'You want me to come too, boss?'

'No, Harry, you stay here. I want to know Roy Short's movements on the day he died. You need to concentrate on finding that phone.'

A disappointed Harry meekly replied, 'Yes, boss,' before turning back to the three thousand pages of computer printouts on his desk.

Chapter SIXTY-TWO

Anna ran straight out of the Major Incident Room, past St John's Church and the ruins where they had found the body of Roy Short, and into the park.

She was followed by Sergeant Harris and two constables. Bringing up the rear, moving as fast as she could, was Emma.

Anna ordered the sergeant and one of his men to go right and check close to the river on the path nearest to the Groves, while she went towards the left with another copper in close proximity. She ran past the hedge where the boys had hidden just two nights ago, scanning left and right continuously for the man and his cart.

Nothing.

She ran on, around the quadrant with its now bare flower beds. There were no leaves on the path she was running along; had he already swept here this morning?

She stopped for a moment, looking all over, but could see no sign of the cart or the man. On her right, the sergeant was running on a path nearer to the river, bordered by trees, his police jacket standing out against the golden yellows and browns of the autumn leaves.

The copper beside her tapped in a few numbers on his Airwave radio. 'Seen anything, Tom? Over.'

A brief crackle followed by, 'Nothing so far, Larry. Over.'

'Ask him if the leaves have been swept on his path.'

The copper repeated the question.

'No, covered in the stuff here. Nobody has swept this today. Over.'

'Right, tell him to follow the path round and we'll meet him at the statue.'

'Roger that,' came the answer before the copper had relayed the message.

Anna ran on, hearing the young constable panting behind her. Weren't they supposed to be fit? Hadn't he just come out of training?

She scanned left and right, looking for the distinctive box-like shape of the man's cart and this bright green high-vis jacket. Still nothing.

She arrived at the statue of Richard Grosvenor, second Marquess of Westminster, a well-known landmark in the park named after him.

As a kid, when she visited the area on a trip with her school in Wales, they had stopped at the statue. One of the girls had pointed to it, saying, 'That man is wearing knickers.'

They had all giggled at the joke, but now, looking at it again, she still thought he was wearing the most ridiculous costume she'd ever seen on a statue.

The words on his plinth, though, still remained.

THE GENEROUS LANDLORD
THE FRIEND OF ALL THE DISTRESSED
THE HELPER OF ALL GOOD WORKS
THE BENEFACTOR TO THIS CITY
ERECTED BY HIS TENANTS, FRIENDS AND NEIGHBOURS
A.D. 1869

The sycophancy of the message had struck her then and it struck her now too. He seemed too good to be true.

Sergeant Harris arrived with another constable. 'We checked along the riverfront at the Groves and in the park. Can't see him.'

Emma came panting up. 'You haven't found him?'

'Not yet,' answered Anna. 'Tom, search along the terrace and Dee Lane, he may be sweeping down there. We'll look through the kids' play area and the miniature railway. We'll meet up at the front gate near the café.'

The sergeant trotted off, while Emma, Anna and the young copper strode towards the play area, scanning left and right.

The park was absent of any early evening strollers; perhaps the news of all the police activity in the area had deterred visitors. The children's area seemed deserted while the miniature railway was closed for the season, only opening at the weekends.

The place was quiet, but all the paths had been swept and were free of leaves.

'It looks like he's been here already,' said Anna.

'So where's he gone? You can't hide a cart in a park this size.'

'Let's go to the front gate. See if Tom Harris has had better luck.'

They strode up the path to the gate and the café next to it. The wind was getting stronger now, a chill sweeping over the mountains of Wales and on to the plains of Cheshire. Here, close to the river, it was stronger and cooler than normal.

Anna wished she had put on her coat before she came running out.

'I'm going to have to go to the gym,' Emma said, slightly breathless. 'Seen him?'

Anna shook her head. 'He doesn't seem to be in the park.'

Sergeant Harris approached. 'We've checked along the river and Dee Lane, he's not there either.'

As he spoke, a stronger gust of wind blew through the trees and Anna turned away to put her back to the breeze.

The road sweeper was walking casually down the path, pulling his cart behind him, entering a small compound on the left where the park keepers kept all their gear.

'Oi, Mr Jackson, stop there! We want a word with you,' shouted Sergeant Harris.

The man's head shot round. A startled, deer-like look appeared in his eyes and he took off, running out on a path leading to the Headlands and Dee Lane.

Without waiting for an order, the two younger coppers and Sergeant Harris chased after him, shouting for him to stop.

'They don't need our help, do they, Anna?' asked a still breathless Emma.

'Shouldn't think so, boss.'

Within thirty seconds the Airwave that Emma was holding squawked into life.

'Got him.'

'Right, caution him and take him to the Town Hall nick. We'll question him there.'

Chapter SIXTY-THREE

Emma stared through the observation window into the interview room at the small, shrew-like man sitting in front of a table with a plastic cup of coffee resting on it.

His eyes kept darting towards the door as if waiting for a monster to walk through it at any moment. His fingers intertwined themselves, occasionally tapping nervously on the table or lifting the now-empty coffee cup to his mouth. He had asked if he could smoke but his request had been refused.

For Emma, this man didn't look like somebody who could murder and put the eyes out of two young men. But what did a murderer look like? Did Harold Shipman look like a killer? Did Peter Sutcliffe look like someone who murdered young women?

'Does he look guilty to you, Anna?'

The detective constable shrugged her broad shoulders. 'He looks nervous.'

'Has he been cautioned?'

'When he was arrested, and it was repeated on booking in.'

'Good. And has he asked for a solicitor?'

'No, said he didn't know any. Never been in trouble before.'

'Strange. No previous at all?'

'I checked, and according to the records, he has no form. Could be using a false name though, so we're running his fingerprints and mugshot through IDENT1.'

Should Emma interview him now or wait for a duty brief to come to the station?

She stared through the window again. If the brief advised him to say 'no comment', they could be here all night. But if she went ahead with the interview and he confessed, he could claim later that he hadn't been represented by legal counsel.

She watched as he nervously lifted the empty coffee cup to his lips once more.

'How long has he been in there?'

'Thirty minutes.'

'Get him another coffee and we'll go inside. He's been cooked enough.'

'You don't want to wait for the brief?'

Emma shook her head. 'This one is going to cough straight away or he's going to keep his mouth shut. Either way, I'd like to find out before the brief arrives. Go and get the coffee and we'll get started.'

Emma found a large file and stuffed it full of spare paper to make it look big, bulky and imposing. She then placed her notepad on top, added three pens and, when Anna returned with the hot coffee, they went into the interview room.

'Good evening, Mr Jackson. My name is Detective Inspector Emma Christie of City of Chester Constabulary, and this is my colleague, Detective Constable Anna Williams. We'd like to ask you a few questions. Before we start, here's some more coffee.'

'I need to call my wife, she'll be worried when I don't come home on time.'

'Soon, Mr Jackson, we just have to ask you a few questions first.'

Emma switched on the tape machine on the desk.

The camera in the corner above her head was also recording both sound and visuals, but it was important to have a recording too.

'The time is 19.05 on Friday 27th October. This is Detective Inspector Emma Christie speaking, of City of Chester Constabulary, and I'm joined by my colleague, DC Anna Williams. With us is Mr Philip Jackson. Could you repeat your name and address for the audio tape, Mr Jackson?'

The man's eyes darted left and right. 'Why? Have I been arrested?'

'You are helping us with our enquiries at the moment. No arrest has been made so far. I would like to caution you that anything you do say may be used in evidence against you. You do not have to say anything. But it may harm your defence if you do not mention when questioned something that you later rely on in court. Is that clear?'

The man nodded.

'I need you to speak into the microphone when you respond please.'

The man leant forward and said, 'I understand, but can I go home now?'

Emma frowned. Was he really understanding her? His fingers were tapping quickly on the table and he appeared agitated, his eyes still darting left and right. Should she have given him more coffee?

'I need you to state your name and address.'

'My name is Philip Jackson and I live at Henry Place.'

'Good, thank you, Mr Jackson. You do understand that you can have a solicitor present during this interview if you want one?'

'I don't have a solicitor. Never needed one.'

'We can get a duty solicitor to come and represent you. There is no cost to you.'

'When can they get here?'

'As soon as they can, but it could be a couple of hours depending on how busy they are.'

Jackson seemed to take this information in before asking, 'You just need to ask me some questions and I can go when I've answered them?'

'I need to ask you some questions and, if the answers are truthful, you can go.' Emma didn't add that if the answers convinced her of his guilt, then he wouldn't be leaving the station for a long, long time.

'Okay. I need to get home to see the wife, she'll be worried.' There was a short pause and then he added, 'I did it.'

Emma glanced across at Anna Williams. Had she just heard correctly?

'Could you repeat that last statement please, Mr Jackson?'

'I did it.'

Emma sat back in the chair. Something didn't feel right. Nobody admits to the murder of two young men so easily. 'You did what, Mr Jackson? Can you explain clearly for the tape?'

'I did it, I just told you.'

'You murdered two young men and placed their bodies in the ruins of St John's Church and in the Roman Gardens?' asked Anna.

The man's eyes narrowed. 'What are you talking about?'

'The murders of two young men; what are *you* talking about?'

'Murder? I didn't do no murder.'

Emma placed her hand on her colleague's arm, stopping her from asking any more questions. 'What did you do, Mr Jackson?'

The man looked down, staring at his hands in front of him. 'I took out the CCTV cameras on the church and the path to the gardens.'

'Why?'

'A man gave me a hundred quid to do it. I thought he was going to nick the lead off the roof of the church. At least, that's what he told me he was going to do.'

'So why immobilise the CCTV on the path behind the Roman Gardens?'

'That was where he said he was going to park his van for the stuff.'

Emma thought for a moment, questions racing through her brain. Was this man telling the truth or was it all a pack of lies?

'How did you disable the CCTV?'

'Easy, I just smashed the cameras with a hammer. Then, to make them a bit more difficult to repair, I unplugged the power supply and then sliced through the cables with a box cutter.'

At least he knew how the cameras had been disabled, but he could have picked up that information easily on his rounds in the park.

'You seem confident you could disable it.'

The man looked down at the ground. 'I got in a spot of trouble when I was young. I was a bit of a tearaway back then.'

'What did you do?'

The man's eyes drifted upwards. 'When I was a kid in Manchester I was caught breaking and entering.'

'You're not on our system?'

'I was fourteen, they gave me a caution but never really forgot about me. Every time something went missing in Wythenshawe, the cops were round my house like a flash. One of the reasons I came to Chester, get away from you lot.'

Emma closed her eyes. She was sure he'd just said something important, but she couldn't put her finger on it. It was like the name of an old friend that was on the tip of her tongue but just wouldn't come out. She gave up forcing the answer and asked a different question.

'Can you tell me what the man who gave you the money looked like?'

'Hard to tell, really. He was wearing a hoodie with a baseball cap pulled over his eyes.'

'His build – was he stocky or thin, muscular or lean, broad or narrow?'

'He was sort of stocky and sort of lean, if you know what I mean.'

Emma didn't. She tried again. 'His height? Was he as tall as you or shorter?'

'Definitely taller.'

'Taller than the sergeant who caught you today?'

Jackson shook his head. 'About the same height, an average sort of height.'

There was that word again, 'average'. Probably the word that annoyed Emma the most right now.

She decided to take a different tack. 'Can you tell us where you were on the night of October 24th?'

'That's easy – at home with the wife and kids. I've got six kids, the wife's a Catholic,' he added as a way of explaining.

Emma noted in her pad. 'And yesterday evening, where were you around nine thirty?'

'Down the pub with the wife and her mother. It was the mother-in-law's birthday and we went out for a few drinks to celebrate.'

'People can corroborate that you were there?'

'About a hundred were there, so I should think so. It was a proper knees-up.'

'You didn't leave the party?'

'I was there all the time. The mother-in-law had an open bar and the old bag doesn't do that very often.'

'Mr Jackson, I have to inform you that a man matching your description and with a dustcart exactly the same as yours was seen last night in the Roman Gardens at nine thirty.'

'It wasn't me. I was getting drunk.'

'Where do you keep your cart and your high-vis jacket?' asked Anna.

'In the potting shed. Put it there when the shift finishes at six o'clock every night and pick it up again every morning before beginning my rounds.'

'And it was there this morning in the same place?'

The man nodded. 'Same as always, and my jacket was hanging on the hook.'

'Same as always? Has anything been different in the last couple of days?' asked Emma.

'Different? In what way?'

'I don't know. Anything unusual happened?'

The man thought for a moment. 'Unusual, not really. In my job, it's the same every day. I sweeps the path and keeps it clear. I gets a bit busier this time of year with the leaves and all, but can't be helped.'

'The rain it raineth every day,' said Emma, remembering her high school Shakespeare.

'The potting shed was broken into four nights ago. I guess you could say that was unusual. Why anybody would break into a potting shed, though, beats me. Must have been kids.'

'Has the lock been fixed yet?'

'You're joking, ain't you? The council might get round to it by this time next year if we're lucky.'

Emma sighed, trying one last question. 'Why did you run when you saw us?'

'I had nicked two bags of compost from the potting shed in the cart. I thought nobody would notice they were missing, what with the break-in recently.' He shrugged. 'I just panicked.'

Emma closed her pad. 'I'm terminating this interview, pending confirmation of the information provided by the witness. The time is now 19.30.'

'Can I go home?'

'Not yet, Mr Jackson.'

'But you said I could go home if I told the truth.'

'We need to check your story with the witnesses. Plus there's the little matter of destruction of church property and the theft of two bags of compost. But I will allow you to call your wife after we have spoken to her.'

The man shook his head. 'You said I could go if I told the truth.'

'Thank you for your honesty, Mr Jackson, we'll be as quick as we can. Do you want anything else to drink or would you like anything to eat?'

'I could murder a bacon sarnie and a cup of tea. I didn't like to say before, but the coffee tastes like it came from the River Dee.'

'Welcome to my world, Mr Jackson. Unfortunately, the tea doesn't taste much better.'

Chapter SIXTY-FOUR

He knew this dealer well. The boy always hung around the same spot under the trees in Queen Street, wearing his usual gear taken from the street gangs of LA – oversized t-shirt and jeans, gold chains, a baseball cap on his head.

Cars would come down the street, parking up in the lay-by. He'd lean in through the open window to find out what they wanted, then take the money and go to his stash nearby before delivering the gear to his customers.

Pedestrians were different. They would approach and he'd signal his lookout to fetch the gear while he took their money.

Either way, it was a regular retail operation that ran as smooth as a McDonald's drive-thru.

A proper little pharmacy supplying the junkies of Chester with their gear: crack, dope, horse and Es, delivered within seconds.

All the time the lookout was watching, ready to warn the boy in case a copper wandered down to the area. If it happened, they'd be on their bikes and away, returning fifteen minutes later when the coast was clear.

But he'd noticed a fault in their system. One that left his target vulnerable.

When they'd had a particularly busy sales period, usually at this time early in the evening, the lookout would have to get on his bike and go to replenish their stash. It was obviously kept nearby, as the lookout would be back within five minutes.

But this absence gave him a window to act. Time to take the boy off the streets. Just one more death and the gangs would be at each other's throats, saving him the problem of killing them.

He watched for ten more minutes. The boy gave a signal to his lookout and the youngster hopped on his bike.

Now was the time. Now he should act.

He checked the street: it was empty. He ran back to the car parked around the corner, started the motor, and drove down Queen Street.

Another punter looking to score.

The boy approached the open window.

'Whaddya wan'?'

He beckoned for them to come closer. 'What do you have?'

The boy leant on the car windowsill, still speaking softly. 'Anything you wan', man, but we waitin' for the re-up. You gotta come back in ten minutes.'

He pulled the money out from inside his jacket. 'One hundred quid in fresh, crisp notes.'

'A nice wad. You wan' crack or H? Order now, deliver in ten.'

'How do I know I can trust you?'

'Listen, man, you wan' the gear or not?'

He pretended to think before finally nodding.

The hand reached for the money. As it did, he grabbed it, pulling the boy into the car. His free hand clamped the chloroform pad over the boy's nose and mouth, jamming his throat against the ledge of the door.

The boy struggled for a few moments, his legs kicking against the side panels of the car, before he stopped struggling and his body went limp. Slowly, the man opened the car door, ensuring the boy didn't hit his head on the metal sill.

He didn't want his prize to be damaged.

Not yet.

He stood up and lifted the boy's body from the open window. The ribs felt thin and emaciated through the oversized cotton t-shirt. Had the boy been using his own gear?

Probably. They all succumbed eventually.

He opened the back door with his free hand and pushed him on to the back seat, making sure he was sat upright. Anyone watching would think he was just a passenger.

Taking out a syringe, he injected a small dose of Rohypnol into the inside of the boy's elbow.

This one would go back to the lock-up like all the others. He wouldn't kill him immediately though. That pleasure would have to wait until later.

He'd take his time with this one, making sure the boy would suffer as much as all those people he'd hooked on smack or crack or any of the poisons he'd sold on the streets of Chester.

A quick look to check nobody had seen him and he slipped back into the driver's seat, putting the car into gear and reversing back down Queen Street to the main road.

He didn't notice the boy on the bike who'd arrived back with the gear. But the boy noticed him and knew something was wrong.

A dealer never got into a car with a customer.

Chapter SIXTY-FIVE

'What do you think, boss?'

They had both retired to the observation room to discuss the case. Philip Jackson was still sitting at the table. A constable was there, having brought a large mug of what was called tea but looked more like estuary mud, and a beaten-up bacon sandwich. Jackson seemed to be enjoying both.

'If he's guilty of murdering two young men and taking out their eyes, I'm a Dutchman. But we need to check. Send a car round to his address to check his alibi with the wife. Better still, you go with the car and call me back as soon as she's confirmed the timings for both nights.'

'Right. What are you going to do?'

'We need to get the CSI team down to the potting shed. See if there's any prints from the break-in, and we need to check out the man's cart too.'

'You think it was used to transport the bodies?'

'What other way of moving a bulky object like a body in plain sight? Nobody notices a street cleaner these days, particularly if he's wearing a high-vis jacket with the council's name on it.'

'You could get our identikit officer to produce an image of the man who paid him off?'

'Good idea. It sounds like he won't be able to describe him but it might give us something for the papers.'

'You want me to organise it with the desk sergeant on my way out?'

'Thanks, Anna. You'd better be off and see his wife. I don't want her getting too anxious about him.'

Anna glanced into the interview room, where Jackson had finished his bacon sandwich and was asking if there were any more to eat.

'Are we going to charge him, boss?'

'That's a decision above my pay grade, Anna. Not for the bloody compost, but destroying CCTV cameras to facilitate a crime is serious and he knew what he was doing. It'll be up to Davy Jones and the CPS whether it moves to a formal charge. Get on your way and see his missus. Call me as soon as you have something.'

'Will do, boss.'

'And don't forget to arrange the identikit officer before you leave. I'll call Jane Eastham to get a team down to the potting shed straight away. Last thing, Anna – be careful, check you're not followed.'

'Why do you ask, boss?'

Emma frowned. 'It's just that every move we've made in this case seems to have appeared in the press. It's like they know what we're doing before we even do it.'

'You think somebody is leaking information.'

'I'm not sure, but if they are, I'll—'

Emma didn't finish her sentence.

'I'll check I'm not followed.'

'Good, off you go. Call me as soon as you confirm his alibi.'

As Anna left the room, Emma picked up her mobile phone and stared through the glass at Jackson. 'Who paid you to destroy the CCTV?' she whispered.

Chapter SIXTY-SIX

Harry Fairweather's eyes began to water and the long rows of numbers he was looking at began to dance in front of his eyes.

He put down the reams of computer printouts and pinched the bridge of his nose.

'Do you want a hand, Harry?'

It was Mark Kennedy offering to help.

Harry shook his head. 'By the time I've explained it all, Mark, I might have found what I'm looking for. Thanks for the offer though.'

'I've just brewed a fresh pot of coffee if you need a break.' He pointed to where a table had been set up in the Incident Room with a coffee machine and an assortment of sugars, milks and biscuits.

'Thanks, Mark. Let me finish this number and I'll get a coffee.'

Harry picked up the thick wad of papers covered in seemingly endless lines of data in extremely small type. The service providers had provided all the data for each of the phones and their numbers which had been sold at the petrol stations close to Roy Short's house.

Harry had been on a course at Edgeley Park in Manchester when he was working for the drugs squad. What he was doing was called geolocation and it was one of the latest tools in the copper's armoury.

These days everybody carried a mobile phone around with them everywhere they went. What most people didn't know was that each of those mobile phones kept up a constant stream of chat with communication towers placed all over the city. It was the equivalent of a man with a bullhorn shouting, 'I'm here, where are you?' every thirty seconds and receiving an answer immediately from the mobile phone. 'I'm here and I'm ready to make a call or send a message.'

At all times, the phone knew exactly where it was, receiving communications from more than one tower and triangulating its position, deciding which tower was the closest when it wanted to make a call.

Luckily for the police forces of this world, the towers sent a constant stream of data back to their service providers on which phone had contacted a tower at a certain date and time. The police could then use the data to track a phone's movements across the city. Whenever anybody made a call or sent a message, they would use the tower which was closest or with the strongest signal and this data was recorded for billing purposes.

The problem for Harry was this technique only worked when he knew the phone number being used by a target.

But in this case, he didn't know Roy Short's number so he had to find out which one it was by isolating it from the list of burner phones he knew had been sold by petrol stations close to where the victim was living.

If Roy had bought the phone from another place or from a petrol station in another part of town, Harry was going to be, in the technical term, banjaxed.

He had to go through every single piece of the data and Tracy Cummings had said Roy bought his phones locally.

At first, he thought it would be easy.

All he had to do was find out which one of these phones had not been used since Roy Short's death.

Except when he checked that data, twenty-four out of the twenty-eight phones had ceased operation within a day of the murder.

Not surprising really. These were burner phones, often used by drug dealers who dumped them regularly, or people with little money who couldn't afford to keep topping them up.

It was back to square one.

Luckily, he had one definite data point for Roy Short's phone; it had been used to make a call at 4 p.m on Sunday, October 22, from Tracy Cummings' home. He had to go through the pages of data for each of the twenty-eight phones and look for that time and date, checking the data against the log numbers of the towers closest to her house.

So far it had taken him three hours to eliminate just four phones. His eyes were now hurting and the long lines of numbers were beginning to blend into each other.

Time for a quick break before he started on the fifth burner. His phone rang. 'DC Fairweather.'

'How's it going, Harry?'

'It's going, but slow, boss. I've still got twenty-four phones left to do.'

'So many?'

'Can't be helped, I need to eliminate them one at a time. How are you doing with Philip Jackson?'

'Not good, my intuition tells me it's not him. Anna is checking his alibi as we speak.'

'Why'd he run then?'

'Stupid, like all of them. He'd nicked a couple of bags of compost.'

'He's not going to get life for those, is he?'

'Anyway, just thought I'd give you a call. I think we need to know where Roy Short was before he disappeared. I have a nagging feeling in my stomach we've missed something, but I don't know what it is.'

'Boots might have a cure for it, boss. Have you tried Milk of Magnesia? My missus swears by it.'

'Thank you, Dr Fairweather. Remind me not to ask you for medical advice, Harry. Keep your nose to the grindstone or, in your case, the paper mill.'

The phone went dead in Harry's hand. He knew the conversation had been light-hearted, but he heard the tension in Emma's voice. She was under immense pressure to solve this and solve it quickly.

Instead of going for a break, Harry picked up the next sheaf of mobile phone data, crossing his fingers, toes and other dangly bits that this would be the right one.

Chapter SIXTY-SEVEN

Anna called Emma ten minutes later.

'It's confirmed, boss, he was at home three nights ago and in the pub with the mother-in-law and her family last night. Both women confirmed his story. They even have pictures on their mobile phones showing them all enjoying a drink together. It looks like a very good night was had by all.'

'Philip Jackson didn't leave the pub at all? Not even for half an hour?'

'Not according to his family. The said he was too drunk to leave. Spent most of the time huddled in the corner, cuddling a pint of bitter.'

Emma scratched her head. She knew this case wasn't going to be that easy to solve.

'Can you put the wife on your mobile, Anna? I'll get him to talk to her.'

'Right. Let me go back inside the house.'

Emma walked into the interview room. Jackson and an older copper were hunched over the photo ID books but it didn't sound like it was going too well.

'Did the eyes look like these or like these or even like these?'

'I told you, I didn't really look at this face, he was wearing a hoodie and a baseball cap. I think he had a beard though.'

'What colour was the beard?'

'I dunno, like a gingery-browny colour. I wasn't really looking, he was waving a wad of notes in my face.'

'Was he wearing gloves too, Mr Jackson?'

The man thought for a moment. 'He wasn't wearing gloves. I remember his hands were soft, not like mine or those of anybody who does a bit of graft.'

'Where did you put the money he gave you?'

Jackson took a deep breath. 'It's in a tin beneath the bed. The wife doesn't know it's there. She'll kill me when she finds out. I was saving up for Christmas.'

Anna's voice came back on the line. 'Mrs Jackson is here now, boss.'

'Before you put her on, can you tell her to get a tin box from under her bed? It's got the money given to Mr Jackson by our killer.'

'Right, boss, I'll tell her.'

'Go with her to make sure she doesn't open it.'

There was the noise of movement for thirty seconds before Anna came back on the line. 'Got it, boss.'

'Right, take it down to forensics and check for prints. Apparently our perp wasn't wearing gloves when he gave the money to Mr Jackson. Is the wife still there? Put her on the line.'

Emma handed her mobile over to the man. 'Amy,' he said quietly.

There seemed to be a loud voice on the other end of the line but Emma couldn't hear what she was saying; all she could hear were Philip Jackson's attempts to get a word in.

'I know, dear… Sorry, dear… But I… It was… I'm still here…'

She turned away. It looked like the man was going to need to do a lot of explaining before the night was out.

Chapter SIXTY-EIGHT

Emma was done for the night, the fact that she hadn't slept for thirty-six hours was finally catching up with her.

She'd already called the Major Incident Room to check in if there were any developments, but there was nothing new.

Philip Jackson had been released on police bail for the wilful destruction of church property. A simple holding charge while the powers-that-be decided whether more serious charges would be laid against him.

Emma hoped they wouldn't. The man had been greedy, stupid and ignorant, but if they were to arrest everybody who displayed those characteristics, the jails would be full to overflowing.

Anna had returned with statements from both the man's wife and mother-in-law confirming his alibi for both nights as well as the notes from the tin beneath the bed. She even had photos from the mother-in-law's phone confirming Jackson's presence in the pub. But if he wasn't the murderer, who was?

It must have been somebody who knew the jacket and dustcart were kept in the potting shed. The CSI team had already taken both objects back to the lab for testing. Emma wasn't hopeful of a result, but they might get lucky. All they needed was one break in this case but so far none had happened.

As her dad said often, 'A good cop is a lucky cop.'

The last thing she'd done was call Davy Jones, telling him what happened in the interview. His response was blunt in the extreme.

'So, you're telling me we have two dead bodies but no suspects, no leads, no forensics, no DNA and our only witness could be charged with nicking two bags of compost?'

'We do have a description from Mr Jackson of the man who paid him a hundred pounds.'

'I've seen it. A picture of a man in a hoodie and baseball cap. It fits half the men in Chester, including me.' A long pause. When Jones spoke again his voice was softer. 'I have most of the newspapers in the UK ringing me up. The bloody *Sun* is blaming the Welsh, the *Express* are leading with a tip-off that the murder was done by illegal immigrants, while the *Mail* has implied there are satanic rituals involving satanists living in Chester? The nearest we have to devil-worshippers are the poor souls who support Chester City.'

'We don't have any evidence that either of those theories is true, sir.'

'I know that, you know that, but in the absence of any real news on the case, the bloody newspapers can print what they like.'

As he became angrier his voice betrayed his Welsh origins.

'We're working as hard as we can, sir.'

'I don't need you to work hard, I need you to work smart. You have one more day before I pass the case on to DI Riggs. He'll make sure he gets a result.'

Without worrying if the right person is arrested, thought Emma, but she didn't say a word.

Into the silence, Jones ended the conversation. 'One more day, DI Christie. I want results.'

She put down the phone and began to pack up her things, putting her notepad in her briefcase. She'd look at her notes later at home over a glass of good Rioja. She'd checked in with Hortensia already. Her father had taken his meds and was sleeping soundly after watching the telly.

She wouldn't disturb him when she went home.

Perhaps tomorrow, she'd have a chat with him. Tell him what was happening.

In the old days, he was great at coming up with advice to help her. But these days, she could never predict what he would say or if he would say anything at all.

God, she missed her dad.

The man she lived with now was a husk of the man who had raised her. A sad, empty husk.

She picked up her bag, walked to the door and then it hit her like a double decker bus. The car was parked at the Major Incident Room.

Damn it to hell and back.

She went to the front desk, where Sergeant Tunney was on duty. 'Hi there, Paul. Thanks for the help identifying the first victim.'

'No worries. We see the little dealing scum all the time in the town centre nick. We usually lock 'em up for the night but they're back on the streets the day after. That one, though, he didn't even spend a night here. Out by two, he was. And we didn't charge him even though he was found with a load of coke.'

'Yeah, it happens far too often for my liking. My dad always thought we should lock op the little scrotes and throw away the key.'

'He was always sound was your dad.'

. Anyway, I'm stuck here. Can I get a lift to the Major Incident Room near St John's to pick up my car?'

'Sorry, Emma, we're short this evening. I just started my shift and it's all kicking off tonight. We've got a pool car in Trinity Street car park if you want to use that. I'll need it back tomorrow, mind.'

Emma sighed. It was one of those nights. 'Thanks, Paul, I'll borrow the car.'

He reached behind the desk for a set of keys. 'Say hello to your dad for me. He was a great copper, old school. He wouldn't have put up with all the crap we have to handle these days…'

'I will. Trinity Street, you said?'

'Yeah, they're always parked on the third level.'

Chapter SIXTY-NINE

'DI Christie, DI Christie.'

Emma glanced across the road at the man racing towards her from the wine bar on the opposite side of Northgate, and quickened her pace down the steps.

'DI Christie,' he shouted as she turned into Princess Street, hurrying towards Trinity Street car park.

She continued to ignore his shouts. She heard the man's footsteps on the paving behind her. She had always wanted direct access from the police station to the car park, but as Trinity Street was probably the most evilly designed car park in the world, she knew this was never going to happen. The place resembled a Dante's *Inferno* for cars. Only worse.

She hurried her pace only to feel a light tap on her shoulder.

'DI Christie.'

It was the young reporter who had accosted her earlier. His breath smelt faintly of stale wine and cigarettes. She couldn't recall his name.

'Didn't you hear me call you?'

'I have a policy of ignoring men who shout my name at this time of the night.'

'Have you any comment on the progress of your investigations into the murders of Roy Short and Altea Marku?'

How did he know their names? They had not been released yet.

'No comment.'

She walked on, towards the hell hole of the car park.

'And do you have any comment on the arrest and subsequent release of a worker in the park, Philip Jackson?'

She stopped and turned back towards him. 'You need to contact the force PR person, Penny Morgan, or the main contact for the investigation, Chief Inspector David Jones, Mr…?

'Newton, Gavin Newton of the *Chester Daily.*'

'I have to go now, Mr Newton, thank you for your time.'

Once again, she turned and walked down Princess Street. The reporter made the mistake of following her.

'DI Christie, how is the investigation going? Is it true that you have no forensics, no clues and no suspects? The police are totally lost, aren't they, DI Christie?'

Suddenly, the tiredness washed over her. The last thing she needed right now was a bloody idiot of a reporter in her face, shouting at her.

She turned back and pushed him against an orange hoarding proudly proclaiming 'Welcome to Chester Market'.

Her arm lay across his windpipe and she leant her weight into his throat. The smell of stale wine and cigarettes was much stronger now.

She spoke through gritted teeth, her anger threaded through every syllable. 'Mr Newton, if you are not careful I will arrest you for harassment. Accosting a lone female on a dark street after ten o'clock is not behaviour I would condone, least of all from a reporter.'

His eyes indicated he couldn't breathe and he grabbed at her arm.

'Where are you getting all your information, you little toerag?'

She leant in towards him, gradually increasing the pressure across his throat before releasing it, letting him slump forward, gasping for air.

'As I said earlier, I have no comment. You need to contact the force PR or Chief Inspector Jones for information in the case. Oh, and I'd get yourself a new jacket. Your lapels have stains from last week's dinner. Spag bol, was it?'

She continued walking towards the entrance to the car park.

'You won't hear the last of this, DI Christie. You're done for, finished. Do you hear me? You've got just one more day and then you're out.'

She carried on walking.

'You're done for, Christie. Finished.'

Chapter SEVENTY

Newton spat into the gutter, feeling the taste of blood in his mouth. The police bitch would pay for what she had done.

He nodded at the photographer hiding in the shadows on the other side of the road. The man stepped forward and put his thumbs up.

'You got the shot, Craig?' asked Gavin.

'Clear as daylight. Nice bit of photojournalism even though I do say so myself.'

Craig Cheeseman crossed the road, showing Gavin the screen at the rear of his Canon. 'I'd use the whole sequence: you running up, asking a question, then her pinning you against the wall and finally letting you go and you sinking to your knees. Tells the whole story visually, don't need any words.'

That was the advantage, and disadvantage, of having more money. The plus side was he could employ a photographer to follow him around taking the pictures; the negative was he'd have to listen to the man's ideas about his bloody art.

Gavin prodded the third picture in the sequence. 'Nah, just one tells the story I want to use.'

It was the shot of the bitch detective with her arm across the reporter's throat.

'You've got her bang to rights. That's assault and battery, that is.'

'You haven't dealt much with the police, Craig. I could put a complaint in to the Office for Police Conduct and she might be charged with misconduct. But she'd probably argue that she was a single female walking in a dark area late at night and thought she was being attacked.'

'That's bollocks, you shouted her name.'

'But, Craig, my son, your pictures don't have sound, do they? All they show is me running up to her, she turns round with fear in her eyes and presses me against the hoarding, releasing me when she realises she has made a mistake. It wouldn't surprise me if she isn't making a note saying exactly that in her notebook as we speak.'

'I didn't think of that.'

'You're paid to take pictures, Craig, not to think. If I wanted a brain instead of a pair of eyes, I'd employ Lassie.'

Craig thought for a moment before asking, 'What do you want me to do then?'

'A couple of things. First, I want you to delete all the shots except that one.'

'The one where she leans on your throat?'

'You got it. That's the money shot.'

'But I thought you said you couldn't use these to charge her with assault?'

'I can't, but I can use them to put pressure on her and her bosses at Police HQ. I can see a nice little exclusive in the *Chester Daily* under the Gavin Newton byline. "Police Have No Clue." Has a nice ring to it. I might even start to call our murderer "the Killer with No Eyes". Not a bad name. Not as good as Jack the Ripper, but hey, it'll do for now. I might even give the idea to Quentin. Where is he, by the way?'

'Still at the wine bar getting pissed.'

'Good. We'll file a story direct to his editor in London and another to the *Chronicle*. Got to make hay while the sun shines. He can find out about it when he sobers up tomorrow.'

'You said you wanted me to do two things.'

'I was getting to that. I want you to get some close-ups of where the body was dumped at the Roman Gardens; tight shots of the crime scene.'

'Okay, I'll do it tomorrow morning.'

'No, you'll do it now.'

'But it's nearly eleven o'clock.'

'You're right, it's not the right time.'

Craig relaxed for a second.

'Wait for an hour and do them at midnight. Photos taken during the witching hours add a nice little ghoulish element for the reader. Plays into the whole satanic angle.'

'But… I… But… What are you going do?'

'I'm off back to the wine bar. It's thirsty work being strangled by a copper.'

Chapter SEVENTY-ONE

Emma poured herself a large glass of Rioja, possibly too large. She shouldn't have reacted to that reporter, but she was tired and he had it coming. She'd have to explain it to Davy Jones tomorrow though. Better to cover her rather large arse in case Newton made a complaint.

She wandered into the kitchen, joining Hortensia. The nurse was drinking a mug of tea and reading a book.

Emma glanced at the title: *The Conquest of Happiness*. 'That's a bit deep, isn't it?'

'Not really, I need to read it for my degree. I'm doing philosophy at the Open University. This Bertrand Russell man is really interesting, he seems to hate everybody and his dog.'

'Rather you than me, I don't have time to read books these days.'

'It's the long nights. I could spend hours watching some drivel on TV or I can stay awake by reading. I prefer reading. Did you take a look in at your father?'

Emma nodded. She'd crept upstairs when she'd arrived home and popped her head around the door. He was curled up in bed wearing his flannelette pyjamas and clutching one of her teddy bears she'd had when she was a kid. The light beside his bed was still on. He couldn't fall asleep in the dark any more so she'd bought a night light for the side of his bed.

She tiptoed in and pulled the cover up so it covered his chest. For a moment, his eyes fluttered and she thought she had woken him. But he licked his lips and went back to sleep, clutching the teddy bear even tighter. She stood over him, listening to his slow, steady breathing. He looked like a child, save for the grey, wispy hair draped over his ears. A wave of sadness swept over her. She dispelled it quickly, whispering, 'Those sorts of feelings help nobody, Emma Christie.'

He licked his lips once more as Emma switched off the light and crept out of the bedroom her parents had shared for more than thirty years.

'Your father sleeps well, doesn't he? Some of my clients are up every couple of hours. As they get older most people need less sleep, but your dad seems to want more.'

'I think it's the dreaming he wants, not the sleep.'

Hortensia looked at her quizzically.

'He didn't sleep too well when he was working. Too much going on in his mind then. Now, I often think he's catching up on the dreams he missed.'

'If you don't mind me asking, how are you sleeping?'

'Not like him, a few hours a night at most. But once the case is over...'

'There'll be another case.' Hortensia finished her sentence for her. 'You need to sleep, you know.'

'So everybody tells me.'

'And that stuff doesn't help.' She pointed to the wine.

'It does for me.'

'Alcohol produces troubled sleep.'

'So says the teetotaller.'

'True, I never drink. I'm not against it, mind, my kids all enjoy a drink, but somehow I never got the taste. It's just another drug to dull the senses.'

'Why do you only work nights?'

'The kids are all working now so they don't need me. I can get my coursework done and I enjoy the silence of the wee small hours. There's something beautiful about the sound of a house at three o'clock in the morning. After I finish here, I go home, make the kids breakfast before they go to work. Then I get my head down and sleep for a few hours.'

'Sounds like you never see the light.'

'Oh, I do. These days I pick and choose my clients. I only work with the patients I like.'

Emma understood that Hortensia liked her father. The duo had somehow hit it off despite their differences and his illness.

Emma picked up her glass and her notepad. 'I'll leave you to your philosopher. I need to read my notes from today.'

'If you don't mind me asking, how's the case?'

'Sorry, I can't talk about it.'

'I know, shouldn't have asked.'

Emma stood up, walking to the door. 'One thing I can say, I can't help feeling I've missed something along the way…'

'Like keys, you know you put them somewhere but can't remember the place.'

'Exactly, and what do you do when you've lost them?'

'You go over the things you did before you lost them.'

She held up her notes. 'Exactly what I'm going to do now.'

In the front room, Emma sat down at the table. It was the same place her father used to sit when he was on a case. She remembered going in to see him before she went to bed. He would look up, his eyes unfocused and in another place, look at her, and immediately a smile would cross his face and she would run over to hug him good night.

But there was nobody there to disturb her now.

Nobody to hug her good night.

She opened her ledger full of notes to the first page. Updates on the case were kept in the computer log by John;

these case notes were hers and hers alone, written in an unruly scrawl that leant heavily to the right.

Her instinct was telling her she'd missed something. She checked her notes for the first killing, Roy Short.

Boy/Man.

Displayed for all to see.

Found at 10 p.m. Body planted between 9–10 p.m. that evening.

Sign around the neck. 'Not in my city.'

How did he get up there?

Was the boy supposed to find him?

Any defensive marks on body?

No tattoos or major identifying marks but small scar on hairline.

Place quiet, but surely the body would have been seen first thing in the morning? Was that when it was supposed to have been found?

Check CCTV.

Where had he been before ending up here?

She relived each memory as she read them. What she was doing and why she had written that particular note. She stared at the drawing of the crime scene. The wall with its small wooden coffin halfway to the gable top. The body upright inside, on display for all to see. The blue chalk lying untouched on the floor.

Nothing seemed to stand out to her. Time to move on to the next page.

Interview with Daniel Sangster.

Check his school mates.

Is he being bullied?

Noises interesting? What could make those sounds? A car? A van? Electric car?

Mother nervous, unhappy.

First impressions of crime scene: dark, quiet, nobody around.

Lucky the body was found tonight. Should not have been found till tomorrow a.m.

Did killer expect it to be found so quickly?

She made a new note about the sound.

Could Daniel have heard the noise of the electric dustcart as he was hiding in the bushes? Is that how the killer transported the body and the ladder he had used? Was that why the examination of ANPR and vehicles in the area had revealed nothing? She needed to get the CSIs to re-check it for fingerprints and DNA. Was this the break she needed?

Before she sent a message to the crime scene manager, she wanted to look at her notes on Altea Marku.

Boy/Man.

Displayed for all to see.

Found at 10 p.m. Body planted between 9–10 p.m. that evening.

Sign around the neck. 'Not in my city.'

How did he get there?

Place quiet, but locked up. How did the killer get in?

More ruins (like Roy Short). Is this about the past?

When was the body supposed to be found?

Check CCTV.

Where had he been before ending up here?

With a few more things added after talking with Dr Anstey:

No defensive wounds.
Handled cannabis before death.
Strangled (same MO as Roy Short).
No DNA, fibres or fingerprints on body.
Killer aware of forensics?
Eyes removed. Why?
Body killed elsewhere (same MO as Roy Short).

She was beginning to notice a few patterns, a signature, as the FBI would call it. The bodies were always young drug dealers or handlers. They were murdered in a kill place and then transported to the dump site. The eyes were removed. They were always placed between 9.30 and 10 p.m. in the evening. There was no forensic evidence on either body.

She looked at what she had written and felt she was making progress. The killer's patterns were emerging. But something was still nagging her, something important she had missed. What the hell was it?

The telephone in the hall rang. Who could be ringing her? Nobody from work called on her landline, they all had her mobile number.

It rang again, seemingly louder this time.

She didn't want it to wake her father.

Could it be a cold caller or a prank call? If it was, she would hang them out to dry, after cutting off both their feet and reducing their brains to the size of chicken nuggets.

She ran out into the hall and checked the number display on the screen.

Nothing.

She picked it up, saying without thinking, 'DI Emma Christie, City of Chester Constabulary.'

'Don't say anything more until I have finished speaking.'

'What? Who is this?'

'If you know what's good for you, just listen. Don't ask questions. Are you the copper investigating the murders in Chester?'

'I am,' Emma said slowly.

'You're barking up the wrong tree. The Liverpool and Manchester gangs had nothing to do with those deaths, do you understand me?'

'Who are you? And how did you get my number?'

'I'll say it one more time so it gets into your tiny little brain, Emma Christie: the Liverpool and Manchester gangs had nothing to do with those deaths.'

'Who are you?' she shouted into the phone, but the line had already gone dead.

She stared into mid-air. *Who was that, and how did they know her home number?*

Walking slowly back into the living room, her mind raced, remembering the man's words exactly.

'The Liverpool and Manchester gangs had nothing to do with those deaths.'

She stopped suddenly in front of her desk.

How did they know what she was investigating? First the reporter and now this man. It was as if everybody knew more about the case than she did.

Chapter SEVENTY-TWO

Should he kill him now or tomorrow morning? That was the question.

The young dealer was lying on the floor of his cell in the lock-up. He hadn't moved for a few hours.

He looked across at the Kilner jars he'd placed on his trophy shelf. There were five of them there, with two already full. The eyes sitting in their bath of pure alcohol stared back at him.

He thought of his father. The man standing over him when he was five years old, eyes red and livid in his face, breath stinking of alcohol and tobacco.

'You've wet the bed again. Will you not learn, how many times have I told you?'

The eyes bearing down on him, dragging him out of bed, wrapping the soiled sheet around his thin body and hustling him off to the bathroom.

His father had been a policeman too, but old school. The type that gave a teenager a clip round the ear when he was caught shoplifting, The type that took a thief aside and broke his hand rather than bother sending him to court. The type that looked forward to Saturday afternoons, policing a football match, hoping it would kick off.

The type who took his son into the bathroom and shoved him under the cold shower with his wet sheet and left him there all night in the middle of winter.

God, how he hated the man. How he hated his eyes.

He looked back towards the young drug dealer.

Had the dose of Rohypnol been too strong? Had he given him too much? He'd seen cases where people whose drinks had been spiked in a club had been out for a day afterwards.

But he needed this one awake.

There was no fun in killing them if they were unresponsive. There was no joy in punishing them unless they realised the error of their ways before they died.

Roy Short had begged to be saved even as the knife was being inserted behind his eyeball. There are none that are blind but those who cannot see.

Roy saw where he had gone wrong before he died.

A shame.

By then it was far, far too late.

The Albanian boy was different. He had spat in his face when he was dying, truculent and stubborn to the last, almost welcoming his death.

Perhaps it was a cultural thing. Those brought up in an agricultural community where death, and seeing death, was normal, accepted it more easily.

How would this boy respond?

Would he beg for his life or would he remain defiant to the end? He couldn't wait to find out.

The boy was still not moving though.

He made his decision. He would kill him tomorrow morning before he went to work. He'd already decided where he was going to display the body. The war memorial at the cathedral was perfect. The body would be there for the worshippers to see when they arrived on Sunday morning.

He might even ring up the stupid reporter and let him know where the body was before it was discovered by the police. That would set the cat amongst the pigeons. He'd even suggest a different supernatural element. What about Roman legionnaires coming back to Chester to punish the miscreants of the town?

He laughed out loud.

That would get the citizens all riled up and worried. Perhaps they would then be tougher, cleanse the place of its drug addicts and dealers.

Roman vigilantes. Gavin Newton was bound to go for the idea. He might even be able to get a thousand quid for the tip-off this time. Not that the money mattered, but the missus would be happy.

Every little helped.

He checked the doors of the cell one last time. You couldn't be too careful these days. Always check everything twice.

He peered through the bars. The young man was still out cold on the floor.

Sleeping ugly, he thought, laughing to himself again.

He'd finish him off tomorrow morning and plant the body just before ten o'clock tomorrow evening.

Death always comes as the end.

In the young man's case, it would be far earlier than he expected.

Chapter SEVENTY-THREE

In the front room, Emma put down her ledger and rubbed her eyes.

She should really get some sleep if she wanted to be awake and active tomorrow morning.

How had her father managed his investigations?

He never seemed to want or require sleep when he was working. Just moving forward constantly with an almost boundless energy.

She buried her face in her hands and released a long sigh. How could she live up to his reputation?

She picked up her notes once more. There was something she was missing. Her father always said it was the small details, the little inconsistencies that solved most crimes. What was it that she couldn't see?

What was she missing?

There was a tap on the door. Hortensia's head appeared. 'I'm making a cuppa, d'you want one?'

She shook her head. 'Thanks for the offer, but I really need to finish looking at these.'

'You know, my professor at university always says the worst place to find ideas is sitting at a desk.'

'I bet he's never investigated a murder before.'

Hortensia smiled, her teeth gleaming. 'Nah, the worst thing he's ever looked into is a bad case of plagiarism. You should take a break though, or go to sleep for a while. Sometimes I go to bed and before I sleep, I ask God in his infinite mercy to send me the answer to my problem in my dream. And you know what?'

'Let me guess…'

'I know he tells me the answer but I can never remember what he said.'

They both laughed.

'That's why I write everything down,' Emma finally replied. 'Sometimes the universe whispers to you and you have to remember what it says.'

'Anyway, are you sure you don't want a cuppa?'

'I'm sure, but thanks for the offer.'

The door closed and Emma was left alone in the room. It was a place she had known intimately since her childhood but, for some reason, it felt alien to her now.

Why had she received the phone call earlier? And who was it from? It sounded like one of the Liverpool gang leaders from his accent. But why call her direct? He was obviously trying to tell her it wasn't a gang war that was causing the killings.

Should she believe him? Or was he just trying to throw her off the scent?

But if it wasn't a struggle between gangs, that left just one option: a vigilante murder.

But why?

The words of her boss came back to her. 'I don't need you to work hard, I need you to work smart. You have one more day before I pass the case on to DI Riggs. He'll make sure he gets a result.'

Just one more day.

She couldn't fail again, couldn't let her dad down another time. She needed to crack this case now.

She picked up the ledger again. Every fibre of her being told her the answer was in there somewhere.

But as she read her notes one more time, the universe wasn't whispering to her.

In fact, there was only one deafening sound.

Silence.

Saturday, October 28.

Chapter SEVENTY-FOUR

Emma stood up in front of her team. Behind her, the wall of information on the two murders had been expanded by John Simpson to include the latest post-mortem report and the identikit picture created last night.

She'd nodded off at her dad's desk last night, reading her notes. Hortensia had shaken her awake at 3 a.m. and sent her off to bed. She'd got up at eight, showered, grabbed a quick bite to eat, said goodbye to her dad and Hortensia and drove to the Major Incident Room.

It felt like she had never left.

'Good morning, people. Listen up. Last night we interviewed a Mr Philip Jackson, a council worker in Grosvenor Park. He told us he was paid by a man, this man —' she tapped the identikit picture '—to destroy the CCTV cameras on the church and in the car park behind the Smokehouse.'

Once again, a strange feeling of déjà vu flooded through her brain as she spoke. What was it she had forgotten?

Richard Gleason put his hand up. 'That picture could be of any male aged between thirty and sixty, boss, including most of the coppers here. The beard could be fake too…'

There was a smattering of laughter throughout the room.

'At the moment it's all we've got.' Emma turned to the force PR person. 'Penny, have you arranged for the flyers to be printed to hand out around town?'

'They'll be here at eleven a.m., Emma.'

'Good. Sergeant Harris, can you make sure your teams have the flyers and give them out to the public?'

'Will do, DI Christie.'

'One more update. The toxicology results have come in from Dr Anstey. Both victims had traces of Rohypnol in their bloodstreams. They were sedated and incapacitated before they were murdered. Harry, anything on the last sightings of the victims?'

'Nothing on Roy Short, boss. He left the house in Everton and seems to have vanished into thin air. I'm still working on the burner phones but I could do with some help. I managed to eliminate six numbers last night before my eyes gave out, just twenty-two left.'

He glanced down at his notes.

'In addition, I talked with the neighbours close to the cannabis farm yesterday. They said it was always very quiet in the area, they weren't even sure anyone was living in the house. One of the neighbours thought it was being used for storage. When I asked why, he said a white van used to come and they'd take stuff out of the house in black plastic bins and put it in the back. He didn't get the number of the van or any sort of description.'

'Shame. Thanks, Harry. How did you do with CCTV, Gerry?'

'Well, not great. As you know, Philip Jackson destroyed the cameras close to the Roman Gardens. But I found footage on CCTV of a man wearing a high-vis jacket on October 26th, pulling a rubbish cart. It's after nine thirty, boss, and it's quite far away. He's heading away from the Roman Gardens towards Grosvenor Park.'

Gerry turned his laptop around to show them the footage.

'Can't we get a clearer picture?'

'The techies are trying, but they're not hopeful. The council hasn't serviced its cameras for donkey's years.'

'I think the artist's drawing is clearer, boss. That CCTV could be any man in Chester over twenty.'

'Actually, it could be most of the women too,' answered Harry.

'If he's heading away from the Roman Gardens, perhaps he's already dumped the body and is heading back to the potting shed in Grosvenor Park,' said Emma. 'Richard, how are we doing with the ANPR?'

'The analysis was finished late last night, boss. All twenty-three cars are accounted for. The owners all have reasons for being in the area. Plus we contacted the eleven owners we'd missed on the first pass. They were eliminated too.'

'Did you expand the search times as I asked?'

'Done. We've eliminated those drivers too. Looks like it was a waste of time and effort.'

'It's never a waste of time, Richard,' Emma corrected him. She paused for a long time, staring at the boards. 'I was going through my notes last night and it occurred to me that Daniel Sangster reported strange whirring sounds near the ruined church. I wonder if that noise was from the dustcart? Did our killer use Philip Jackson's cart to transport the bodies of Roy Short and Altea Marku? Is that why our tracking of the vehicles in the area has given us no results?'

'The killer could also have used it to transport the ladder too. There's no way Roy Short's body could have been put there without one,' said Anna.

'Right. Jane, did you go over the cart last night? Any fingerprints or DNA from any of our victims?'

'Already on it, Emma. I'll check with the team to see if there are any results yet.'

'Dr Anstey has confirmed that the victims were killed at least twelve hours before they were found, and that the church ruins and the Roman Gardens were not the places where they were killed. If that is true, the bodies would still have to be transported to the shed where the dustcart was kept.' She walked over to the map of Grosvenor Park on the boards. 'This is where the cart was kept after Philip Jackson finished work at six p.m. If we're right, somebody must have brought the bodies here.' She tapped the map.

'But they would need a key to open the park gates,' said Harry. 'Surely, we would have caught them on CCTV?'

Richard Gleason blushed. 'We didn't check for any CCTV at the park gates or that far down on Grosvenor Park Road. But anyway, with the one-way system, we would have picked them up later when they turned left coming out of the gate.'

'Perhaps they didn't turn left.' Harry stood up and joined Emma at the map. 'If they exited via the Headlands and the top of Dee Lane, they could have turned right to go north through the city rather than use the one-way system.'

'But that would mean crossing over the island in the middle of Foregate Street.'

'Not a real problem, I've done it myself a few times, it's only a couple of inches high. There's a pedestrian crossing next to that junction. There's sure to be CCTV there.'

Richard Gleason remained silent.

'Find that footage, Richard. Hopefully it hasn't been deleted. Just concentrate on vans coming out of the junction between nine forty-five to eleven p.m on the evening of October 24th.'

'Me again. Why can't Harry do it seeing as it's his brilliant idea?'

Emma took three deep breaths before she spoke quietly. 'You will do as you are ordered, DC Gleason, is that clear?'

Silence.

'Is that clear?'

'Yes, ma'am,' was the sullen reply. 'You're the boss.'

'You're correct, I am. Report back to me at noon.'

Gerry Rafferty put his hand up. 'If they entered through the main gate to the park, St Werburgh's Church has CCTV covering that area. Perhaps the van was picked up by the cameras. Do you want me to check the footage, boss?'

'Do that, Gerry. Again, report to me at noon too.'

'On it, boss.'

Gleason's mate, Alan Holt, coughed. 'I've heard rumours DI Riggs is being brought in on the case, is that true?'

Emma stared at him for a long time. 'I am in charge of this case until further notice. Understood? If you have a problem with that, DC Holt, please talk to me after this meeting and I will re-assign you. I've heard a rumour traffic are looking for a new car park inspection officer.'

'No disrespect meant, ma'am. Just a rumour I heard.'

'Our job is to gather evidence, not gossip, DC Holt.'

John Simpson appeared in her eyeline. 'What is it, John?'

'A word, boss.'

'If it's about the case, share it with everyone, John.'

'It's the *Chester Daily*.'

He held up a newspaper. On the front a big, bold headline screamed:

POLICE DON'T HAVE A CLUE

John passed it to her. Beneath the headline was the byline of the 'special correspondent' Gavin Newton and a large, slightly unfocused picture of Emma pushing the reporter against the advertising hoardings.

She read the article:

Police today remain baffled in the case of the murder of two young men, Roy Short and Altea Marku. Last

night, they arrested a Mr Philip Jackson, a council worker in Grosvenor Park, before releasing him at 10 p.m.

This reporter spoke to Mr Jackson on his release. 'They questioned me inside the police station, two of them, both aggressive women, accusing me of murdering two people. I've never been so scared my whole life. They wouldn't let me make a phone call to my wife and I didn't have a solicitor. It was very scary. Imagine if you had suddenly been accused of murder, how would you feel?'

Father-of-six Mr Jackson is today filing a formal complaint against the police for their treatment of him. When this reporter confronted the police detective involved, her only answer was to attack me and threaten me with arrest for 'harassment'.

City of Chester Constabulary have been under investigation in recent times by His Majesty's Commissioner of Police for failing in many of the areas required of a modern police force. This reporter also thought about filing a complaint with the Office for Professional Conduct but, given the past record of this force at investigating itself, decided that such an action would be a waste of time and effort.

Concerning the case of the No Eyes Killer, the police seem totally lost, with no apparent clues, forensics or suspects. Last night's arrest of an innocent council worker is just another instance of them clutching at straws in an investigation that is floundering in a morass of ineptitude and incompetence.

When are City of Chester Constabulary going to finally bring in some professionals to investigate? Or do we have to wait for another young man's body to be found before they finally take action?

City of Chester Constabulary was asked to comment on this article before publication. Unfortunately, no response was forthcoming before press time.

'It doesn't look great, John.'

'A hit job, boss, nothing more, nothing less. He doesn't like you at all.'

They were joined by Penny Morgan. 'Can I see it?'

She scanned the article. 'The bastard,' she whispered. 'I got a text at three a.m. when I was asleep last night, asking for an update on the investigation. I didn't realise this was what he was going to write. I'll have him for breakfast.'

'What's done is done. You handle the press side, we need to stop the negative stories.'

'I need to warn you, Emma, the nationals are becoming interested in the story. I received enquiries from the *Sun* and the *Mail* this morning, and the others won't be far behind. This is just child's play compared to what those vipers are capable of.'

Emma turned to the team and held up the newspaper. 'Listen, everybody. You are to ignore all this. Our job, our one job, is to focus on the investigation. Nothing else matters. We have to stop this killer before he strikes again, is that clear?'

A chorus of yesses and grunts from the team.

'You all know what you have to do, time to get on with it.'

'Anything you want me to do?' asked Anna.

Before Emma could answer, there was a sharp rap on the door and Sergeant Harris entered.

'We've just had a report in from Central Nick. Another drug dealer has gone missing.'

Chapter SEVENTY-FIVE

'Why didn't you report your friend, Denzel Brown, as missing earlier?'

Emma was interviewing the witness, Eamonn Flanagan, in Room 3 of Central Station. At least being there meant she had managed to return the car she had borrowed last night.

'I dunno. I don't have that many dealings with the police.'

'But you have dealings with the public, don't you?'

'I don't know what you mean?'

'Come on, Mr Flanagan, you and your friend, Denzel, were dealing drugs on Queen Street, weren't you?'

'I don't know nothin' about that. I was just hangin' round the area, riding me bike.'

Emma decided not to pursue it. 'So why have you come forward now?'

'It's like all those young people being murdered in the city. I seen the flyers, the lads in the ruins and the Roman Gardens. And now Denzel…' Hi voice trailed off. 'The car, it was reversing down the street. Denzel, he was sitting in the back but he weren't moving, just sat there.'

'So you waited for him to come back and he didn't come.'

'That's right, he was a no-show.'

'Couldn't he have been getting a lift somewhere?'

'Denzel don't get in the back of cars with no strangers.'

'What did this stranger look like?'

'I didn't see him clear. It all happened so quickly. I remember he had a beard though.'

Emma pulled out the flyer with the image the identikit officer had drawn from Philip Jackson's description. 'Like this man?'

'That's him, that's exactly him. But I think the beard was fake.'

Emma frowned. 'Why did you think it was fake?'

'It was all wrong, man, bits hanging off. No beard looks like that.'

Emma thought for a moment. If the beard was fake, all the flyers they had sent out were useless. 'So what did you do then?'

'I followed the car, didn't I? But I lost him at the Bars, he turned off along the A51.'

'Did you get the number of the car?'

'I didn't think, did I? By the time I thought about it the car was too far away.'

'So what did you do then?'

'I was hungry so I went for some chicken.'

'You didn't ring anybody?'

Eamonn was suddenly defensive. 'Who would I ring? There's nobody to ring.'

Emma smiled. So he had rang somebody. Probably his supplier. Was that why she had received a warning call late last night? 'I would have thought you would ring his phone, see if he was okay.'

Eamonn relaxed. 'Yeah, I rang it straight away but he didn't answer. Denzel always answers his phone.'

'He has to for business, doesn't he?'

The young man's face went sullen. 'I don't know what you mean.'

'Didn't you also ring his family?'

'I rang them at eleven. They said they hadn't heard from him, thought he was with me.'

'So then what did you do?'

'I went home, didn't I? Slept on it overnight and then woke up early and came here to report him missing.'

'Nobody told you to come?'

Defensive again. 'Who would tell me to come? I don't know what you gettin' at.'

Emma stood up. 'Thank you, Mr Flanagan, a constable will come in to take your statement.'

'That's it? You ain't gonna look for Denzel? What if the No Eyes Killer has taken him?'

Emma revealed no emotion on her face. 'Mr Flanagan, we will look for Mr Brown. Thank you for coming in today. Please go into all the details in your statement to the constable.'

Emma stood up and left the room with Emma.

Outside, they stood in the corridor. 'What do you want to do, boss?'

'Get on to the boy's family. Find out all you can about him. Lifestyle, school, habits, who he hung around with. Get his telephone number and see if you can track it. Finally, contact police intelligence, see if Denzel is on their files and who he was dealing for.'

'You think he's been taken by our killer, boss?'

'I know he's been taken, Anna, it's just a question if we can get to him before our killer murders him, putting his body on display somewhere in Chester.'

Chapter SEVENTY-SIX

Harry picked up the eleventh sheaf of data printouts from the desk in front of him. So far, this morning had been a total bust. He'd tracked the numbers of the phones and their communication with the towers but none of them went anywhere near the one he was looking for on Bolton Road.

He picked up the ruler and followed the data line by line until he came to the date he was looking for: October 22. Then he went across until he could see a time: 15.56. He took a deep breath and checked the latitude and longitude of the tower.

It matched.

He let out a stifled shout. The rest of the team in the Major Incident Room looked up from what they were doing and stared at him.

He blushed and went back to looking at his Excel spreadsheet. Somebody had sent an SMS message from a mobile phone in the same area as Bolton Road at 15.56 on the right date.

He didn't know if this was Roy Short, it could have been anybody living in the area. But it was the first phone on his list which matched the correct cell tower.

Now the real work began. He brought up a map of Chester with all the communication towers and their respective latitudes and longitudes marked. In the city, these towers were spaced about 400 metres apart. In the countryside, they could be separated by up to five miles.

He checked the next use of the phone ten minutes later. A call had been made to another number and it had registered on one of the towers. He took a red pen and drew a line between the first tower and this one. The phone was moving closer to the city.

He continued to track the phone as three more SMS messages were sent and one more call was made. He'd love to see what the SMS messages said, but unfortunately that data was not included on this Excel spreadsheet.

One more call was made at 17.05 p.m. and after that no messages were sent or calls made.

The phone had gone dead.

He checked the latitude and longitude of the last call and triangulated the three towers it had communicated with.

There it was. The perfect meeting place.

Outside the front gates of Grosvenor Park.

Bingo.

'Gerry,' he shouted, 'can you come over here for a sec?'

'Coming, Harry, I need to show you something too.'

The young police constable picked up his laptop and walked over to Harry's desk. 'Remember Emma asked me to look at footage for the front gate of the park on October 24th? Well, here it is.'

He pressed a key on his laptop and footage from the CCTV at St Werburgh's Church appeared.

A white van came into view and stopped in front of the park gates. A man wearing a black hoodie stepped out of the van, ran to the gates and fiddled with the lock for a few seconds before driving through and locking them again after himself.

'That's the only van that entered the park during our time span, it must be our killer. I've checked and he doesn't come out this way. But Richard sent me this footage from an hour later.'

Gerry brought up a new lot of footage. The same white van appeared at the top of Dee Lane, turned right, crossed over the low traffic island in the middle of the road and accelerated past the traffic lights, heading down Grosvenor Park Road towards the A51.

'So I was right, the van did leave the park from the Headlands. No wonder we didn't find it on any of the CCTV closer to the ruins and the Roman Gardens. Now, I have a job for you, Gerry.'

'Go on...'

'Do you have footage of the front gate from two days earlier? Around 17.00 on the Sunday?'

'Yeah, I downloaded everything St Werburgh's had. You want me to check it for that time?'

Harry stared at him. 'Is the Pope Catholic?'

'Yeah, but what's he got to do with it? He wasn't in St Werburgh's on Sunday, my bet is he was probably in Rome.'

Harry closed his eyes and muttered, 'Lord give me strength,' under his breath. Then he spoke slowly and clearly. 'Can you show me the footage?'

'Sure, no problem.'

Gerry Rafferty tapped the keys on his laptop and the master roll of footage appeared. He selected a date and fast-forwarded the footage. 'You wanted five o'clock, right?'

'Yesssss...'

'I only ask because I'm always getting those twenty-four-hour clocks wrong.'

'It's simple, just minus twelve from the number and you'll get the time.'

Gerry stopped what he was doing. 'I never thought of it like that, Harry, but you're right, it works.'

'I'll send you the bill for the lesson later.'

'Here it is. Five o'clock.'

The footage began to run. Both of them watched as a young man strode impatiently in front of the gates. The weather was cold and wet but the young man was only wearing a thin jacket. Except for the occasional passing car, the street appeared to be empty.

'Is that Roy Short, our victim?'

Harry nodded, not taking his eyes off the screen.

'But he's still alive.'

'Well spotted, Sherlock.'

They continued to watch as, for the next three minutes, Roy Short walked up and down in front of the gates, occasionally checking his watch. At 17.05, Roy pulled out a phone from his pocket and made a call. As he did, a white van pulled up and stopped at the kerb.

Gerry pointed at the screen. 'That's the same van as Tuesday.'

On screen, the van door opened and a man in a black hoodie got out, walking around the front towards Roy.

The man in the hoodie pulled something out of his back pocket and showed it to the young man. Roy backed away, his hands in the air, and attempted to run but the man was too quick for him. A brief struggle ensued before Roy was pushed to the ground. His hands were pinioned behind his back and a pair of handcuffs locked in place efficiently. The young man was then bundled into the back of the van and it drove off. The whole scene hadn't lasted longer than thirty seconds.

'Go back, reverse the footage.'

'What? Okay…'

The footage on the screen went backwards.

'Stop it here,' shouted Harry.

The footage stopped. Just as the struggle was nearly over, the man's hoodie was pulled from his face.

'Freeze it there.'

The footage stopped and the man's face could be seen clearly.

'Jesus, is that who I think it is?' said Gerry.

Harry picked up his phone. 'Boss, I think you need to come back here, you've got to see this.'

'Is that really necessary, Harry? Another drug dealer has just gone missing and I'm leading the search for him.'

'Boss, you really want to see this. Now.'

Chapter SEVENTY-SEVEN

Should he kill him now or later?

A line from one of those awful Shakespeare plays he was forced to read at school popped into his head. 'To be or not to be, that is the question.'

Should this drug dealer continue to be for a little while longer?

At least the young scrote was awake now. A little groggy and disoriented but obviously aware of what had happened to him.

He'd begun shouting as soon as he sat up. 'Let me out of here, let me go.'

When that hadn't worked, he had reverted to threats. 'I'm gonna kill you, mate, just you see. When I get out of here, your life ain't gonna be worth living. You a dead man...'

The threats had soon petered out though, when he realised exactly who was in a position of power here. Then, of course, the wheedling began. 'Please let me out. I done nothing wrong. Why am I here?'

It was extremely satisfying to see the look of surprise on the young man's face when he had revealed himself without the beard.

'You? What are you doing here? Are you gonna let me go?'

He hadn't replied, simply thrown the man a bacon sandwich laced with Rohypnol. At least the drug dealer would now be quiet until he made his decision.

He didn't understand why he was vacillating so much over killing this one. The others had been easy. A small dose of Rohypnol to keep them docile, then strangulation using a choke hold.

He laughed to himself. The choke hold was another thing he had learnt at school. This time in the playground rather than the classroom. The boys used to practise putting each other to sleep in their break time. Oh, the joys of an English education.

The knowledge had come in useful later, of course.

He checked the time. 11.35 a.m.

He was due in to work soon. Kill him now or later?

He didn't want to rush this one. His death was going to be enjoyed, to be savoured. He'd already chosen a location to place the body. Somewhere everybody would notice, and a call to Gavin Newton would ensure pictures appeared in all the newspapers. They would be censored, of course, but the full impact would still be felt as they found their way on to the internet for the delectation of his followers all around the world.

He couldn't use Philip Jackson's cart any more though. His use of it before would have been discovered by now. As soon as he heard the man had been arrested, he knew that particular method of moving the bodies around town was no longer open to him.

Shame, it was so very convenient.

Philip Jackson wouldn't be able to recognise him though, he had made sure of that. The man was too interested in the money to see that the beard was fake or to notice anything about his features. He'd seen the identikit drawing already. It looked like most of the men in Chester – and half the women.

He stared through the two-way glass at his prisoner, lying on the floor of the cell, his head already nodding forward as the Rohypnol began to take effect.

He took a long look at Denzel Brown and decided to act. Enough wasting time, let's get this one over and done with.

He could take more time with the next one, but this one was ready and he'd run out of patience.

He'd strangle him now and then he could place him in the cathedral gardens on the war memorial this evening, just before ten o'clock. A lovely place to enjoy your last hours; the eyeless eyes of Denzel Brown staring out at the works of a God whose commandments he had broken almost every day of his short life.

On a Saturday night, the place would be empty.
Perfect.

He opened the door and Denzel looked up at him through glassy eyes. The young man tried to form words but they wouldn't come out.

'It's okay, Denzel, I understand. You're not feeling yourself at the moment. It's the drugs I gave you. Personally, I would never accept food and drink from strangers, you never know what's inside them.'

He moved behind the young man and knelt down, placing his muscular right arm around the man's throat with the left coming round to force the head forward.

Denzel didn't react at all or struggle.

'Say a last prayer, Denzel. And if you do happen to meet God at the pearly gates of heaven, put in a good word for me. After I've finished with my work, I'm going to need it.'

He then began to apply pressure.

Chapter SEVENTY-EIGHT

Gavin Newton was reading his article in the *Chester Daily*. He loved seeing his byline, now in an even larger typeface. He particularly enjoyed the line about the police not having a clue. He did love a good pun.

Quentin Forde was sat in front of him at Greasy Joe's. The redness of his eyes and the sallowness of his skin betrayed the presence of a large hangover. One that had probably lasted for over twenty years.

'Shouldn't have done that, you know.'

'Done what?' Gavin answered innocently.

'Contacted my editor directly. It's not the done thing. I'm the reporter here, not you.'

Gavin took a loud, long slurp from his mug of tea. 'What are you worried about? I made sure you got the byline even though you had nothing to do with the story. I did try to get in touch with you, but you were well gone. In fact, most of you was draped over that reporter from the *Express*, what's-her-name?'

'Maggie, her name is Maggie, and I've known her for at least twenty years.'

'Is that in the biblical sense? Because from where I was standing, you seemed to have been examining her tonsils from the inside.'

'We're just good friends, ex-colleagues, in fact.'

'I'm sure your wife knows you are such good "friends", doesn't she? I asked my photographer to take a couple of shots when you and Maggie were both at your most friendly.' He passed over his phone. 'These photos are almost explicit in their friendliness. I'm sure your wife would be delighted to see how many old friends you are seeing again in Chester.'

'You wouldn't dare…'

Gavin scrolled down his list of numbers. 'This is her mobile number, isn't it? You know, these numbers are so easy to obtain if you know where to look – or you can get a friendly copper to look them up for you.'

Quentin Forde was sober now. In fact, he hadn't been this sober for twenty years. 'What do you want?'

Gavin smiled. 'I'm not a greedy man, but I think the daily stipend you're paying me is a little pusillanimous, isn't it? As a reporter you probably don't know what pusillanimous means. It's stingy, mean and cheap. A bit like you, really. I think we should increase it to 750 quid a day, just for starters, of course.'

Quentin Forde's eyes flickered for a second before he finally nodded. 'Agreed, 750 quid it is.'

'There is one other thing I will need.'

'What's that?'

'A joint byline. Your name first, of course, but mine immediately afterwards in the same size typeface and point size, both in bold would be fantastic. It will look good on my resumé.'

'I don't know if my editor will agree.'

'I'm sure you can convince him, you have such startling powers of persuasion. After all, you did persuade the sultry Maggie to spend the night in your room last night.'

'How did you know…?'

'Hotel employees are always so poorly paid, any opportunity to earn a little extra is accepted. No pictures of you two together, unfortunately, I'm sure they wouldn't be safe for your children. However, I do have a signed copy of your bill for champagne at three in the morning, with a picture of the bottle and two glasses. As my artistic photographer would say, put them together and you have a story that doesn't need any words.'

'I'll talk to the editor.'

'He'll agree?'

'If I convince him.'

'Good, I'm so glad that is settled satisfactorily. Now, I have a few things for you. Firstly, my photographer took a few pictures of the crime scene at the Roman Gardens at midnight last night. He has done a good job. I particularly like the way he has used the shadows to suggest menace. They should go down a storm with your readers in East Cheam.'

Quentin Forde stared at them. 'They're good, very good. We can really push the satanic angle with these pictures.'

'I'm glad you agree. There's one other little titbit between us girls and this full English.'

'What?'

'Another drug dealer has gone missing. The police are looking for him as we speak.'

'What? When? Who is it? Do you have pictures?'

Gavin put on an accent. 'Be patient, Grasshopper. All will be revealed in time.'

'I want an exclusive, none of the other parasites must know about this. Agreed?'

'I'm sure we can come to some arrangement, Quentin. A daily fee of a thousand quid, perhaps?'

'A grand? We never pay our stringers a grand a day.'

'There's always a first time, Quentin. But just to whet your appetite, his first name is Denzel…'

Chapter SEVENTY-NINE

Emma Christie strode into the Major Incident Room looking for Harry, but he was nowhere to be seen.

She frowned. She'd rushed here from Central Nick because of his phone call and now he'd vanished. Probably off to get a bacon roll and a coffee, typical.

'John, have you seen Harry?'

Her civilian researcher scanned the room. 'He was here a minute ago, must have popped out. Do you want me to ring him?'

'It doesn't matter. I'll give him a piece of my mind when I see him.'

At the door on the opposite side of the room, Gerry Rafferty appeared. He gestured with his hand for her to come towards him. The he repeated the gesture more urgently.

'What is it, Gerry? I've got a bloody case to run, another young dealer has gone missing, and now you're playing silly buggers.'

He gestured again towards her, putting his finger across his mouth and whispering, 'You need to come with me, boss.'

'Can't we do it here? I've got to go through the resource logs with John.'

'Come over here, boss. Harry wants a word.'

She shook her head but walked to the door. The last thing she needed right now was somebody bloody messing about. If this was one of Harry's little jokes, she'd string him up by his own shoelaces. 'What is it?' she snapped at Gerry Rafferty

Gerry Rafferty pushed her out of the door and down the corridor to a small room on the right-hand side. He knocked on the closed door and it was opened by Harry.

'Well done, Gerry, you've brought her. Did anybody see?'

'I don't think so. John was doing something on his laptop.'

'Good, come in, boss.'

'Harry, what's with all the cloak and dagger? If you're messing about, I swear I'm—'

'I've got something important to show you, boss.' On a desk in the small room was a single laptop. 'Look at this.'

He pressed a key and Emma watched as footage of the front gates of Grosvenor Park came into view.

'What am I seeing here? You discovered the footage of the van entering the park on the night we discovered Roy Short's body?'

Harry shook his head. 'Look at the time and date code.'

Emma stared at the flickering numbers at the top right of the screen. 'But this footage is from two days earlier, on Sunday evening.'

'It was taken from St Werburgh's Church, boss,' interrupted Gerry Rafferty.

Into frame walked a young man carrying a blue bag.

'Is that Roy Short?' asked Emma.

'It's him, boss, carry on watching.'

The young man walked up and down in front of the gates, occasionally checking his watch impatiently. He picked up his phone to make a call...

Harry reached in and stopped the playback. The time code on the right said 17.05.23.

'This is how we managed to find him, through his burner phone.'

'You isolated which one it was?'

Harry nodded. 'But carry on watching what happens next.'

He pressed another key and the footage began rolling forward. A white van came in and stopped in front of the gates. The driver, in a black hoodie, walked around the front to talk with Roy Short.

Suddenly, there was a short struggle, Roy Short's legs kicking in the air.

Emma leant in to get a better look.

The young man stopped struggling and his hands were handcuffed behind his back. The driver shoved the body roughly into the rear of the van. As he did so, the hood slipped off his face and he looked around to check if anyone had seen what happened. He closed the back door, got back in the driver's seat and the van moved off out of camera.

Emma took a deep breath. 'Did I really just see that?'

Harry didn't say a word but brought up a still shot of the driver's face.

'Is that who I think it is?'

'It's Paul Tunney, boss.'

'You're sure, Harry?'

'You only have to look. I've worked with him for more than ten years, I'd know him anywhere.'

And then it hit Emma. The little detail that had been nagging at her for the last few days but she had been unable to put her finger on, until now.

'Harry, I've just thought of something. Remember that Roy Short had a mark on his hairline—'

'You think it could have been caused in the struggle, boss?'

'Perhaps, but that's not the important point. Paul Tunney said he noticed the mark when Roy Short was taken to Central Nick six months ago, but I remember the doctor said the mark had been caused less than a week before Roy died.'

Harry closed his eyes. 'I get it, boss.'

Gerry Rafferty piped in. 'How did Paul Tunney know about the mark six months ago when it was only made last week?'

Harry smirked. 'This one is going to go far. Aiming for chief constable, are you, Gerry?'

'But he's right, Harry. Paul Tunney must have met Roy Short just before he died and this video proves it.'

'There's one more thing. Tunney shows our victim something before he handcuffs him. We've looked at the footage again and again, boss, and we think it could be his warrant card.

'So that's how he traps his victims?'

'We think so.'

Emma ran her fingers through her hair. Paul Tunney was an old friend of her father's. She had been chatting with him just last night. He was a copper, and a bloody good one.

'Right, Harry, get Anna to come here immediately.'

'On it.'

'Gerry, I want you to pull John Simpson out of next door and bring him here too.'

'Anna's on her way, boss.' Harry was still on the phone.

'Get her to find out when Sergeant Tunney's shift ends today.'

Harry spoke into the phone and then waited.

Emma continued giving orders to Gerry. 'If Mark Kennedy is there, drag him along as well, but do it quietly. I don't want anybody else to know, we need to keep this under wraps.'

'Are you sure you want to involve Merseyside, boss?' asked Harry as he waited for a response from Anna.

'I think it might be useful to have somebody who's neutral in all of this, in case any awkward questions are asked later on.'

'What if he's already killed Denzel Brown?' asked Gerry Rafferty.

'There is that possibility already. I would prefer our vic to be alive, but if he's already dead, the way we honour his memory is to put Paul Tunney away for the rest of his life. I want this case so cut-and-dried not even the CPS could screw it up.'

'Tunney's shift finishes at eight p.m. this evening, boss.'

Emma knew then that Denzel Brown was already dead. She stared into mid-air for a long time, thinking of the right plan. 'Right, if he follows his usual MO, he's going to place the body somewhere this evening after he's finished work, between nine thirty to ten p.m. When the rest of the team gets here, I'll take you through what we are going to do.'

'Aren't we going to arrest him?' asked Harry.

'Not yet.'

'Why, boss? What's the problem?'

'We don't have enough on Tunney.'

'What? We've got him bang to rights.' Harry began to count on his fingers. 'One. He's in the same car we know was in the area on the night Roy Short was murdered. Two. We have him meeting and attacking Roy Short on the Sunday. Three. He drives off with Roy Short in the back of the car and the young man was never seen alive again. Surely we've got enough to arrest him?'

'Remember, Tunney is a copper.'

'So?'

'What if he says it's not him in the video?'

'But we can see it's him.'

'No, we can see somebody who looks like him. What if Tunney produces an alibi and a witness who says he was somewhere else on Sunday at five p.m? He's not a stupid man and he knows exactly how we work. After twenty years on the force, there must be thousands of cons that owe him a favour.'

'What about the van?'

'What about it? My bet is we'll never tie it to Tunney.'

'The plates are false,' said Gerry.

Emma used a parody of a criminal's voice. 'Never seen that motor in my life, guvnor, I swear on my old mother's grave.'

Harry stroked his chin. 'I see what you're getting at, boss.'

'We have no DNA, no fingerprints and no forensic evidence tying Paul Tunney to any of the two murders, or to the missing Denzel Brown. The Crown Prosecution Service would laugh us out of their offices.'

'What do you want to do, boss?'

'There's only one thing we can do. We need to find him with his latest victim, alive or dead.'

Chapter EIGHTY

When Liam Gilligan arrived in Chester, he was met in the bar of the Grosvenor Hotel by Mickey.

He ordered drinks for both of them. A pint of lager for Mickey and an old-fashioned for himself. He'd started drinking this after watching a few episodes of *Mad Men*, where the lead character seemed to down at least four every lunchtime without any effect. Liam discovered a taste for them and had drunk them ever since.

Thank you, Don Draper.

They retired to a corner where they wouldn't be overheard. 'Tell me what's going on, Mickey.'

Mickey pointed to a newspaper. 'It's like it says here, boss, the police don't have a clue. According to my source in Chester Constabulary, Roy was killed on October 24th and placed in a coffin in the ruins with his eyes plucked out. He was last seen on Sunday, October 22nd. The police believe he was killed somewhere else and then dumped in the ruins. Altea Marku was killed on October 24th and placed in the Roman Gardens. Last night, another dealer, Denzel Brown, was picked up from his corner in the town centre.'

'One of ours?'

Mickey nodded. 'One of our best. He'd been dealing that corner for a couple of years and built up a regular clientele of smackheads and dopeheads. Always paid on time did Denzel. Not the brightest tool in the box but a good soldier, you know what I mean?'

It was Liam's turn to nod. 'No chance he was nicking stuff from us like Roy?'

'Not a chance, boss. I'd swear on my mother's life, Denzel is straight.'

'I wouldn't swear so easily, Mickey. You never know what some of our chancers get up to. How'd we find out?'

'Our source in the police let us know, plus his runner, Eamonn Flanagan, gave us the same story.'

'He's not involved?'

'Nah, he's another one who's not too bright. We turned over Denzel's gaff just to make sure. It was clean as an Amsterdam sewer. The lads are going to be looking for some sort of payback, boss. Since this bastard has been targeting our dealers, they've not been able to work, takings are down eighty per cent over the last week. Denzel was the last straw. They're scared, boss, looking for protection from whoever is doing the killing.'

Liam Gilligan ignored the man's whining. 'Where's Flanagan now?'

'I let him tell what he saw to the local bizzies, he's not come out yet.'

'Was that wise?'

'Eamonn's a straight up lad, boss, I'd stake my life on it.'

There was a long silence from Liam Gilligan as he thought everything through. 'Do you have our soldiers out looking for Denzel?'

'As we speak, they're out scouring the city. We'll find him, boss.'

'Alive or dead?'

Mickey shrugged his shoulders. 'Your guess is as good as mine.'

'I want Denzel found, Mickey. Put everybody we have in Chester on it, don't hold back.'

'Got it, boss. What about Cheetham Hill, did you sort them out?'

'That's sorted, don't worry about it.'

He wasn't going to tell his second-in-command too much at this stage. There had been far too many slip-ups in Chester recently. Had Mickey lost his touch?

'Look,' he prodded Mickey in the chest, 'I want Denzel found, okay? I don't really care if he's alive or dead, but I want him found before the police get to him. Clear? Your future in our organisation depends on you sorting this out, Mickey, get it?'

As Liam Gilligan's threat penetrated his tired brain, the message alert sounded on Mickey's phone.

He glanced down at the name that came up on the screen. 'It's the source, boss.'

'See what he says.'

'The source has come through with a name.' Mickey was reading a message on his phone. 'It's a cop. The man who's been killing our dealers is a sergeant in the Chester Constabulary. His name is Paul Tunney.'

'Are you sure?' Liam said doubtfully.

'That's what the message says.'

'Give it to me.'

Mickey handed over his phone and Liam Gilligan read the message himself. There it was in black and white type. The killer was a policeman.

'What about Denzel, Mickey? What about our dealer?'

'The source didn't say anything, boss. What are we going to do, Liam?'

Liam Gilligan stared out of the window. He didn't really care what his dealers wanted in this poxy city at the arse-end of the world, but he did care what his brothers thought. What happened if the police cocked this up? Or worse, got it completely wrong and this sergeant had nothing to do with it. Then their business would continue to suffer. If it did, his brothers would blame him, nobody else.

'Right, here's what we're going to do. Message the source and find out what the police are up to. We'll keep watching them using all our resources in Chester. If anything goes wrong, we sort it out for ourselves. Copper or no copper. I'll even do him in myself. So either the police get him or we get him. Either way, he's going down. Got it, Mickey?'

'You'd do in a copper?'

Mickey was suitably impressed, as Liam had intended.

'Of course, anybody who attacks our dealers has to deal with me. A bullet works just as well against a copper's flesh as against any other.'

Liam had no intention of killing anybody, but Mickey didn't know that. Instead, his number two would repeat his words back to the minions. Leading a gang was often about the perception of toughness, not the actuality.

Personally, Liam hated violence unlike his brothers, who revelled in it. He was a businessman not a thug. He believed that sometimes, just sometimes, the threat of violence worked far better than the act itself.

He took another large swallow of his old-fashioned.

'The source is giving us details of the police plan now, boss.'

'Right, once we know what they are doing, we'll work out our plan of action. But I definitely want to find Denzel before they do. A grand to whoever comes up with the info, Mickey. I want to find him. Now.'

He had to be seen to care about his dealers even if he didn't give a monkey's toss. A grand was a cheap price to pay.

Chapter EIGHTY-ONE

Gavin Newton was enjoying an early happy hour, paid for by his new favourite newspaper owner. He'd spent most of the afternoon running around Chester looking for more details on the abduction of Denzel Brown, but it had been a singularly unsuccessful day.

Quentin Forde hadn't joined him in the work though. As he said, 'For a grand a day, you can do the legwork, not me. The editor is going to be looking for results, especially when he sees the bills.'

Their little disagreement from this morning, otherwise known as blackmail, seemed to be forgotten.

'I thought you said you would tell him about the increase in my per diem?' Gavin said.

'Listen, me old cock, a word in your shell-like. In the newspaper game, everything is a cost until it isn't.'

'What does that mean?'

'It means you can spend what you like as long as you get a front-page splash from it. That was the old days. Now, it's clicks. If your article on the website gets a shitload of clicks, the editor is as happy as a dildo in a harem. No clicks? Sad, very unhappy editor. Lots of clicks? Happy, smiling editor who signs off expense forms without even looking at them. *Capisce?*'

'So yesterday we did well with the photos and the article?'

'We did very well. The big problem is that success has to breed more success. The story isn't over and we're still here spending his money. We need another big story to build on what we had. If we can do that, our happy little editor might even sling us both a bonus. So, how did it go today? Did you get anything?'

The waitress arrived at their table. 'Here's another bottle of the Chateau Fleet Street you ordered, Mr Forde.'

'Just keep 'em coming, lovely, and there's a rather big tip for you at the end of the night.'

'You said that last night, Mr Forde.'

'I did, didn't I? Never mind, I'll double it tonight.'

'Promise?'

'My word is my bond. And everybody knows a reporter never breaks their word.' He winked extravagantly at Gavin Newton. 'Now, if you could open this soldier and fill up my friend's glass, I'm sure he will be very happy. He may even add to your tips this evening. He can afford it now he's blackmailed me into paying him more.'

So perhaps this morning wasn't completely forgotten.

After the waitress had filled his own glass with a liquid the colour of the deepest ruby, Quentin Forde continued his questions. 'You still haven't told me how you did this afternoon. Discover anything?'

Gavin weighed up telling the man the truth or feeding him a line. The police were keeping a tight lock on all information this time. He hadn't heard anything since this morning.

'I'm getting there, following up a few leads.'

The reporter moved in closer, prodded him in the chest and snarled, 'Listen, me old cock, you can't bullshit a bullshitter. You got anything or not?'

Gavin recoiled from the alcohol-stained breath. 'Not yet... but I will do.'

'You'd better. I don't pay a grand a day for nothing.' Then his demeanour changed and he smiled broadly as a woman entered the wine bar. 'The lovely Maggie, how's my favourite female reporter person? Had a wonderful day enjoying the bright lights of sunny Chester, have we?' He waved his paw at the waitress. 'Another glass for my darling competitor.'

Maggie joined them at the table, leaning in to Quentin Forde and whispering, 'Looks like we're going to be here longer. Another drug dealer has gone missing.'

Forde threw death stares at Gavin Newton. 'Where did you hear that, Maggie, down the local Women's Institute?'

Maggie checked over her shoulder to make sure that nobody was listening. 'It's kosher, Quentin, I just thought I'd let you know.'

'Thanks for that, darling.' He raised his glass in salute. 'The readers of the worst newspaper in the world thank you from the bottom of their hearts.'

Just then, the message alert on Gavin's phone beeped. He looked down to check it but didn't recognise the number. It wasn't from his usual police source.

Be at the war memorial outside the cathedral at 10.15 this evening. You'll see something that will interest you.

Who was it from? And how did they get his number?

And then it clicked. Quentin Forde or one of the other reporters was winding him up, playing one of their childish public-school pranks on him.

He checked around the wine bar.

Quentin Forde was deep in conversation with Maggie, staring down her cleavage as she talked to him.

The rest of the bar was the usual hubbub of customers. Nobody was looking at him, nobody watching his reaction to the message.

Could this be real?

Was this the killer letting him know another victim was going to be put on display this evening? He thought about telling Quentin Forde but decided against it. He would just go there with the photographer and get a picture exclusive. Perhaps sell it to one of the other big national red-tops.

Hadn't Quentin said it was a dog-eat-dog world in Fleet Street? It was time he enjoyed his share of the pie.

Chapter EIGHTY-TWO

Emma Christie and Harry Fairweather sat in their car a short distance from the exit to Central Police Station, close to the hoarding that shouted 'Welcome to Chester Market'.

She knew Paul Tunney would walk this way to his car, which was parked on the third level of the car park.

The time on the dashboard said 19.57.

Both were nervous, neither saying anything on the short drive from the Major Incident Room. Anna was in the station, ostensibly to follow up on Eamonn Flanagan's witness statement, but in reality to keep an eye on Tunney.

Mark Kennedy and Gerry Rafferty were in the car park with eyes on Tunney's motor. John Simpson was back at the Major Incident Room co-ordinating the operation. The rest of the investigative team thought they were on a special off-site to re-assess the case and its implications.

Emma had been blunt as she briefed the small team before they began.

'I'm going to ask you to do something difficult for me, which, because it could affect your careers, you will have to volunteer for. If you don't think you can do it, don't worry, I won't hold it against you.'

'What do you want us to do?' asked Anna.

'As I explained earlier, we don't have enough evidence to charge Paul Tunney, so we have to discover him with one of the victims.'

'How are we going to do that?'

Emma took a deep breath and composed herself. 'Tunney always follows a pattern. He takes his victims, kills them somewhere else, and then always – and this is key – places the body with the eyes missing between nine thirty and ten p.m. in a public place.'

'But we don't know where he is going to place his latest victim. And there's just six of us, we can't cover the whole of Chester.'

'I agree. But we do know he finishes work at eight p.m —'

'So sometime between eight and nine thirty, he needs to pick up the body and take it to his chosen dump site.'

'Exactly, Anna.'

'You think Denzel Brown is already dead, boss?'

Emma dropped her gaze to the floor. 'I do, Gerry. If Tunney follows his usual pattern from the other two victims, which I think he will, it means Denzel was killed this morning and his eyes removed. I hope I'm wrong and we can save him, but we won't be able to do that until we know where Tunney keeps his victims, his killing zone. So this is what we are going to do.'

Emma took them all through her plan.

'It's deliberately simple. The fewer complications, the better.'

'Are you going to keep our boss, Davy Jones, informed?'

Emma thought long and hard. What would her father do?

'Not at this moment. We act first and ask for permission later. And because Tunney is police, I want to keep this a secret till we have all the evidence we need. We know Tunney is our killer, now we have to make certain that knowledge stands up in a court of law.'

'Davy Jones is going to be furious, boss.'

'I know, but if I'm right, he will also be the person who has put a terrible serial killer, a member of his own force, behind bars. That's why I need all of your agreements to what I've asked you to do. This is above and beyond the call of duty, people. Are all of you in?'

Everybody nodded or said yes.

'Right. Centre of operations is this room. Can you set it up quietly, John? We begin at seven p.m.'

'What are you going to do now, boss?'

'I'm going to ring Davy Jones and update him on the progress of the investigation.'

'You're going to lie to him, boss?' asked Anna.

'Not at all, it's gross misconduct to lie to a senior officer. I'm simply not going to tell him the truth. Wish me luck.'

Emma retreated into the corner of the room and called Davy Jones.

'I've been expecting your call, DI Christie.'

'Sorry, sir, we've been busy.'

'Have you found Denzel Brown yet?'

'Not yet, sir, but we have a plan and I hope to give you some good news shortly.'

'You've been saying that, DI Christie, for the last four days since the first victim was found, but I haven't seen any progress at all. And now, another young man has disappeared from the streets of Chester. The public and the press are asking questions, but I can give them no answers, DI Christie.'

'I know, sir, I'm sorry, but if you could just give me a little more time, I'm sure we'll have some good news soon.'

'Unfortunately, you don't have more time, DI Christie. I've made my decision. From tomorrow morning at nine a.m., DI Riggs will be running this investigation as senior officer. You, of course, will remain on the case, reporting to DI Riggs and giving him any aid and assistance he needs. Is that clear, Detective Inspector Christie?'

'Yes, sir, crystal clear. From tomorrow morning, I will be reporting to DI Riggs, sir.'

The chief inspector lowered his voice, adopting an almost regretful tone. 'You've done your best, Emma, unfortunately it wasn't good enough. You haven't let your father down and I won't let him know. Put this failure behind you. I'll arrange some new courses for you to attend in the next six months or so. Alternatively, I hear Greater Manchester Police are hiring. They need more women in their ranks, an equality drive, apparently...'

He left the rest of his sentence unsaid, but the inference was clear. It would be better if she found employment elsewhere.

'I understand, sir. Thank you for all your support. I'll give your words the attention they deserve.'

'Good, I'm glad to hear that, Emma.'

'One last thing, sir. I am in charge of the investigation until DI Riggs comes aboard tomorrow morning?'

'You are, Emma. I wanted to give Stew Riggs some time with his family before he takes over the case. Apparently there is some big rugby game today.'

'I understand and I think that was very wise of you, sir,' said Emma, with just a hint of irony. 'I'll prepare the case files to hand over to him. Should I bother you if anything comes up this evening, sir?'

'No, don't bother ringing me, my wife was most upset last time you called. Let Riggs know all about it tomorrow morning.'

'Thank you, sir, and have a good night.'

'I am sorry, Emma. I wish, just for your father's sake, you had managed a successful outcome and conclusion to this case.'

'There's still this evening, sir.'

'I suppose so, Emma, but I would go home if I were you. After you have updated the files for DI Riggs, of course.'

'Of course, sir, good night.'

She ended the call and looked across at the team, who were all staring back at her. 'What? I did offer to keep him updated this evening, but he doesn't want to be disturbed.'

'He's going to hang you out to dry, boss,' said Harry.

'Not before we put Tunney away. We've still got this evening.'

So here they now were, sitting in an old unmarked police car waiting for a killer to leave a police station.

The numbers of the clock turned over to read 20.00.

Chapter EIGHTY-THREE

He handed over to the duty desk sergeant. 'There you go, Bruce, all the logs up to date. It's pretty quiet so far for a Saturday. Just one drunk in cell 3 sleeping it off.'

'It'll kick off when the pubs close, we'll be full in here by the end of the night. What are we supposed to do with cell 3?'

'He's some Taff from the Valleys. He's been seen by the doctor and the duty inspector wants you to give him breakfast at seven tomorrow morning then throw him out on the streets. It's all in the logs.'

'Thanks. What shift are you on next week?'

'Switching over to nights from Tuesday.'

'Luckily, I'm just finishing, Got a long leave coming up soon. I'm off to Spain to play a bit of golf for a week.'

'Lucky lad.'

'What about you?'

'Nah, don't like golf, never got into the swing of it. Boom, tish. Won't be going away this year, too much on my plate, too much to do.'

'All work and no play…'

'Makes Paul an awfully dull boy. I get it. Anyway, I'm off – see you the week after next.'

'Not if I see you first.'

He went to the changing rooms and peeled off his uniform. The thing was sticking to him after an eight-hour shift. Police stations were never the cleanest places in the world at the best of times, but today seemed to be one of those times when the great unwashed of Chester had decided they should visit the station.

He spent a long time washing his hands in the sink, making sure they were scrubbed clean, particularly under the nails. As he washed, he went over the plan in his head. At 20.15, he'd ring the wife and tell her he would be late back. It would be the usual excuse: they were short-handed and I need to work a few hours overtime. She would moan as usual but the thought of the extra money would bring her round. It was one of the reasons he'd started selling tips to the press in the first place. The extra money always came in handy if his wife wanted to do a bit of designer shopping at Cheshire Oaks.

After the phone call, at 20.20, he'd drive directly to the lock-up in Boughton. He'd already washed and prepared Denzel Brown's body and the eyes were sitting on the shelf in their Kelvin jar. He'd take a long look at those before he left. But he wouldn't enjoy staring at them too long, his timings were exact to the minute.

After changing into his work clothes, he'd wrap the body in a sheet and place it in the back of the van, leaving the lock-up at exactly 21.15.

It was only a ten-minute drive back into the town centre, entering the city through North Gate and turning off to St Werburgh's Road next to the cathedral.

He'd already placed four police bollards in the parking bays at the top of Godstall Lane along with a trolley he'd nicked from Tesco. It was amazing how people obeyed these bollards with their stern warning of 'Police. No Parking.'

At exactly 21.30, he would begin to unload the van, using the trolley to transport the body across the road. The streets were usually empty in that area on a Saturday night. And anyway, he'd chosen the war memorial because it was set back from the road and dominated by the Cathedral. The gate might be locked, but that was probably better as he had a copy of the key given to the police from the Cathedral in case they needed to enter.

For exactly five minutes, he'd arrange the body on the plinth of the war memorial, making sure it was forensically clean, before finally hanging the sign around its neck.

He'd take a picture and then he'd walk casually back to the van, leaving the shopping trolley by the side of the road, and drive back to the lock-up.

He'd change once more, dumping the clothes in a trash bin to be burnt later and then he'd drive home, arriving back at exactly 23.00.

Job done.

It was all planned to the minute, with contingency in case of problems on the roads. But he'd checked with the traffic division before he left and the city's thoroughfares were clear that evening.

He checked the time. 20.15, time to ring the wife. He made the call and at exactly 20.20 put his bag over his shoulder and walked out of the station.

It was time to go to work.

Chapter EIGHTY-FOUR

'There he is.'

Harry nudged Emma in the ribs. Their target was walking up the street in civilian clothes with a blue bag over his shoulder.

Immediately, Emma was on her Airwave. 'Mark, target walking towards you, we think he's heading to pick up his car. Over.'

'Roger. We'll keep a look out for him and let you know when he's close to us. Over.'

Emma watched as he entered the car park and ran up the steps.

'Shall we run back to the car, boss?'

'Not yet, Harry, in case he comes back. Let's wait until Mark Kennedy picks him up.'

Right on cue, the Airwave squawked. 'We see him. Getting into his car now. We're about to follow. Over.'

'Don't get too close, I don't want him to spot you. Over.'

'Roger. Over.'

Kennedy left the Airwave on as he relayed the instructions to Gerry Rafferty who was driving.

Emma heard the motor of the car start up, shifting into second before she heard the scream of brakes followed by the loud squawk of a car horn.

'We've just been cut off by a couple of boy racers. Lost track of the target. Over.'

'Get a move on, Harry. We need to get over to the exit of the car park.'

They began running back to where their car was parked on a double yellow line.

Another garbled and distorted shout from the speaker of the Airwave:

'Don't cut in you, old fool. Get a move on. Jesus Christ, you can't pay with a credit card, you have to have a bloody ticket.'

Another loud honk on the horn followed by more shouting from Mark Kennedy and a long stream of Scouse expletives.

'We're stuck behind some idiot who hasn't got a ticket. The target turned right out of the car park but we don't know whether he turned left or right at St Martin's Way.'

Emma jumped in the car. 'Move it, Harry, he's getting away.'

From the Airwave came the sound of a car being reversed quickly, then put in gear again and crashing through a barrier.

'We're in pursuit now. Still no sight of the target. Right or left on St Martin's Way? Over.'

'You take the left, we'll follow the right in case he's heading towards Fountains Roundabout. Over.'

'Roger. Over.'

Harry accelerated onto St Martin's Way, moving as fast as he could. He didn't want to use the lights or sirens in case Tunney heard them.

'Which exit, boss?'

'Slow down, Harry.' Emma checked the Parkgate and Liverpool Road exits as they slowly went around Fountains.

'Go off at St Oswald's Way, I'll check the exit at Hoole Way.'

Harry accelerated again until they reached the next roundabout and slowed again, exasperating the car behind them.

'Nothing. Keep going to the Bars, Harry, I think he's using the A51.'

'That would make sense, boss, we've spotted his white van on that road too.'

They went round the Bars, coming off onto the main road.

Still nothing.

Emma picked up the Airwave. 'Can you see him, Mark? Over.'

'Negative, Emma.'

It felt like the whole world was sitting on her chest. She couldn't breathe and a wave of panic flooded her body. She'd taken a gamble and screwed it up.

'Pull over on the left, Harry. We've lost him.'

He signalled left and pulled into a Waitrose. 'What do we do now, boss?'

She scratched her wrist. Her eczema had suddenly flared up. 'I have to call Davy Jones.'

'You going to tell him everything?'

'I have to, no point in dissembling now.'

Where had Tunney gone? She knew he was probably going to pick up the body of Denzel Brown and then take it to the place where he would display it.

She had messed it all up by using too few cars to follow Tunney. She should have used the whole team, then they wouldn't be in this mess.

Her father wouldn't have made that mistake. He would have made sure there was ample resources to follow Tunney properly.

After this, she would have to take Davy Jones' not-so-subtle hint and apply for another force. But with her record, which operation would take her?

'Probably the Met, they'll take anybody, even you,' a nasty little voice in her head told her.

Then a horrible thought hit home.

What if Denzel Brown wasn't dead?

What if Tunney hadn't followed his usual plan of killing his victims well before he placed them?

What if he was going to kill the young man now?

She closed her eyes. Her screw-up had let a killer escape, Where was he now?

She had to ring Davy Jones. Tunney's pattern was to place the bodies at well-known Chester landmarks. What if they had coppers near all the main ones? They could have a chance of catching him with the body.

Before she picked up the phone, it began to ring.

Had Davy Jones heard about the whole fiasco already?

Chapter EIGHTY-FIVE

'This is what we've got on Tunney, Liam.' Mickey whistled through his teeth. 'He's a weird one.'

'What?'

'The local toms know him quite well. He often picked them up for a ride in his van but never had sex, just talked to them about changing their lifestyle. Goes on about dirt, and pollution and filth and all sorts of strange shit. With our dealers he's completely different. Not afraid to give them a good kicking after their arrest. He's been desk sergeant down at Central for two years now. The toms tell me he always treats them decently but the dealers say he's a right bastard.'

'Got a thing about drugs, has he?'

'That's not all. The toms said he wants to stare into their eyes when he's talking to them. If they look away, they get nicked, but if they just look back at him, he lets them go. He told them it's because the eyes are the window of the soul. By looking into their eyes, he knows if they have a pure heart.'

'Weird.'

'He also gives them a couple of tenners for their time so they don't mind. They come running straight to our dealers with the money, so we aren't complaining.'

'Why didn't I know this before, Mickey? I could have used it.'

'You know the toms, Liam, they quite liked him so nobody ever said anything. The dealers though, they were afraid of him.'

'Is the car following him?'

'A couple of the young lads, boy racers. They won't lose him.'

'Okay, but that doesn't get us any closer to finding Denzel, does it?'

'Give me a couple of minutes, boss, I've just sent Tunney's photo to one of the toms.'

'Where did you get the picture?'

'Off the police website, where else? Anyway, one of her mates was round the back of some advertising hoardings looking after a punter when she saw Tunney coming out of a lock-up. I'm just waiting for a response.'

As he spoke, the phone rang. 'Yeah, it's him. Great.' Another call came in which Mickey answered. 'What? Hang on, let me talk to the boss.' He covered the phone with his hand. 'It's the two lads who followed Tunney. He's just gone into a lock-up in Boughton. And guess what?'

'It's the same one the tom saw him using.'

'Right first time. What do you want them to do. Bring him in?'

Gilligan didn't answer. He was furiously working out the options in his head. He made a decision. This could end up a win-win position, and if Denzel was still alive it could be win-win-win.

'What's the address of the lock-up?'

Mickey wrote it down.

'I don't want the lads to do nothing. Just get out of sight and watch, okay?'

He picked up his phone.

Chapter EIGHTY-SIX

Emma checked the caller ID.

No number.

Whoever was calling had probably dialled 141 blocking the number display before making the call. At least it wasn't Davy Jones. He wasn't tech-savvy enough to do that.

'DI Emma Christie, City of Chester Constabulary.'

'Don't talk, don't say a word, just listen. I know exactly what you are doing, DI Christie.'

'Who is this? Who am I talking to?'

'The man you are looking for, Sergeant Paul Tunney, has just gone to this address: 46 Laken Street, Boughton. It's a lock-up. He's there now. 46 Laken Street, Boughton. Got it?'

'Who is this? I need to know who this is.'

'Oh, you'll know soon enough. You owe me a favour, Emma Christie. One day, I'm going to call it in.'

The phone went dead in Emma's hand.

'Who was it, boss?'

Emma just stared out through the windscreen Should she believe the caller? How did they know she was looking for Paul Tunney? How did they know where he was?

'Harry, go to 46 Laken Street, Boughton.'

'I know it, boss, but why?'

'Apparently, Paul Tunney is there. Get on to Anna and Mark Kennedy. I want them there too, plus back-up. Get control to send whatever vehicles they have in the area to that address. Now.'

'Right, boss.'

Emma could hear Harry on the Airwave to the rest of the team and then on his mobile to Control.

'The back-up ETA is five minutes, boss. Anna and Mark will be not long after that.'

'Let's move, Harry. How long for us?'

'Less than three minutes.'

'Move it, I want to get there first. No blue lights. I don't want Tunney to know we're coming.'

Harry put the car in gear and pulled out from the Waitrose car park. He accelerated down the A51 and just after the Christleton Road junction turned right into the warren of streets in that area.

'Laken Road is just down here on the left' He turned into the road and slowed down. 'Number 46 is up here. If I remember it's a row of six lock-ups built just after the war. Prefabs, I think they were called.'

'There's Tunney's car parked outside one of them.'

'What are we going to do?'

Emma checked her watch. Should they wait for back-up? 'We're going in, Harry, Denzel Brown might still be alive.'

'Which one?'

Emma looked along the row of lock-ups. All had a single door on the right with a roll up metal door on the left large enough for one car.

'Let's try the one where his car is parked.'

Before Harry could try to kick down the door. A trio of police cars arrived, disgorging six officers. The blocked the street with their cars and then ran to her.

Emma flashed her warrant card. 'Kick down the door,' she ordered.

'That won't be necessary, Emma.' Paul Tunney had opened the door and was standing in the dark with his hands above his head.

'Come out where I can see you, Paul.'

The man stepped into the yellow glare of the street lights and the headlamps of the police cars.

'That's Sergeant Tunney, I'm arresting him?' said the copper who was about to kick the door in.

'No, Sunny Jim,' said Emma. '*I'm* arresting him.'

The copper took a step back.

'Paul Tunney, I am arresting you on suspicion of the murder of Roy Short and Artea Marku. You do not have to say anything. But it may harm your defence if you do not mention when questioned something which you later rely on in court. Anything you do say may be given in evidence. Do you want to say anything to me?' Emma took delight in handcuffing Tunney's hands behind his back.

Another squeal of tires as a car slid to a stop at the entrance to the lock-ups. Anna Williams, Gerry Rafferty and Mark Kennedy jumped out of the car and ran to where they were standing.

'I see the cavalry have arrived.'

'Where's Denzel Brown?'

Tunney indicated with his head. 'Inside, but you're too late. He's dead. I killed him this morning. I do think you should move back a little, you see there's quite a lot of inflammable material in there.'

As he spoke, there was a whoosh of flame inside the lock-up, followed by a strong yellow glow. The fire took hold almost immediately with the flames licking the inside walls and slinking though the gaps in the metal shutters.

'Everybody move back across the street!' shouted Emma. 'Harry, call the fire brigade.'

'Will do, boss.'

They ran away from the lock-up as the sound of broken bottles and brief flashes of flame appeared begins their backs.

Tunney was being held by two burly coppers. He was staring at the flames as they leapt even higher, exploding out through the roof and spreading across to the lock-up next door.

Emma could see he had tears in his eyes.

'All my work, gone. I had so much work left to do.'

'Take him down the nick and charge him, Harry. No special treatment.'

'Will do, boss.'

As Tunney was being led away, a large explosion erupted from the middle of the lock-up, throwing glass and metal high into the air.

They all ducked down behind the parked cars as the flames rose higher over the streets of Chester.

Only Paul Tunney remained standing, looking back over his shoulders. 'My eyes, they are gone,' was all he had to say.

Chapter EIGHTY-SEVEN

'Gross dereliction of duty that's what it is, DI Christie.'

DCI Davy Jones was pounding the table, his face red and getting redder.

In front of him, Emma Christie sat with her hands in her lap, not saying a word.

'First, you arrest a serving police officer without keeping anybody in senior management informed of what you were doing.'

'But I did ask you, sir, and you said you didn't want to be disturbed.'

'Don't come the crap with me, DI Christie. You know in such a case, senior officers should always be informed,'

Emma didn't answer.

'Secondly, you instituted an operation without informing senior management, or logging it correctly on the system, or informing all the members of your team.'

'There had been a series of leaks in the investigation, sir. Given the seriousness of the allegations concerning Sergeant Tunney, I decided to restrict the information we had on him to those people I could trust.'

'Does that mean you didn't trust me?'

Emma didn't answer again.

'Thirdly, you involved a serving officer from another force in your operation without informing his senior management.'

'Mark Kennedy volunteered for the assignment, sir.'

'I don't care what Mark Kennedy does or doesn't do, there are protocols to be followed, and these you ignored.'

Emma kept silent.

'Fourthly, your management of this investigation has been disastrous from the beginning. Two young men have died and another is missing...'

'Sergeant Tunney has admitted to killing both of them, sir, and he confessed that the body of Denzel Brown was still in the burning lock-up. The fire brigade hasn't yet got the fire under control. I'll send in forensics to go through the embers as soon as it's safe.'

'*You* will do nothing of the sort.' Davy Jones took a deep breath, composing himself. His face still remained red but at least his voice no longer had a strident, accusatory quality. 'DI Christie. You have failed yourself, your father, me, the people of Chester and this police force, I want your —'

Before Davy Jones could complete his sentence, the office door opened and the chief constable stepped in. Both Emma and Davy Jones stood up.

'I hope I'm not disturbing anything. I just wanted to congratulate DI Christie on her sterling and speedy work solving this case. I heard Tunney has coughed to the murders.'

The chief constable's public-school voice always sounded strange and forced when he used police slang.

'He has, sir,' answered Emma. 'Apparently, he had two more kidnappings and murders planned but we managed to find him before he carried them out.'

'Very good. I'm holding a press conference at noon, I'm sure you'll be free to join me and explain the investigation to the press, DI Christie. Can I call you Emma?'

'You can call me whatever you want, sir. And yes, I'll make myself available.'

He held up the latest issue of the Chester Daily. The headline was big and bold:

CITY OF CHESTER CONSTABULARY NABS KILLER

'The reporter, a chap called Gavin Newton, even admits he was contacted last night to go to the war memorial where he was would find something the killer had left for him. I believe *you* stopped that from happening, Emma.'

'It wasn't just me, sir, this case was a team effort. I'd like to commend DCs Fairweather and Williams, as well as our civilian researcher, John Simpson. Sergeant Tom Harris and PC Gerry Rafferty did most of the leg work. Without them we couldn't have moved as quickly as we did. I mustn't also forget the intelligence given to us by DI Mark Kennedy of Merseyside.' She paused for a moment before turning to Davy Jones. 'And not forgetting the constant support and advice of my superior, DCI Jones. Without his constant help and guidance, we couldn't have arrested Tunney as quickly as we did.'

'That's as may be, but I am a big believer in the mantra that leadership is everything. It was your leadership of the team, Emma, that ensured the successful conclusion to this sorry episode. Wasn't your father a serving officer in the City of Chester Constabulary too?'

'He was sir, twenty-two years in the force.'

'Before my time, I suppose. A chip off the old block, then. I always wondered if the ability to solve crimes was genetic. Anyway, I must run. Well done, again, and I'll see you at 11.30 for the pre-press conference briefing. The fact that Tunney was a serving police officer will cause us a few problems, but every force has it's bad apples. Look at the Met, they seem to have a whole orchard of them.'

'Tunney may have used his warrant card to detain at least one of the victims, sir.'

'Yes, that was unfortunate, but the press don't know anything about it. Luckily for us, Tunney was just about to be kicked off the force for gross misconduct. The Independent Office for Police Conduct had been investigating him for striking a detainee.'

'Why wasn't he suspended, sir?'

'Everybody, including a police officer, is innocent until proven guilty, Emma, you should know that. But the investigation may have been one of the catalysts that caused him to act as he did.'

'To murder young drug dealers?'

'Precisely. I'll see you at 11.30, Emma. I have to run now. Thank you, Davy, great work from your team.'

He saluted them by tipping his swagger stick against the peak of his cap. Within seconds he was gone, and they heard his booming, cultured voice thanking the secretary for all her hard work, the sound becoming lower as he moved further away.

'You were about to tell me something before the chief constable interrupted us, sir. What was it?'

'Don't bother sitting down, DI Christie, you've got away with this one. But I won't forget how you nearly screwed everything up. Now get out of my sight, before I change my mind. I won't forget this, and nor should you.'

'I promise I won't, sir. And thank you for your support.'

She left the office, closing the door quietly behind her. She couldn't be bothered hiding the broad smile spreading across her face.

But inside, she was still troubled. Not by Davy Jones; he was just a stale fart trapped inside a bag of bones. What worried her was the phone call.

How did the man know what she was doing?

How did he know about Paul Tunney?

Was there a mole on her team feeding information to him?

And who the hell was he? The words came back to her. 'You owe me a favour, Emma Christie. One day, I'm going to call it in.'

She'd go to the press conference at 11.30 as she'd promised. But she knew this case wasn't over.

In fact, it was only just beginning.

The next book in the DI Emma Christie crime series, Death on the Dee, is available from September, 2024. It can be ordered here: https://www.amazon.com/Death-Dee-Christie-Crime-Thriller-ebook/dp/B0CW1GHJWH

If you enjoyed The Coffin in the Wall, please leave a review on Amazon. It will help other readers discover my books.

Plus to keep in touch with me and find out the latest news, there are three options.

Follow my Amazon page - https://www.amazon.co.uk/stores/author/B013TJLJ8A

Or my Bookbub page - https://www.bookbub.com/authors/m-j-lee

Or subscribe to my author newsletter at https://www.writermjlee.com

Thank you for reading.

Printed in Great Britain
by Amazon

42543060R00208